The events in this book are real.

Names and places have been changed to protect the Lorien,
who remain in hiding.

Other civilizations do exist.

Some of them seek to destroy you.

The Rise of Nine

PITTACUS LORE

MICHAEL JOSEPH
an imprint of
PENGUIN BOOKS

MICHAEL JOSEPH

Published by the Penguin Group

Penguin Books Ltd, 80 Strand, London WC2R 0RL, England

Penguin Group (USA) Inc., 375 Hudson Street, New York, New York 10014, USA

Penguin Group (Canada), 90 Eglinton Avenue East, Suite 700, Toronto, Ontario, Canada M4P 2Y3
(a division of Pearson Penguin Canada Inc.)

Penguin Ireland, 25 St Stephen's Green, Dublin 2, Ireland (a division of Penguin Books Ltd)

Penguin Group (Australia), 250 Camberwell Road, Camberwell, Victoria 3124, Australia
(a division of Pearson Australia Group Pty Ltd)

Penguin Books India Pvt Ltd, 11 Community Centre, Panchsheel Park, New Delhi – 110 017, India

Penguin Group (NZ), 67 Apollo Drive, Rosedale, Auckland 0632, New Zealand
(a division of Pearson New Zealand Ltd)

Penguin Books (South Africa) (Pty) Ltd, Block D, Rosebank Office Park,
181 Jan Smuts Avenue, Parktown North, Gauteng 2193, South Africa

Penguin Books Ltd, Registered Offices: 80 Strand, London WC2R 0RL, England

www.penguin.com

First published in the United States of America by Harper, an imprint of HarperCollins Publishers 2012
First published in Great Britain by Michael Joseph and Razorbill 2012

001

Copyright © Pittacus Lore, 2012

The moral right of the author has been asserted

All rights reserved

Without limiting the rights under copyright
reserved above, no part of this publication may be
reproduced, stored in or introduced into a retrieval system,
or transmitted, in any form or by any means (electronic, mechanical,
photocopying, recording or otherwise), without the prior
written permission of both the copyright owner and
the above publisher of this book

Set in 13.5/16 Garamond MT Std
Typeset by Jouve (UK), Milton Keynes
Printed in Great Britain by Clays Ltd, St Ives plc

A CIP catalogue record for this book is available from the British Library

HARDBACK ISBN: 978–0–718–15649–7
TRADE PAPERBACK ISBN: 978–0–718–15969–6

www.greenpenguin.co.uk

Penguin Books is committed to a sustainable
future for our business, our readers and our planet.
This book is made from Forest Stewardship
Council™ certified paper.

ALWAYS LEARNING

PEARSON

I

6A. Seriously? I look at the boarding pass in my hand, its large type announcing my seat assignment, and wonder if Crayton chose this seat on purpose. It could be a coincidence, but the way things have gone recently, I am not a big believer in coincidences. I wouldn't be surprised if Marina sat down behind me in row seven, and Ella made her way back to row ten. But, no, the two girls drop down beside me without saying a word, and join me in studying each person boarding the plane. Being hunted, you are constantly on guard. Who knows when the Mogadorians might appear.

Crayton will board last, after he's watched to see who else gets on the plane, and only once he feels the flight is absolutely secure.

I raise the window shade and watch the ground crew hustle back and forth under the plane. The city of Barcelona is a faint outline in the distance.

Marina's knee bounces furiously up and down next to mine. The battle against an army of Mogadorians yesterday at the lake, the death of her Cêpan, finding her Chest – and now, it's the first time in almost ten years that she's left the town where she spent her childhood. She's nervous.

'Everything okay?' I ask. My newly blond hair

falls into my face and startles me. I forgot I dyed it this morning. It's just one of many changes in the last forty-eight hours.

'Everyone looks normal,' Marina whispers, keeping her eyes on the crowded aisle. 'We're safe, as far as I can tell.'

'Good, but that's not what I meant.' I gently set my foot on hers and she stops bouncing her knee. She offers me a quick apologetic smile before returning to her close watch of each boarding passenger. A few seconds later, her knee starts bouncing again. I just shake my head.

I feel sorry for Marina. She was locked up in an isolated orphanage with a Cêpan who refused to train her. Her Cêpan had lost sight of why we are here on Earth in the first place. I'm doing my best to help her, to fill in the gaps. I can train her to learn how to control her strength and when to use her developing Legacies. But first I'm trying to show her that it's okay to trust me.

The Mogadorians will pay for what they've done. For taking so many whom we've loved, here on Earth and on Lorien. It's my personal mission to destroy every last one of them, and I'll be sure Marina gets her revenge too. Not only did she just lose her best friend, Héctor, back at the lake, but, like me, her Cêpan was killed right in front of her. We will both carry that with us forever.

'How is it down there, Six?' Ella asks, leaning over Marina.

I turn back towards the window. The men below

the plane begin to clear away their equipment, conducting a few last-minute checks. 'So far, so good.'

My seat is directly over the wing, which is comforting to me. On more than one occasion I've had to use my Legacies to help a pilot out of a jam. Once, over southern Mexico, I used my telekinesis to push the plane a dozen degrees to the right, only seconds before crashing into the side of a mountain. Last year I got 124 passengers safely through a vicious thunderstorm over Kansas by surrounding the plane with an impervious cloud of cool air. We shot through the storm like a bullet through a balloon.

When the ground crew moves on to the next plane, I follow Ella's gaze towards the front of the aisle. We're both impatient for Crayton to board. That will mean everything is okay, at least for now. Every seat is full but the one behind Ella. Where is he? I glance out at the wing again, scanning the area for anything out of the ordinary.

I lean down and shove my backpack under my seat. It's practically empty, so it folds down easily. Crayton bought it for me at the airport. The three of us need to look like normal teenagers, he says, like high school students on a field trip. That's why there's a biology textbook on Ella's lap.

'Six?' Marina asks. I hear her buckle and unbuckle her seat belt nervously.

'Yeah?' I respond.

'You've flown before, right?'

Marina is only a year older than I am. But with her solemn, thoughtful eyes and her new, sophisticated haircut that falls just below her shoulders, she can easily pass for an adult. Right now, however, she bites her nails and pulls her knees up to her chest like a scared child.

'Yes,' I say. 'It's not so bad. In fact, once you relax, it's kind of awesome.'

Sitting there on the plane, my thoughts turn in the direction of my own Cêpan, Katarina. Not that I ever flew with her. But when I was nine years old, we had a close call in a Cleveland alley with a Mogadorian that left us both shaken and covered in a thick layer of ash. Katarina moved us to Southern California after that. Our crumbling, two-story bungalow was near the beach, practically in the shadow of Los Angeles International Airport. A hundred planes roared overhead every hour, always interrupting Katarina's teaching, as well as the little free time I had to spend with my only friend, a skinny girl next door named Ashley.

I lived under those airplanes for seven months. They were my alarm clock in the morning, screaming directly over my bed as the sun rose. At night they were ominous ghosts telling me to stay awake, to be prepared to rip off my sheets and jump in the car in a matter of seconds. Since Katarina didn't let me stray far from the house, the airplanes were also the sound track of my afternoons.

On one of those afternoons, as the vibrations from an enormous plane overhead shook the lemonade in our plastic cups, Ashley said, 'Me and my mom are going to visit my grandparents next month. I can't wait! Have you ever been on a plane?' Ashley was always talking about all the places she went and things she did with her family. She knew Katarina and I stayed close to home and she liked to brag.

'Not really,' I said.

'What do you mean, "Not really"? You've either been on a plane, or you haven't. Just admit it. You haven't.'

I remember feeling my face burn with embarrassment. Her challenge hit its mark. I finally said, 'No, I've never been on an airplane.' I wanted to tell her I've been on something much bigger, something much more impressive than a little airplane. I wanted her to know I came to Earth on a ship from another planet called Lorien and the trip had covered more than 100 million miles. I didn't, though, because I knew I had to keep Lorien secret.

Ashley laughed at me. Without saying good-bye, she left to wait for her dad to come home from work.

'Why haven't we ever been on a plane?' I asked Katarina that night as she peered out the blinds of my bedroom window.

'Six,' she said, turning to me before correcting herself. 'I mean, Veronica. It's too dangerous for us to travel by plane. We'd be trapped up there. You know what could happen if we were thousands of miles in the air and *then* found out Mogs had followed us on board?'

I knew exactly what could happen. I could picture the chaos, the other passengers screaming and ducking under their seats as a couple of huge alien soldiers barreled down the aisle with swords. But that didn't stop me from wanting to do something so normal, so human, as to fly on a plane from one city to the next. I'd spent all my time on Earth unable to do the things other kids my age took for granted. We rarely even stayed in one place long enough for me to meet other kids, let alone make friends – Ashley was the first girl Katarina even allowed over to our house. Sometimes, like in California, I didn't even attend school, if Katarina thought it was safer.

I knew why all this was necessary, of course. Usually, I didn't let it bother me. But Katarina could tell that Ashley's superior attitude had gotten under my skin. My silence the following days must have cut through her, because to my surprise she bought us two round-trip airline tickets to Denver. The destination didn't matter – she knew I just wanted the experience.

I couldn't wait to tell Ashley.

But on the day of the trip, standing outside the airport, Katarina hesitated. She seemed nervous. She ran her hand through her short black hair. She had dyed and cut it the night before, just before making herself a new ID. A family of five walked around us on the curb, dragging heavy luggage, and to my left a tearful mother said good-bye to her two young daughters. I wanted nothing more than to join in, to be a part of this everyday scene. Katarina watched everyone around us while I fidgeted impatiently by her side.

'No,' Katarina finally said. 'We're not going. I'm sorry, Veronica, but it's not worth it.'

We drove home in silence, letting the screaming engines of the planes passing overhead speak for us. When we got out of the car on our street, I saw Ashley sitting on her front steps. She looked at me walking towards our house and mouthed the word *liar*. The humiliation was almost too much to bear.

But, really, I *was* a liar. It's ironic. Lying was all I had done since I'd arrived on Earth. My name, where I was from, where my father was, why I couldn't stay the night at another girl's house – lying was all I knew and it was what kept me alive. But when Ashley called me a liar the *one* time I was telling someone the truth, I was unspeakably angry. I stormed up to my room, slammed the door, and punched the wall.

To my surprise, my fist went straight through.

Katarina slammed my door open, wielding a kitchen knife and ready to strike. She thought the noise she'd heard must be Mogs. When she saw what I had done to the wall, she realized that something had changed with me. She lowered the blade and smiled. 'Today's not the day you get on a plane, but it is the day you're going to start your training.'

Seven years later, sitting on this plane with Marina and Ella, I hear Katarina's voice in my head. 'We'd be trapped up there.' But I'm ready for that possibility now, in ways that Katarina and I weren't.

I've since flown dozens of times, and everything has gone fine. However, this *is* the first time I've done it without using my invisibility Legacy to sneak on board. I know I'm much stronger now. And I'm getting stronger by the day. If a couple of Mog soldiers charged at me from the front of the plane, they wouldn't be dealing with a meek young girl. I know what I'm capable of; I am a soldier now, a warrior. I am someone to fear, not hunt.

Marina lets go of her knees and sits up straight, releasing a long breath. In a barely audible voice, she says, 'I'm scared. I just want to get in the air.'

'You'll be fine,' I say in a low voice.

She smiles, and I smile back at her. Marina proved herself to be a strong ally with amazing Legacies on the battlefield yesterday. She can breathe under water, see in the dark, and heal the sick and wounded. Like all Garde, she also has telekinesis. And because we're so close in order – I'm Number Six and she's Number Seven – our bond is special. When the charm still held and we had to be killed in order, the Mogadorians would have had to get through me before they could get to her. And they never would have gotten through me.

Ella sits silently on the other side of Marina. As we continue to wait for Crayton, she opens the biology book on her lap and stares at the pages. Our charade does not demand this level of concentration and I'm about to lean over and tell her, but then I see she isn't reading at all. She is trying to turn the page with her mind, trying to use telekinesis, but nothing's happening.

Ella is what Crayton calls an Aeternus, someone

born with the ability to move back and forth between ages. But she's still young and her Legacies have not yet developed. They will come in their own time, no matter how impatiently she wills them to develop now.

Ella came to Earth on another ship, one I didn't know existed until John Smith, Number Four, told me he saw it in his visions. She was just a baby, which means she's almost twelve now. Crayton says he is her unofficial Cêpan, since there wasn't time for him to be officially appointed to her. He, like all of our Cêpans, has a duty to help Ella develop her Legacies. He told us that there was also a small herd of Chimæra on their ship, Loric animals capable of shifting forms and battling alongside us.

I'm happy she's here. After Numbers One, Two, and Three died, only six of us remained. With Ella, we number seven. Lucky number seven, if you believe in luck. I don't, though. I believe in strength.

Finally, Crayton squeezes down the aisle, carrying a black briefcase. He's wearing eyeglasses and a brown suit that looks too big for him. Under his strong chin is a blue bow tie. He's supposed to be our teacher.

'Hello, girls,' he says, stopping next to us.

'Hi, Mr Collins,' Ella responds.

'It's a full flight,' Marina says. That's code for everyone on board looks okay. To tell him everything on the ground appears normal, I say, 'I'm going to try to sleep.'

He nods and takes his seat directly behind Ella.

Leaning forward between Marina and Ella, he says, 'Use your time on the plane wisely, please. Study hard.'

That means, don't let your guard down.

I didn't know what to think of Crayton when we first met. He's stern and quick tempered, but his heart seems to be in the right place and his knowledge of the world and current events is incredible. Official or not, he has taken his Cêpan role seriously. He says he would die for any one of us. He will do anything to defeat the Mogadorians; anything to exact our revenge. I believe him on all counts.

However, it's with reluctance that I'm on this plane headed to India at all. I wanted to get back to the United States as soon as possible, to get back to John and Sam. But yesterday, standing on top of the dam overlooking the carnage at the lake, Crayton told us that Setrákus Ra, the powerful Mogadorian leader, would be on Earth soon, if he wasn't here already. That Setrákus's arrival was a sign that the Mogadorians understood we were a threat, and we should expect them to step up their campaign to kill us. Setrákus is more or less invincible. Only Pittacus Lore, the most powerful of all the Lorien Elders, would have been able to defeat him. We were horrified. What did that mean for the rest of us then, if he was invincible? When Marina asked this, asked how any of us could possibly stand a chance of defeating him, Crayton told us even more shocking news, knowledge that all the Cêpans had been entrusted with. One of the Garde – one of us –

was supposed to hold the same powers as Pittacus. One of us was supposed to grow as strong as he had been, and would be able to beat Setrákus Ra. We just had to hope that that Garde wasn't One, Two, or Three, that it was one of the ones still alive. If so, we had a chance. We just had to wait and see who it was, and hope that these powers showed themselves soon.

Crayton thinks he's found him – the Garde who holds Pittacus' powers.

'I've read about a boy who seems to have extraordinary powers in India,' he told us then. 'He lives high up in the Himalayas. Some believe him to be the Hindu god Vishnu reincarnated, others believe the boy is an alien imposter with the power to physically alter his form.'

'Like me, Papa?' Ella had asked. Their father-daughter relationship took me by surprise. I couldn't help but feel a touch of jealousy – jealousy that she still had her Cêpan, someone to turn to for guidance.

'He's not changing ages, Ella. He's changing into beasts and other beings. The more I read about him, the more I believe he is a member of the Garde, and the more I believe he may be the one to possess all of the Legacies, the one who can fight and kill Setrákus. We need to find him as soon as possible.'

I don't want to be on a wild goose chase for another member of the Garde right now. I know where John is, or where he is supposed to be. I can hear Katarina's voice, urging me to follow my instincts, which are telling me we should connect with John first before anything else. It's the least risky move. Certainly less risky than flying around the world based on Crayton's hunch and rumors on the Internet.

'It could be a trap,' I said. 'What if those stories were planted for us to find so we would do exactly this?'

'I understand your concern, Six, but, trust me, I'm the master of planting stories on the Internet. This is no plant. There are far too many sources pointing to this boy in India. He hasn't been running. He hasn't been hiding. He's just *being*, and he appears to be very powerful. If he *is* one of you, then we must get to him before the Mogadorians do. We'll go to America to meet up with Number Four as soon as this trip is over,' Crayton said.

Marina looked at me. She wanted to find John almost as much as I did – she'd been following the news of his exploits online and she'd had a similar feeling in her gut that he was one of us, a feeling I had confirmed for her. 'Promise?' she asked Crayton. He nodded.

The captain's voice breaks through my reverie. We're about to take off. I want so badly to redirect the plane to point it towards West Virginia. Towards John and Sam. I hope they're okay. Images of John being held in a prison cell keep entering my mind. I never should have told him about the Mog base in the mountain, but John wanted to get his Chest back and there was no way I could convince him to leave it behind.

The plane taxis down the runway and Marina grabs my wrist. 'I really wish Héctor was here. He'd have something smart to say right now to make me feel better.'

'It's okay,' Ella says, holding Marina's other hand. 'You have us.'

'And I'll work on something smart to say,' I offer.

'Thanks,' Marina says, though it sounds like something between a hiccup and a gulp. I let her nails dig into my wrist. I give her a supportive smile, and a minute later we're airborne.

2

I've been in and out of consciousness for the past two days, rolling back and forth in a hallucinating sickness. The effects from the blue force field outside the Mogadorians' mountain have lingered far longer than Nine told me they would, both mentally and physically. Every few minutes, my muscles seize and sear with pain.

I try to distract myself from the agony by looking around the tiny bedroom of this decaying, abandoned house. Nine couldn't have picked a more disgusting place for us to hide. I can't trust my eyes. I watch the pattern on the yellow wallpaper come to life, the design marching like ants over patches of mold. The cracked ceiling appears to breathe, rising and falling at frightening speeds. A large jagged hole in the wall separates the bedroom and living room, as if someone tossed a sledgehammer through it. Smashed beer cans are strewn around the room, and the baseboards have been torn to shreds by animals. I've been hearing things rustling in the trees outside the house, but I'm too weak to be alarmed. Last night I woke to find a cockroach on my cheek. I barely had the energy to swat it off.

'Hey, Four?' I hear through the hole in the wall. 'You awake or what? It's time for lunch and your food's getting cold.'

I heave myself to my feet. My head spins as I stumble through the doorway into what used to be the living room, and I collapse on the dingy gray carpet. I know Nine's in here, but I can't keep my eyes open long enough to find him. All I want is to lay my head in Sarah's lap. Or in Six's. Either one. I can't think straight.

Something warm hits my shoulder. I roll over to see Nine sitting on the ceiling above me, his long black hair hanging down into the room. He's gnawing on something and his hands are greasy.

'Where are we again?' I ask. The sunlight coming through the windows is too much and I close my eyes. I need more sleep. I need something, anything, to clear my head and regain my strength. My fingers fumble over my blue pendant, hoping to somehow gather energy through it, but it remains cold against my chest.

'The northern part of West Virginia,' Nine says between bites. 'Ran out of gas, remember?'

'Barely,' I whisper. 'Where's Bernie Kosar?'

'Outside. That one is *always* on patrol. He is one cool animal. Tell me, Four, how did *you* of all the Garde end up with him?'

I crawl into the corner of the room and push my back up against a wall. 'BK was with me on Lorien. His name was Hadley back then. I guess Henri thought it would be good to bring him along for the trip.'

Nine throws a tiny bone across the ceiling. 'I had a couple of Chimæras as a kid too. Don't remember their names, but I can still see them running around our house tearing stuff up. They died in the war, protecting my family.' Nine is silent for a moment, clenching his jaw. This is the first time I've seen him act anything other than tough. It's nice to see, even if it's short lived. 'At least, that's what my Cêpan told me, anyway.'

I stare at my bare feet. 'What was your Cêpan's name?'

'Sandor,' he says, standing up on the ceiling. He's wearing my shoes. 'It's weird. I literally can't remember the last time I said his name out loud. Some days, I can barely picture his face.' Nine's voice hardens, and he closes his eyes. 'But that's how it goes, I guess. Whatever. They're the expendable ones.'

His last sentence sends shockwaves through me. 'Henri was not expendable, and neither was Sandor! No Loric was ever expendable. And give me back my shoes!'

Nine kicks my shoes into the middle of the floor, then takes his time walking first along the ceiling and then down the back wall. 'All right, all right. I know he wasn't expendable, man. Sometimes it's just easier to think of him that way, you know? Truth is, Sandor was an amazing Cêpan.' Nine reaches the floor and towers over me. I forgot how tall he is. Intimidating. He shoves a handful of what he's been eating in my face. 'You want some of this or not? Because I'm about to finish it off.'

The sight of it makes my stomach churn. 'What is it?'

'Barbecued rabbit. Nature's finest.'

I don't dare open my mouth to respond, afraid that I might get sick. Instead, I stumble back towards the bedroom, ignoring the laughter that follows me. The bedroom door is so warped it's nearly impossible to close, but I wedge it into the doorframe as tightly as I can. I lie down on the floor, using my sweatshirt as a pillow, and think about how I ended up here, ended up like this. Without Henri. Without Sam. Sam is my best friend, and I can't believe we left him behind. As thoughtful and loyal and supportive as Sam is – traveling and fighting alongside me for the last several months – Nine is so very not. He's reckless, arrogant, selfish and just flat-out rude.

I picture Sam, back in the Mog cave, a gun rocking against his shoulder as a dozen Mogadorian soldiers swarmed him. I couldn't get to him. I couldn't save him. I should have fought harder, run faster. I should have ignored Nine and gone back to Sam. He would have done that for me. The immense amount of guilt I feel paralyzes me, until I finally fall asleep.

It's dark. I'm no longer in a house in the mountains with Nine. I no longer feel the painful effects of the blue force field. My head is finally clear, although I don't know where I am, or how I got here. When I shout for help, I can't hear my voice even though I feel my lips moving. I shuffle ahead, hands out in front of me. My palms suddenly start to glow with my Lumen. The light is dim at first, but quickly grows into two powerful beams.

'John.' A hoarse whisper says my name.

I whip my hands around to see where I am, but the light reveals only empty darkness. I'm entering a vision. I angle my palms towards the ground so my Lumen will light my way, and start towards the voice. The hoarse whisper keeps repeating my name over and over. It sounds young and full of fear. Then comes another voice, gruff and staccato, barking orders.

The voices become clearer. It's Sam, my lost friend, and Setrákus Ra, my worst enemy. I can tell I'm nearing the Mogadorian base. I can see the blue force field, the source of so much pain. For some reason, I know it won't hurt me now, and I don't hesitate to pass through it. When I do, it's not my screams I hear, but Sam's. His tortured voice fills my head as I enter the mountain and move through its mazelike tunnels. I see the charred remains of our recent battle, from when

I tossed a ball of green lava at the gas tanks at the mountain's bottom, sending a sea of fire raging upwards. I move through the main cavernous hall and its spiraling ledges. I step onto the arched stone bridge Sam and I so recently crossed under the cloak of invisibility. I keep going, passing through tributaries and corridors, all while being forced to listen to my best friend's crippling howls.

I know where I'm going before I get there. The steady incline of the floor lands me in the wide room lined with prison cells.

There they are. Setrákus Ra is standing in the middle of the room. He is *huge* and truly revolting looking. And there's Sam. He's suspended inside a small spherical cage next to him. His own, private torture bubble. Sam's arms are stretched high above his head and his legs are splayed, held in place with chains. A series of pipes are dripping steaming liquid onto various parts of Sam's body. Blood has pooled and dried under the cage.

I stop ten feet away from them. Setrákus Ra senses my presence and turns around, the three Loric pendants from other Garde children he has killed dangling from his massive neck. The scar circling his throat pulses with a dark energy.

'We missed each other,' Setrákus Ra growls.

I open my mouth but nothing comes out. Sam's blue eyes turn in my direction, but I can't tell if he sees me.

More hot liquid drips from the pipes, hitting Sam in the wrists, chest, knees and feet. A thick stream flows onto his cheek and rolls down his neck. Seeing Sam tortured finally gives me a voice.

'Let him go!' I shout.

Setrákus Ra's eyes harden. The pendants around his neck

glow and mine responds, lighting up as well. The blue Loralite gem is hot against my skin, and then it suddenly bursts into flames, my Legacy taking over. I allow the fire to crawl along my shoulders.

'I'll let him go,' he says, 'if you come back to the mountain, and fight me.'

I glance quickly over at Sam and see that he has lost his battle with the pain and has blacked out, chin resting on his chest.

Setrákus Ra points to Sam's withered body and says, 'You must decide. If you don't come, I'll kill him and then I'll kill the rest of them. If you do, I'll let them all live.'

I hear a voice yelling my name, telling me I have to move. Nine. I sit up with a gasp and my eyes snap open. I'm covered in a thin layer of sweat. I stare through the jagged hole of broken drywall and it takes me a few seconds to get my bearings.

'Dude! Get up!' Nine yells from the other side of the door. 'There's a ton of stuff we need to do!'

I get to my knees and fumble around my neck for my pendant. I squeeze it as hard as I can, trying to get Sam's screams out of my head. The bedroom door swings open. Nine stands in the doorway, wiping his face with the back of his hand. 'Seriously, bro. Get your shit together. We need to get out of here.'

3

The air is thick and heavy as we leave the airport in New Delhi. We walk along the curb, Marina's Chest under Crayton's arm. Cars inch past on the congested roadways, horns blaring. The four of us are on the alert for signs of trouble, even the slightest indication we're being followed. We reach an intersection and are jostled on all sides. Women shove by with tall baskets balanced on their heads; men with buckets of water draped over their dark shoulders shout for us to get out of the way. The smells, the noise, the physical proximity of the busy world around us could overwhelm us. We stay vigilant.

There's a bustling market on the other side of the street that looks like it stretches for miles. Children crowd us with trinkets for sale, and we politely turn down their wood carvings and ivory jewelry. I'm amazed by the organized chaos of it all, happy to see life moving along in what seems to be routine, happy for this moment away from our war.

'Where do we go now?' Marina asks, raising her voice to be heard above the noise.

Crayton scans the crowd crossing the street. 'Now that we're away from the airports and its cameras, I suppose we can find a –' A taxi skids to a stop in front of us, a cloud of dirt billowing from its tires, and the driver pushes the passenger door open. 'Taxi,' Crayton finishes.

'Please. Where can I take you?' the driver asks. He's young and looks nervous, like this is his first day on the job. Marina must either relate to his mood or be desperate to get away from the crowds, because she jumps right into the back of the car and scoots all the way over.

Crayton gives the driver an address as he folds himself into the front seat. Ella and I pile into the back, next to Marina.

The driver nods, and then promptly slams his foot down on the accelerator, throwing us all back against the cracked plastic seat. New Delhi becomes a blur of bright colors and fleeting sounds. We zip past cars and rickshaws, goats and cows. We take corners so fast I'm surprised it isn't on two wheels. We miss clipping pedestrians by a hair's breadth so many times I lose count. Then I decide it's probably best if I don't look so closely. We're tossed back and forth against each other. The only way we keep ourselves from falling onto the car's dirty floor is by clinging to one another and anything else we can grab.

The taxi jumps a curb at one point, shooting down a stretch of narrow sidewalk to avoid stalled traffic. It's totally crazy and I admit it I love every second of it. Years of running, hiding, and fighting have turned me into a total adrenaline junkie. Marina plants her hands on the headrest in front of her, refusing to look out the windows while Ella leans over her, trying to take it all in.

With no warning, the driver jerks the taxi violently down a road that runs behind a long row of warehouse buildings. The street is flanked by dozens of men with AK-47s. Our driver nods at them as we fly past. Crayton looks over his shoulder at me. His concerned face makes the knot in my stomach grow larger. The road is suddenly and noticeably absent of traffic.

'Where are you taking us?' Crayton demands of the driver. 'We need to go south and you're headed north.' Marina's head jerks up and she and Ella look over at me questioningly.

All of a sudden the car screeches to a halt and the driver dives out the door, rolling away from the taxi. A dozen vans and covered trucks surround the car. Each vehicle has a similar smudge of red paint on the doors, but I can't quite make out what it is. Men in street clothes jump out of the vans, machine guns ready.

Now the adrenaline really starts to flow. It always kicks in before a fight. I look over at Marina and see the terrified look on her face, but I know she will take her cues from me. I keep myself calm. 'You guys ready? Marina? Ella?' They nod.

Crayton puts his hand up. 'Wait! Look at the trucks, Six. Look at their doors!'

'What?' Ella asks. 'What's on their doors?'

The men come closer, their shouts growing urgent.

I'm too focused on the imminent danger to consider what Crayton is talking about. When people with guns threaten me, or the ones I love, I'll make sure they regret it.

Marina looks out the window. 'Six, look! Are those number –'

I finally see what they're all staring at just as the door next to Marina is whipped open. The red smudges on the truck doors are all eights.

'Out!' the man yells.

'Do as he says,' Crayton says under his breath, voice calm. 'For now, we do what they want.'

We carefully get out of the taxi, our hands up, all four of us transfixed by the red numbers painted on the truck doors. We must be moving too slowly because one of the men leans forward and impatiently yanks Ella forward. She loses her balance and falls down. I can't help myself. I don't care if they're with Number Eight or not, you don't knock a twelve-year-old girl to the ground. I heave the man into the air with my mind, tossing him onto the roof of a warehouse across the street. The other men panic, whipping their guns around and screaming to one another.

Crayton grabs my arm. 'Let's find out why they're here and if they know where Number Eight is. If we need to, we'll strike with full force then.' Still furious, I shake off his hand but I nod. He's right – we don't know what they want with us. Better to find out before they're unable to explain.

A tall bearded man wearing a red beret steps out

of one of the covered trucks and slowly walks towards us. His smile is confident, but his eyes are wary. A small pistol sticks out of his shoulder holster.

'Good afternoon and welcome,' he says in thickly accented English. 'I am Commander Grahish Sharma of the rebel group Vishnu Nationalist Eight. We come in peace.'

'Then what are the guns for?' Crayton asks.

'The guns were to convince you to come with us. We know who you are and would never engage in a battle with you. We know we'd lose. Vishnu told us you are all powerful like him.'

'How did you find us?' Crayton demands. 'And who is Vishnu?'

'Vishnu is the all-pervading essence of all beings, the master of the past, present and future, the Supreme God, and Preserver of the Universe. He told us you would be four in total, three young girls and one man. He asked me to convey a message to you.'

'What's the message?' I say.

Commander Sharma clears his throat and smiles. 'His message is: "I am Number Eight. Welcome to India. Please come and see me as soon as you can."'

4

The sky is gray and heavy. The woods are dark and cold. Most of the leaves have fallen from the trees and lie dead on the ground. Nine walks ahead of me, scanning the landscape for game. 'You know, that rabbit was better than I thought it would be.' He produces a short piece of vine from his pocket and pulls his shaggy black hair into a ponytail. 'I'll make it again tonight if you're interested.'

'I think I'll figure something else out.'

He looks surprised at my squeamishness. 'Scared of fresh kill? You have to eat if you want to get your strength up. I don't know why, but our healing stones don't do jack shit for your pain. And, you know, this sickness thing of yours is a real drag. Time's a-wasting, dude. We need to get you better and we've got to get out of here.'

I know how weak my body is by how tired I feel as we walk. We're only a couple of hundred yards from our ramshackle house and I'm exhausted already. I want so badly to be back there, sleeping. But I know I won't feel normal again if I don't get off my butt and move.

'Hey Nine, let me tell you about this dream I just had,' I say.

He snorts. 'A dream? No thanks, man. Well, unless it was about girls. *That* you can tell me *all* about; in detail.'

'I saw Setrákus Ra. I talked to him.' Nine pauses, then keeps walking. 'He offered me a deal.'

'Oh, yeah? What kind of deal?'

'If I go back to him and face him, he said he'll let everyone else live, including Sam.'

Nine snorts. 'That's a load of crap. Mogadorians don't make deals. At least, they don't make deals with any intention of keeping up their end of the bargain. And they don't show mercy.'

'I figure, why not just pretend I'm taking him up on it? I have to go back to the cave anyway to get Sam out.'

Nine turns to me, his face a mask of disinterest. 'Hate to break it to you, dude, but Sam's probably dead. The Mogs don't care about us, and they don't care about humans. I think you had a bad dream, and I'm sorry you got all scared and felt the need to bore me with it. But even if you did channel Setrákus Ra, that kind of offer is obviously a trap and you'll die walking into it. In fact, you'll die going within ten miles of that place. I guarantee it.' He spins around and walks away from me.

'Sam's not dead!' I say, anger welling up inside of me, giving me a strength I haven't felt in days. 'And the dream *was* real. Setrákus Ra was torturing him! I watched his skin sizzle from boiling liquid dropping onto it! I'm not going to just sit around here and let it continue to happen.'

He laughs again, but this time it isn't with a sneer. Not exactly reassuring, but definitely more gentle. 'Listen, Four. You're too weak to even run in place, never mind fight the most powerful being in the galaxy. I know it sounds heartless, dude, but Sam is *human*. There's no way you can save them all, so stop wasting your time and energy. It's not like you have an unlimited supply of either.'

The Lumen in my palms starts to light up. I'm in control of it now, a definite improvement. I'm hoping the glow is a sign

28

the effects of the blue force field are wearing off. 'Look. Sam is my best friend, Nine. You need to get that and keep your opinions about my *energy* to yourself, okay?'

'No, you look,' says Nine. His voice sounds flat. 'This isn't playtime. We're at war, dude: *war*. And you can't make this about your feelings for Sam, if it makes everyone else less safe. I will not let you abandon the rest of us to face Setrákus Ra, just for Sam. We're going to wait until you feel better, whenever the hell that is, and then we're going to meet up with the others and train until we're ready. If you don't like it, then you'll have to fight me to get out of here. And I'm *so* ready for a fight, so, really, bring it on. I could use the practice.'

He lifts his hand and aims it at something through the trees. A second later I hear a quick yelp.

'Got it.' Nine smiles, clearly proud of his telekinetic hunting skills. I follow him, refusing to give up.

'Isn't there anyone you would die for? Anyone you'd risk your life to help?'

'I'm risking my life to help Lorien,' Nine says, fixing me with a stare that makes me listen. 'I'll die for Lorien and anyone who's Loric. And if I die, and that's a big "if," I plan on doing it with two Mog heads smashed between my palms and another one under my foot. I'm not looking forward to feeling your symbol burned into my leg just yet, so grow up, stop being so naïve and think about more than yourself already.'

His words hit me hard. I know that Henri would agree with him, but I will not turn my back on Sam again. I don't know if it's Nine's arrogance or the urgency of the vision I just had or the fresh air and the walking, but my mind seems to be clear and strong for the first time in days.

'Sam saved my ass more than once, and his dad was there to meet our ship when we landed on Earth. His dad may even have died for us, for Lorien. You owe it to both of them to go back to the cave with me. Today.'

'Not a chance.'

I step towards him and Nine doesn't hesitate. He grabs me and throws me against a tree. I pull myself to my feet and I'm about to swing at him when we hear twigs cracking behind us. Nine turns towards the noise. I flatten myself against the tree, dimly lighting my palms to be ready to blind whoever it is with my Lumen. I hope I haven't overestimated how much of my strength is truly back.

Nine looks over at me, and whispers, 'Sorry about you and the tree. Let's go find whoever's tracking us and kill them before they kill us.'

I nod, and we step forward. The noise came from a patch of pines, thick with needles and offering excellent cover. If it were up to me we'd wait and see who or what we're facing, but not Nine. He's wearing a strange little smile as we move towards the pines, ready to destroy whatever emerges. The pines rustle again, and one of the lower branches moves. But what we see isn't a Mogadorian cannon or gleaming sword. Instead, the small black nose of a brown and white beagle emerges.

'Bernie Kosar,' I say, relieved. 'Good to see you, buddy.'

He trots over and I bend down to pet his head. He's the one creature who has been with me since the beginning. Bernie Kosar tells me he's happy to see me back on my feet.

'He took long enough, right?' Nine says. I'd forgotten Nine had also developed the Legacy to communicate with animals. I know it's immature, but it bothers me to share that power with him. He's already the biggest and strongest Garde I've ever seen, has the ability to transfer powers to humans, an antigravity Legacy, super speed and hearing, telekinesis, and whatever else he hasn't told me yet. My Lumen sets me apart from the rest, but unless I find a source of fire to combine it with, it's practically useless. My ability to talk to animals was something I was looking forward to developing further, but now I'm sure Nine will find a better use for it before me.

Bernie Kosar must see the disappointment on my face because he asks if I want to go for a walk with him. Alone.

Nine hears him and says, 'Go for it. You're all BK talks about anyway. Whenever he wasn't patrolling the perimeter, he was in the bedroom looking after you.'

I keep petting his head. 'That was you, huh?'

Bernie Kosar licks my hand.

'My other best friend,' I say. 'I'd die for you, too, BK.'

Nine groans at the display of emotion. I know we're supposed to have each other's back in this massive intergalactic war, but sometimes I wish it *were* just BK and me. And Sam. And Sarah. And Six. And Henri. Really, I'd take anyone but Nine.

'I'm going to find whatever it was I killed out there, make sure we have some food for tonight,' Nine says as he walks away. 'You guys go have your special walk. When you get back, we need to talk about finding the rest of the Garde. Now that you're functioning.'

'And how exactly are we going to find them? The address Six gave us for a meeting point was in Sam's pocket. For all we know, the Mogs have it and are waiting for Six to show up. That sounds like even more reason to find Sam, if you ask me,' I say pointedly.

Bernie Kosar agrees. It sounds like he wants to look for Sam almost as much as I do.

'We'll talk about it over dinner. I'm thinking possum, maybe a muskrat,' he says, already heading into the woods to find his prey.

Bernie Kosar tells me to follow him and he leads me through the trees and down a tall grassy hill. The land levels out for a few feet before rising again. We move quickly and the exercise feels amazing now that my strength is returning. Two huge trees lean into each other up ahead. I focus and push them apart with my mind. As soon as there's a space between them, BK jumps through and I chase after him, remembering our early-morning runs to school back in Paradise. Life was so much easier then, when my days were spent training with Henri and my free time was spent with Sarah. It was exciting, finding out what I was capable of, how my powers would help me do what needed to be done. Even when I was frustrated or scared, there was so much *possibility* and I could just focus on that. I had no idea how good I had it.

My back is sticky with sweat by the time we reach a small peak. I'm better, but still not one hundred per cent. The view is spectacular, a panoramic scene of the Appalachian Mountains wrapped in fir trees, bathed in the late afternoon light. I can see for miles.

'I gotta say, buddy, this is pretty awesome. Is this what you wanted me to see?' I ask.

Off in the distance, down on the left, he says. *Do you see it?*

I scan the landscape. 'In that deep valley?'

Beyond it, he says. *Do you see that glow?*

32

Squinting, I look past the valley. There's a cluster of thick trees and the faint outline of a rocky riverbed. Then I see it. Through the bottom of the trees on the far left is a glowing sliver of blue light. It's the force field at the bottom of the Mog's headquarters.

It can't be more than two miles away. Bernie Kosar says we can go back right now if I want. He'll join me inside this time, now that Sam and I disabled the system that sent a deadly gas to animals through the mountain.

A shiver runs down my body as I stare at the blue light. Sam is in there. And Setrákus Ra. 'What about Nine?'

Bernie Kosar circles my legs twice before sitting at my feet. *It's up to you,* he says. *Nine is strong and fast, but he's also unpredictable.*

'Have you taken him up here?' I ask. 'Does he know how close we are?'

Bernie Kosar cocks his head as if to say, *yes.* I can't believe he knew and didn't tell me. That's enough. I'm done with Nine.

'I'm going back to the house. I'll give Nine the option of coming with us, but whatever he says, it's time for me to face Setrákus.'

5

We bounce along a pothole-riddled road in a military transport truck. We're on the outskirts of the city and I look around. I see a massive mountain range looming in the distance, but that doesn't tell me much. Vehicles full of soldiers are in front of us and behind us. My Chest is at my feet and Six is sitting next to me. That makes me breathe a little easier. After the battle in Spain, the only time I feel even slightly safe is when Six is near.

I didn't think I would ever miss the Sisters of Santa Teresa, but right now, I'd give anything to be back at the convent. For years, all I thought about was escaping their rules and punishments, but now that I have escaped, all I want is something familiar, even if it comes in the form of religious discipline. My Cêpan, Adelina, is dead, murdered by Mogadorians. My best and only friend, Héctor Ricardo, is also dead. The town and convent are both gone, obliterated by the Mogs. The deaths weigh heavily on me; I was the one Adelina and Héctor were fighting to protect. God, I hope I'm not a curse. I hate the idea that my inexperience and lack of training might hurt anyone else. I don't want to put this mission in India in jeopardy just by my presence.

Finally Commander Sharma turns around to give us the lay of the land. 'This trip will last a few hours. Please, get comfortable. Help yourself to water in the cooler behind you. Don't draw attention to yourselves; don't engage with anyone. Not even to smile and nod. We're wanted.'

Crayton nods.

'So what do you think about all this?' Six asks Crayton. 'You think he's really up there?'

'I do. It makes sense.'

'Why's that?' I ask.

'The mountains are the ideal place for a Garde member to hide. For years, people have been scared to go near the glaciers north of China. Stories of alien sightings are enough to frighten the locals, and the Chinese military have been unable to investigate the reports because a mysterious lake appeared in the valley and blocked their access. Who knows what's true, and what's a rumor, but either way it's an excellent place to hide.'

'Do you think there are other aliens up there beside Number Eight?' says Ella. 'You know, like, Mogadorians?'

I was wondering the same thing.

'I don't know who else is up there, if anyone, but we'll find out soon enough,' says Crayton. He wipes sweat from his brow and touches my Chest with the tip of his finger. 'In the meantime, we should start learning how to use what's in here to help prepare us, if Marina is kind enough to share.'

'Sure,' I say quietly, lowering my eyes to the Chest. I'm not opposed to sharing my Inheritance, but I'm embarrassed by how little I understand what I have. My Chest was supposed to be shared between me and Adelina. It was her job to explain how to use everything, how it could save my life. But that never happened. After a beat, I say, 'I don't know what any of it does, though.'

Crayton reaches forward and touches my hand. I meet

36

his solemn, yet encouraging eyes. 'It's okay that you don't know. I'll show you whatever I can,' Crayton says. 'I'm not just Ella's Cêpan now; I'm all of yours. As long as I'm alive, Marina, you can count on me.'

I nod, and place my palm against the lock. Now that Adelina is dead, I can open my Chest on my own and it's a bittersweet power. Six watches me, and I know she understands exactly how I'm feeling, having also lost her Cêpan. The cold metal lock shakes against my skin. With a click, it falls to the floor of the truck. The dirt road we're driving on is covered with potholes and debris, constantly jostling me and making it hard for me to steady my hand as I reach inside the Chest. I'm careful not to touch the glowing red crystal in the corner that caused me so much trouble in the orphanage's belfry, the one I worried was a Loric grenade, or worse. I reach for a pair of dark glasses.

'Do you know what these are for?' I ask Crayton. He examines them for a second but hands them back to me, shaking his head.

'I don't know for sure, but they may give you the power to see through things, like X-ray vision. Or they could be thermal detectors, good for seeing at night. There's only one way to find out, you know.'

I place the glasses on my face and look out the window. Aside from dulling the brightness of the sun, nothing else seems to happen. I check my hands but they're just as solid as before, and when I look up at Crayton's face, there aren't any thermal hot spots.

'So?' asks Six. 'What do they do?'

'I don't know,' I say, checking the barren landscape out the window again. 'Maybe they're just ordinary sunglasses.'

'I doubt it,' Crayton says. 'They have a use that you will discover, just like everything else in there.'

'Can I see them?' Ella asks. I hand them over.

She slides the glasses up her nose, then twists around and looks out the back window.

I turn back to my Chest.

'Wait – everything looks a little different somehow but I can't figure out why. It's almost like seeing everything a little delayed . . . or maybe sped up . . . I can't decide.' Suddenly Ella gasps, then shouts, 'Rocket! Rocket!'

We follow her line of vision, but I don't see anything but crystal-blue sky.

'Where?' Crayton yells. Ella points up at the sky. 'Get out of the truck! We have to get out right now!'

'There's nothing there.' Six squints into the horizon. 'Ella, I think those glasses are messing with you, because I don't see anything.'

Ella doesn't listen. She scrambles over me with the glasses still on and opens the door. The shoulder of the road is lined with sharp rocks and dead shrubs. 'Jump! Now!'

Finally we hear it, a faint whistling in the air, and a black speck suddenly comes into view, right where Ella was pointing.

'Get out!' Crayton yells.

I grab my open Chest, and jump. My feet hit the hard dirt road and sweep underneath me, and the world instantly becomes a swirl of browns and blues and sharp pains. The back tire of our truck grazes my arm, and I barely change direction in time to roll out of the way of the next speeding truck. My head hits a sharp stone and I flip over one last time, landing on my Chest. The impact knocks the wind out of me, and the contents of my Chest have scattered in the dirt. I hear Ella and Six coughing somewhere nearby but I can't see them in the haze of dust that surrounds us. A second later the rocket smashes into the ground just behind the speeding truck we dived from. The explosion is deafening, and with Commander Sharma still inside, the truck flips forward onto its roof in a cloud of smoke. The careening jeep behind it is unable to swerve. It hits the edge of the chasm caused by the rocket, and dives right into the tremendous hole. Two more rockets hit the convoy. The air is so thick with dust that we cannot see the helicopters overhead, but we can hear them.

I blindly grope the area around me, trying to gather everything that spilled out of my Chest. I know I'm probably collecting just as many stones and twigs as pieces of my Inheritance, but I can sort through it later.

I've just grabbed the red crystal when I hear the sound of gunfire tear through the air. 'Six! You okay?' I shout. Then I hear Ella scream.

6

I'm frantic, pulling open closet doors, looking under what little furniture there is, when I hear someone come noisily into the house. I assume it's Nine because Bernie isn't growling.

'Nine,' I yell. 'Where'd you hide my Chest?'

'Look under the kitchen sink,' he calls back.

I walk into the kitchen. The curling linoleum floor looks like a decrepit chessboard someone's spilled coffee all over. The handles to the cupboard under the sink are loose, and when I pull on them I hear a click.

'Wait, Four!' Nine yells from the other room. 'I made a –'

The cupboard doors blow open and I fly backwards.

'Trap!' Nine finishes.

A dozen sharpened sticks are shooting straight at me. They're inches away when my instincts kick in and I'm able to deflect them with my telekinesis. The sticks ricochet left and right, stabbing the walls.

Nine stands in the doorway laughing. 'So sorry, dude. I totally forgot to tell you I rigged that up.'

Furious, I jump to my feet. Bernie Kosar skids in and growls at Nine. While he berates Nine for his stupidity, I focus on pulling the sticks out of the walls. I will them to hover in the air, aimed at Nine. 'You don't sound sorry.'

I'm seriously considering launching the little spears at him when he uses telekinesis to break the sticks into two, four and then eight pieces and they fall to the floor.

'Hey, I really did forget,' he says, shrugging. He turns around to head into the other room. 'Anyway, grab your Chest and get in here. We have to jet, so start pulling your stuff together.'

My Lumen lights up the moldy cupboard and I carefully stick my head under the sink. At first I don't see anything and think Nine is messing with me. I'm about to march into the living room to demand he return my Chest to me when I notice something. The left side of the cupboard goes deeper than the right. I feel my way around and pull away the false plywood wall. Jackpot. There it is. I grab the Chest and carry it out of the kitchen.

In the living room Nine's digging in his own Chest, the Chest we rescued from the Mog cave. 'Good to see you, old friend,' he says when he pulls out a short silver staff. Next he grabs a round yellow thing covered with small bumps. It looks like a strange fruit and I half expect him to squeeze it to produce juice. He sets it in his palm, and before I can ask what it is, he whips it down at the floor and quickly backs himself up against the wall. It bounces high after hitting the carpet and changes from yellow to black, expanding to the size of a grapefruit. When it reaches shoulder height the small bumps explode, turning into razor-sharp spikes. I duck and roll in BK's direction to avoid getting impaled.

'What the hell?' I shout. 'You could have warned me! This is the second time in less than five minutes that you've almost killed me.'

Nine doesn't flinch when the spikes retract violently back into the ball just before it returns to his palm.

'Hey, hey, hey, would you please relax?' Nine says. He holds the ball close to his eye, causing me to hold my breath. 'I

42

knew nothing would hit you. I can control it with my mind. Well, I can control it partly. Usually.'

'Partly? Are you kidding me? I didn't see a lot of control just now. I had to jump out of the way.'

Nine takes the ball away from his eye, looking a little chagrined. Not enough, though. 'Right now, I can only control the color.'

'That's it?' I'm incredulous. He shrugs.

BK tells him to stop fooling around.

'Hey, I'm just checking to make sure I remember how everything works. Everything I know how to use, at least,' Nine says, dropping the ball back into the Chest. 'Because you never know.' He pulls out the strand of green stones he used back at the Mog cave and flings it into the air. It hovers in a perfect circle and sucks debris off the ground like a black hole. It spins towards a back window and glows white, and when Nine snaps his fingers the debris explodes out of the circle, breaking whatever was left of the window.

'Check that one off,' he laughs.

I open my own Chest. Nine thinks that there's something in our Chests that can help us find the others. The first thing I see is the blue coffee can holding Henri's ashes and I suck in my breath. I'm instantly transported back to the forest in Paradise, walking with Sarah through the melting snow to see Henri's dead body. I promised Henri I would take him back to Lorien, and I still plan on it.

I carefully move the coffee can to the floor next to the Chest and grab the dagger with the diamond blade, letting the handle extend and wrap itself around my fist. I turn it over, looking at the blade. I release the dagger and continue to sift through the items. I try not to dwell on the objects

I don't know — the star-shaped talisman, the collection of brittle leaves tied with twine, the bright red oval bracelet — and I stay away from the crystal that's double-wrapped in towels and stuffed into a plastic bag. The last time I touched that crystal, my stomach convulsed and acid climbed up my throat.

I push aside the smooth yellow Xitharis rock that transfers Legacies and pick up an oblong crystal that is full of memories. Its surface is waxy with a cloudy inside, and it's the first thing Henri ever pulled out of the Chest to show me. When the cloud swirled, it meant my first Legacy was developing. This crystal was the beginning.

Then I see Sam's dad's glasses and the white tablet Six and I found in Malcolm Goode's office in the well. That's enough to snap me back to reality.

I look over at Nine. 'Maybe something in our Chests can get us through the blue force field. I think the effect of it is weakened, anyway. There may be a chance we can get to Sam tonight.'

'Would be nice if something in the Chest would help us do that, that's for sure,' Nine says in a casual tone, his eyes focused on the purple pebble he is balancing on the back of his hand. It disappears.

'What's that?' I ask.

He turns over his hand and the pebble reappears on his palm. 'I have no idea, but it would be a killer conversation starter with the ladies, don't you think?'

I shake my head and slide the red bracelet from my Chest over my hand. I hope it will propel me into the air or shoot a ring of lasers, but it just hangs there on my wrist. I wave my arm over my head, asking it to work, begging it to reveal its powers. Nothing happens.

44

'Maybe you should try licking it?' Nine laughs, watching me.

'I'll try anything,' I mutter, frustrated. I keep it on and hope something will just *happen*. Everything in my Chest came from the Elders. Everything has a purpose, so I know it must do something. My hand brushes against the velvet bag holding the seven orbs that make up Lorien's solar system. I pull open the bag and drop the stones into my hand and show them to Nine, remembering the day that Henri first showed them to me. 'Are these what you're looking for to find the others? Henri had these. This is how we figured out another member of the Garde was in Spain.'

'I've never seen those before. What do they do?'

I blow softly on the stones and they glow, coming to life. Bernie Kosar barks at the sight of the orbs hovering over my palm. They have become planets and orbit the sun. Just as I'm about to shine my Lumen onto Lorien to see it in its lush, green state as it was the day before the Mogadorian attack, the orbs once again speed up and brighten and I can no longer control them.

Nine comes closer and we watch as the planets collide one by one with the sun until there is just a large single ball in front of us. The new globe rotates on its axis and flashes a light so bright we have to shield our eyes. Eventually, the globe dims and sections of its surface rise and recede until we're looking at a perfect replica of Earth.

Nine is mesmerized. The Earth rotates and we immediately see two pinpricks of pulsing light one on top of the other. Once we can orient ourselves, we see they are in West Virginia.

'There we are,' I say.

The ball continues to rotate and we see there's another

pulse of light in India; a fourth is moving north quickly from what looks like Brazil.

'When I was showing Six and Sam our solar system a few days ago in the car, the same thing happened. It turned into a globe of the Earth. It was the first time it ever did that,' I say.

'I'm confused,' Nine says. 'There are only four dots on this thing and there are supposed to be six of us left.'

'Yeah, I'm not sure about that. When this happened before, a dot showed up in Spain,' I say. 'Then the globe went all fuzzy and we heard someone who sounded panicked yelling the name Adelina. We assumed she was another member of the Garde. That's when Six decided to go to Spain, to try to find her. I figured this was how you planned to contact the others, but I guess not if you've never seen it before.'

Nine's eyes go wide. 'Wait. Oh my God, man. I haven't seen this thing before, but I think Sandor told me about it. To be honest, when we opened my Chest the first time, the silver staff and the yellow porcupine ball were so amazing I only half listened to anything he said after. But now I remember, he told me some of us had a red crystal – which I do, and that's what I thought I'd use to communicate with the others – and some of us have the solar system.'

'I don't get it.'

He turns to his Chest, grabs a glowing red crystal the size of a cigarette lighter, slams the lid of his Chest, and turns back to me. I glance at the solar system and gasp. One of the blue dots in West Virginia has disappeared.

'Whoa, hold on. Open up your Chest again. I want to see something.'

Nine obeys and a second blue dot reappears on the globe in West Virginia.

46

'Okay. Now, close it.'

He closes it and the dot disappears again. 'This is boring,' he says. When Nine speaks, the Earth globe grows fuzzy and vibrates with a half-second delay of his voice. 'Wait, what was that? Why is my voice echoing?' The Earth vibrates again.

'This is not boring. *This* is incredible,' I say, staring at the globe. 'The reason we don't see all six of the Garde members on the globe is because the orb only reveals the members of the Garde who have their Chests open at that exact moment. Watch.' I lift the lid of Nine's Chest.

Nine whistles. 'Very cool, Four, very cool.' Half a second later we hear his voice through the globe again. Nine puts his crystal down, having figured it out.

'But judging by the speed of this guy here,' I say, pointing to the dot in motion, 'whoever is in South America has to be on a plane. It's covering too much ground too fast to be doing anything else.'

'Why would they have their Chest open on a plane?' Nine asks. 'That's stupid.'

'Maybe they're in trouble. Maybe they're hiding in the bathroom trying to figure out what all this stuff actually does, just like we are.'

'Can they see us right now, too?'

'I don't know, but maybe they can hear us. I think if you hold on to that red crystal, any of us with this macrocosm Earth can hear you.'

'If half of us have a crystal, and the other half have the power to get this big glowing globe up and running, then —'

'The only way for us to actually communicate back and forth would be if a couple of us teamed up first,' I interrupt. 'Well,

47

now that we're together, maybe we should try to talk to the others. You know, in case their macrocosms are going,' I say. 'Maybe another pair has gotten together like us.'

Nine grabs the red crystal and holds it near his mouth like a microphone. 'Hello? Testing one, two, three.' He clears his throat. 'Okay, if any of you Garde members are out there standing in front of a glowing ball, listen up. Four and Nine are together and we're ready to meet up with you. We want to train and end all this bullshit and get back to Lorien. Pronto. We're not going to say exactly where we are in case any Mogs are listening in, but if you have your macrocosm going you'll see two dots together, and they are, uh, us. So, um . . .' Nine looks at me and shrugs his shoulders. 'That is all. Over and out and stuff.'

The skin on my wrist suddenly feels numb under the bracelet. I shake it and my arm begins to tingle. 'Wait. Say we're about to get out of here and for them to make their way to the United States. That's where Setrákus Ra, the Mogadorian leader, is. Tell them we're going after him and we're going to rescue our friends as soon as we can.'

The Earth in front of me buzzes to life with Nine's echoing voice. 'Everyone come to America ASAP. Setrákus Ra has shown his ugly face over here and we're aiming to smash it in and take him down *real* soon. We'll send out another message tomorrow. Stay tuned.'

Nine drops the red crystal back into his Chest, looking way too pleased with himself, then kind of embarrassed that he just talked into a ball. I frown. My right arm has gone ice cold, and I'm about to rip off this bracelet before putting the orbs back into the velvet bag when the Earth grows fuzzy again. Then there's the sound of an explosion, followed by a voice

48

I know well. It's the same girl I heard before, the girl Six went to Spain to seek out. She's yelling. 'Six! You okay?'

We hear a scream and two more explosions rock the fuzzy edges of the globe. I grab Nine's crystal out of his chest, frantic to try to communicate with her.

'Six!' I yell. I would jump into the thing if I could figure out how. 'It's me, John! Can you hear me?'

There's no response. We hear the faint sounds of the blades of a helicopter before the globe goes silent again and the Earth's edges grow solid. The pulsing light in India is now gone. Suddenly, the globe shrinks and reforms into the seven orbs, each of which falls to the ground.

'That did *not* sound good,' Nine says, scooping up the stones. He drops them back into my Chest, and takes his crystal out of my frozen hand.

Six is in trouble — the kind of trouble that involves explosions and helicopters and mountains. And all of this is happening now, halfway around the world. How am I going to get to India? Where can I get on a plane?

'Six is the chick who gave you the map to the mountain? The one who abandoned you and your boy to jet off to Spain?' Nine asks.

'That's her,' I say, kicking my Chest shut, fists clenched tight. My head is swimming. What's wrong with Six? Who is the other girl, the one I've now heard twice? I notice my arm feels strange. Hearing her voice distracted me so much I forgot about the growing discomfort there. I try to remove the bracelet from my wrist, and it burns my fingers. 'Something's going on with this thing. I think something may be wrong with it.'

Nine shuts his Chest and reaches over. 'The bracelet?' As

49

soon as he touches it he rips his hand away. 'Damn! It zapped me!'

'Well, what do I do?' I try snapping my arm out, hoping I can fling the bracelet off.

Bernie Kosar trots over to smell the bracelet, but stops midstride and jerks his head up to stare at the front door. His ears rise and the fur on his back bristles.

Someone's here, he says.

Nine and I look at each other and start to back slowly into the room, away from the door. We'd been so engrossed in everything in our Chests, and in hearing the voice through the globe, that we'd let our guard down, and weren't paying attention to our surroundings.

Suddenly, the door is blown off its hinges. Smoke bombs fly through the windows sending glass shards everywhere. I want to fight, but the pain from the bracelet is now so intense I can't move. I fall to my knees.

I see a flash of green light and hear Nine shout out in pain. He falls down next to me. I've seen that green light before. That is the unmistakable green light of a Mogadorian cannon.

7

Bullets whistle by, exploding in the dirt all around us. Ella and I take cover behind the wreckage of one of the trucks. The bullets seem to be coming from everywhere, from every direction, from every angle. Ella's been hit. The air is so thick with dust from all the commotion, I can't even see her wounds. I gently run my hands over her body until I feel the wet, sticky blood and find a bullet hole in her lower thigh. When I touch it, she cries out in pain.

I use the most soothing voice I can muster, given the circumstances. 'It's going to be okay. Marina can help you. We just need to find her.' I pick Ella up and start carefully moving away from the truck, shielding her with my body. I almost trip over Marina and Crayton, who are huddled behind another piece of debris.

'Come on! Ella's hurt! We have to get out of here!'

'There are too many of them. If we try to run now, they'll kill us. Let's treat Ella first, then fight back,' Crayton says.

I set Ella down next to Marina. She's still wearing the dark glasses. I can see her wound clearly now; her blood is flowing steadily. Marina places her hands on Ella's leg and closes her eyes. Ella inhales sharply, her chest beginning to rise and fall at a rapid pace. It really is amazing to see Marina's Legacy in action. Another explosion sounds nearby and a blast of dust sweeps over us just as Ella's wound contracts, pushing the bullet out of her flesh. The gash turns from black and red back to the color of her pearly-white skin. An outline of a small bone shifts just below the surface of her skin and Ella's body slowly begins to relax. I rest my hand on Marina's shoulder, relieved, and say, 'That was incredible, Marina.'

'Thanks. It was pretty cool, wasn't it?' Marina removes her hands from Ella, who slowly props herself up onto her elbows. Crayton gives her a hug.

A helicopter roars overhead and decimates two trucks with a spray of bullets. A chunk of metal lands close to me; it's a piece of smoldering truck door, the red number eight just barely visible. The sight of it fills me with anger. Now that Ella is healed, I'm ready to fight back.

'Now we move on them!' I yell at Crayton.

'Is it the Mogadorians?' Marina asks, clicking the lock of her Chest shut.

Crayton looks over the top of the debris heap we've been hiding behind, and ducks back down to report. 'It's not the Mogs. But there are a lot of them and they're coming closer. We can fight here, but it would be better to take it to the mountains. Whoever they are, if they aren't here to attack us but are battling Commander Sharma, I see no reason to reveal your powers.'

An explosion behind us pushes another cloud of

dirt our way, and I watch the helicopter circle back around and head straight for us. Marina and I look at each other and we can tell we're both thinking the same thing. There's no way to honor Crayton's request that we not use our Legacies and do what we need to do. She takes control of the helicopter and reverses its flight path. Its passengers will never understand what happened but we know it's out of our way. And regardless of who's inside, we don't want anyone to be in danger's path unnecessarily. Ella and I cheer with relief as we watch the spinning blades disappear into the distance while Crayton watches with a frown. Then Commander Sharma dives behind our cover.

'Thank God, you're alive,' he says. I'm tempted to say the same thing to him. I thought he was killed when that first rocket struck. Blood trickles from a large cut on his temple, and his right arm hangs awkwardly at his side.

'I'm holding you responsible for this,' I say, glaring at him.

He shakes his head. 'Those are soldiers of the Lord's Resistance Front. They are who we were trying to avoid.'

'What do they want?' I ask.

Commander Sharma scans the horizon before looking me in the eyes. 'To kill Vishnu. And destroy all of his friends. Like you. More are on their way.'

I move to a crouching stance and carefully peer over the demolished truck. A large brigade of heavily armed vehicles is moving towards us, several

53

helicopters hovering above them. Tiny flashes of light appear from the long line of the trucks and jeeps, and seconds later I hear the bullets zip past us.

'Let's go kick some ass,' I say.

'It's not possible to defeat them here,' Commander Sharma says, picking up a machine gun with his good hand. 'No more than twenty of my men are still fighting. We must take it to higher ground if we want a chance to survive this.'

'Just let me handle it,' I say.

'Wait, Six,' Crayton says, scooping up Marina's Chest. 'He's right. The mountains will give us more cover. You can still take out every single one of them. It just won't be as visible, which is good for us. We don't need the Mogs picking up on this right now.'

Marina puts her hand on my arm. 'Crayton's right. We need to be smart. Let's not draw more attention to ourselves than we have to.'

'The Mogs?' Commander Sharma asks, confused. We'll need to be more careful around him.

Before anyone can answer, two low-flying helicopters zip in with their guns blazing. Several of the commander's soldiers are mowed down, their weapons blown to useless shards of metal. If we're going to run, it's now or never. I use my telekinesis to pull on the tail of one of the helicopters, tipping the nose down. It looks like a rodeo horse trying to buck its rider as the pilot struggles furiously to level the copter out. We watch the pilot give a particularly hard yank to the joystick and two men bounce right out of the cabin. They weren't very high in the air, so the fall shouldn't injure them – much.

I look over at our fleet of stalled SUVs and see smoke rising faintly from one of the tailpipes. An engine is still running! I shout, 'Let's go! Now!'

Everyone rushes from behind the cover; Commander Sharma yells for his few remaining men to retreat. The brigade is less than a hundred yards away. As we run I feel a bullet zip through my hair. Another one rips through my forearm, but before I can scream, Marina is right next to me, her icy hands tending to my injury as we run. All but one of the commander's soldiers follows his orders to retreat. That lone soldier follows the commander, running with us.

We reach the SUV and get inside – the four of us, plus Commander Sharma and the one soldier. Crayton steps on the gas and whips us onto the road. Bullets tear through the tail end of our truck, shattering the back windshield, but we're able to manoeuvre around a small rock formation and evade the relentless gunfire.

This is not a road built for speed. It's full of potholes, rocks and other debris, and Crayton struggles to keep us from careening off the shoulder. The SUV is overflowing with guns – I find a shotgun and crawl into the back, waiting for a target. Marina follows suit, leaving her Chest with Ella.

Now that I have a moment to gather my thoughts, I'm angry. We thought if Number Eight remained in the mountains, we would be safe here, under the radar. Instead, we're being attacked because of him. If we survive this, I am *so* going to tear Eight a new one.

'Where are we going?' Crayton yells over his shoulder.

'Just stay on this road,' the commander says. I look over my shoulder and see the Himalayan Mountains through the windshield. They are slowly getting closer, their jagged tops growing more menacing. Up ahead, the brown desert ends, and a curving band of green surrounds the base of the mountains.

'Why do these guys want to kill Number Eight?' I ask Commander Sharma, the barrel of my shotgun bouncing off the frame of the back window.

'The Lord's Resistance Front does not believe he is Vishnu. They believe we are blasphemous, accepting this mountain boy as the Supreme God. They want to kill us in his name.'

'Six!' Ella yells. 'Incoming!' She's still wearing the glasses.

I look out the back window in time to see something fire out of the helicopter. It's a missile of some sort heading straight for us. I use my telekinesis and send it directly into the desert floor, where it explodes. The helicopter fires two more missiles.

'Time to take these dudes out!' I yell. 'Let's do this one together, Marina.' She nods and instead of directing the rockets into the ground this time, we loop them so they're heading directly back at the copter. We watch grimly as the helicopter explodes in a giant fireball. We never try to kill; but, given a choice between killing versus being killed, I will pick us every time.

'Awesome work, Six,' says Ella.

'Yippee-ki-yay, and all that,' I reply with a grim smile.

'Do you think they'll leave us alone now?' asks Marina.

'I don't think it's going to be that easy,' says Commander Sharma.

'She has all the same type of powers as the boy you call Vishnu,' says Crayton, motioning towards me. 'Will that be enough to dissuade them? Do you think they'd still try to fight him?'

'They would if they could find him,' says the commander.

'How many are there in the Lord's Resistance Front?' I ask Commander Sharma.

'In total? Thousands. And they have wealthy donors who support them in any way they need.'

'Hence the helicopters,' Crayton says.

'They have worse than that,' the commander adds.

'The best plan for us is to outrun them,' Crayton says to the commander. 'I'll drive as fast as I can. If we have to fight, we'll fight; but I'd like to avoid it.'

Five minutes pass in tense silence. Marina and I monitor the brigade in the distance, and whenever we pass something large enough, we use our telekinesis to drop it in the path behind us. The tall trees that have begun to dot the sides of the road quickly form a thick line of defense. The car dips into an extremely narrow valley before beginning to ascend the mountain. We have just come to the base when Commander Sharma tells Crayton to stop. I lean forward in my seat and see dozens of small mounds in the dirt.

'Land mines?' I ask.

'I'm not sure,' the commander says. 'But they weren't there two days ago.'

'Is there another route to wherever we're going?' Crayton asks.

'No, this is the only path,' Commander Sharma says.

Suddenly, we hear the sound of helicopter blades, but I don't see them yet. They're hidden behind the tall trees. Of course, that means they can't see us, either, though it sounds like they aren't very far off anymore.

'We're sitting ducks if we stay here,' I say, my mind racing to figure out our next best move.

Crayton opens his door and steps out with a machine gun under his arm. 'Okay, this is it.' He points up and to our right. 'We either go up there and get behind a line of trees and fight, or we keep running straight up the mountain.'

I follow him out. 'I'm not running.'

'Neither am I,' says Marina, standing next to me.

'Then we fight,' says Commander Sharma. He points into the hills. 'Half of us set up on the left while the other half takes position on the right. I will take these two with me.' He indicates Ella and me.

Crayton and I look at each other and nod.

Ella turns to Crayton. 'You okay without me, Papa?'

Crayton smiles. 'Marina's legacy will make sure whatever they do to me won't last long. I think I'll be okay.'

'I'll keep an eye on him, Ella,' Marina adds.

'Are you sure we should do this, Commander?' the soldier asks. 'I can go to fetch Vishnu, bring him back to help.'

'No, Lord Vishnu should stay where he's safe.'

Crayton turns to Ella. 'Keep those glasses on. Maybe you can be our eyes up there in the trees. I'm still not sure how they work, but let's hope they'll help now.'

I hug Marina and whisper into her ear. 'Be confident in your abilities.'

'I should heal Commander Sharma before you go,' she says.

'No,' I whisper. 'I don't trust him yet and he's less dangerous to us if he's injured.'

'You sure?'

'For now.'

Marina nods. Crayton taps her arm and beckons her to join him and the young soldier. The three of them scramble up the left wall of the valley, disappearing behind a boulder.

Commander Sharma, Ella, and I move up the right side of the hills, carefully avoiding the bumps on the ground as we move. We find a position behind some massive boulders, and settle in to wait for the brigade to arrive.

I turn to Commander Sharma. I feel slightly guilty about not letting Marina heal him, but for all I know, he's set this up as an elaborate trap. 'How's your arm?' I whisper to him.

With a grunt, Commander Sharma lies down and sets the barrel of his gun on a flat rock. He looks up and winks. 'I only need the one.'

Out of the corner of my eye I can see a helicopter buzz overhead but it leaves almost immediately. Either Marina took care of it, or the pilot couldn't penetrate the thick canopy of the valley. I look through the trees, hoping to manipulate the clouds surrounding the peaks of the mountains, but the afternoon sun has burned them off. With no wind, and no clouds, there aren't any elements to control. I can turn invisible if I need to, but I prefer to keep that hidden from the commander for now.

'What do you see?' Ella asks.

'A whole lot of nothing,' I whisper. 'Commander, how far away is Number Eight?'

'You mean Vishnu? Not far. A half day's walk, maybe.'

I'm about to ask him to tell me where, exactly. We should know in case something happens to the commander and we need to move forward without him. But I'm distracted when a rusty pickup truck swings into the narrow valley at full speed with a man standing in the open bed. Even from a distance, I can see he's nervous as well as armed. He jerks his gun from side to side, frantically trying to be everywhere at once. As soon as our SUV comes into view, the pickup skids to a stop and the soldier in the back hops out. More vehicles appear and pull up behind the pickup. A soldier drops out of a red van and sets a rocket launcher onto his shoulder. I see an opportunity.

I nudge the commander with my foot. 'I'll be right back.'

I don't give him a chance to argue as I run quickly into the woods. When he can't see me any longer, I use my invisibility Legacy to disappear and sprint down into the valley. The soldier has our truck in his crosshairs, but before he can pull the trigger I rip the rocket launcher off his shoulder and slam one end into his belly. He doubles over and goes down with a scream. Hearing the commotion, the driver of the truck rushes over with a pistol in his hand. I point the rocket launcher at his face. The soldier takes a split second to decide if the free-floating launcher is about to do its thing, then turns and runs away with his arms above his head.

I aim at the now empty, rusty pickup and pull the trigger. The rocket flies out of my launcher and a wave of fire explodes under the pickup, blowing it thirty feet into the air. The burning truck lands hard, and bounces and rolls quickly forward, the momentum sending it into the back of our SUV with a crash. I watch it lurch forward, rolling slowly over the small mounds in the road that had stopped us from advancing. The next thirty seconds are filled with ear-splitting, rapid detonations, as soldiers fire blindly around them and the mounds in the road explode. Thousands of birds burst out from the trees all around us, their sounds quickly drowned out by the snap, crackle and pop of munitions doing their thing. I was right; they *were* land mines. And now our SUV is nothing more than a smoldering pile of metal.

Evidently, this was just the opening act. The main attraction — armored vehicles, small tanks, mobile missile units — is closing in on the mountain. There have to be a couple of thousand soldiers on foot. Five or six attack helicopters hover overhead. I hear a whirring and turn to see a missile launcher rising and rotating, going into operational mode. The tips of five white missiles turn up and towards the area where Marina and Crayton have taken cover. There's movement in the tree line, and the commander's young soldier runs down into the valley. He's unarmed and headed right for the missile launcher. At first I think he's going to sacrifice himself some-how to save my friends, but no one fires at him. He stops when he reaches the launcher and starts pointing higher up the side of the mountain, to where Crayton and Marina are hiding. The launcher rises another few feet and adjusts its aim.

He's a traitor, part of the group trying to kill us! The next thing I know, he is flying into the air, yanked upward by telekinesis. Marina must have realized the same thing. But it might be too late. He's already revealed her location.

I look towards the missile launcher and gather my strength so I can alter the flight of the missiles once they're fired. As I start to focus on it, another launcher whirs to life and aims its missiles directly at me. Though I'm invisible, the army knows a shoulder rocket was fired from where I'm standing. I only have the power to deal with one of them, and there's no time to run. I have a choice. Save Crayton and Marina or save myself.

The launcher pointed toward the mountain starts firing. The missiles come screaming out, heading straight for the hills. I get control of them and redirect them into the ground, where they explode, just as the second launcher fires. I turn and see their white tips moving towards me. I don't have time to do anything, but suddenly the missiles loop up and turn back towards the launcher that fired them and the brigade. They barrel into five different vehicles, all of which explode.

Marina. She saved my life. We are working together, just as we were meant to do, and the thought makes me feel more determined than before to get this pit stop over with and find Eight. I want to send a message to the remaining soldiers of the brigade so I stop using my invisibility Legacy and show myself. I focus and start to control the flames rising from where the missiles exploded with my telekinesis. I spread the fire down the road to engulf the rest of the brigade. One by one, the flames move down the row of vehicles and it's like exploding dominos. Message received. The remaining soldiers of the Lord's Resistance Front begin to retreat. For a second, I'm tempted to indulge in a little retribution. But that's cruel and unnecessary and exactly the kind of thing the Mogadorians would do. I know my fantasies of going medieval on their retreating asses are not going to help us now.

'That's right! Run! Because if you don't, that fire is just waiting to finish the job off!' When the last one disappears from view, I turn and start walking back towards the hills. I need to find my friends.

8

The smoke is thick but beginning to dissipate. From where I am on the floor, I can see dozens of legs and black boots. I raise my eyes and see almost as many rifles, all of them aimed at my head.

My eyes move from the heavy boots up to the gas masks, relieved to see they belong to humans and not Mogadorians. But what kind of humans have Mogadorian weapons? A gun barrel is pushed into the back of my skull. Normally, I'd use my telekinesis to rip it away and toss it a mile into the mountains, but the pain from the bracelet is too intense for me to be able to focus my energy on that. One of the men says something to me, but I can't concentrate enough to make out what he's saying.

I search for a focal point to help get me through the pain, and see Nine groaning on the carpet. From where I am, it looks as if he's having trouble breathing; it also looks like he can't move his arms and legs. I want to help him, and struggle to get up, but I'm kicked back down as soon as I start to move. I roll onto my back and immediately a long cylindrical tube is pressed into my left eye. There are hundreds of lights inside the tube, and I watch them swirl together to become one solid green beam. It's definitely a Mogadorian cannon, the same kind that paralyzed me outside our burning house in Florida. I focus my other eye past the side of the weapon and see a man in a khaki trench coat. He pulls back his gas mask to reveal a ring of white hair and a fat, crooked nose that looks like it's been broken more than once. I find myself looking forward to breaking it again.

'Don't move,' he growls at me, 'or I'll pull the trigger.'

I glance over at Nine, who seems to be recovering. He's sitting up, looking around, struggling to shake off his dazed expression. The man with the cannon pressed to my face looks over at him. 'What do you think you're doing?' he says.

Nine smiles up at him, clear eyed and calm. 'Trying to decide which one of you I'm going to kill first.'

'Shut him up!' a woman yells as she enters the house, also carrying a Mog cannon. Two men press their boots against Nine's shoulders and force him back to the floor. The woman motions at me, and someone takes me by the shoulders and pulls me onto my feet. Another man grabs my wrists to put me in handcuffs.

'Son of a bitch!' he cries as he touches my red bracelet. I may not know everything the bracelet does, but I like this part of it.

Once upright, I get my bearings. There are ten or twelve men in masks, all holding rifles. The man and woman who were speaking seem like they're in charge. I look for Bernie, but don't see him. Even so, I can hear him inside my head.

Just wait. Let's see what they want and what they know.

'What do you want with us?' I ask the man with the broken nose.

He laughs and looks over at the woman. 'What do we want, Special Agent Walker?'

'For starters, I want to know who your friend is over there,' she says, pointing the tube back at Nine.

'I don't know this kid,' Nine says. He blows his hair out of

66

his face and offers a smile. 'I just stopped by to sell him a vacuum cleaner. The place looked like a dump and I thought he could use it.'

The man circles over to Nine. 'Is that what you have in these fancy chests here? Vacuum cleaners?' He nods to one of the other officers and says, 'Let's have a look at these vacuum cleaners, shall we? I may be interested in one myself.'

'Be my guest.' Nine's smile is menacing. 'I'm having a sale. Two for the price of three.'

For a split second, Nine and I make eye contact. Then Nine sweeps his eyes over to the wall, where a moth is hovering near the ceiling. Bernie Kosar. I'm sure Nine also heard BK's orders to wait to see where this is going. I wonder if he'll be able to control himself. One of the soldiers slaps a pair of handcuffs on Nine, and he quickly sits up again. I can see the handcuffs around his wrists are already broken. He's only holding his hands together to keep up the charade.

Nine's just waiting for the right time to attack. I don't know if he ever intended to do as BK asked. I pull my arms apart behind me, quietly and easily breaking my own handcuffs. Whatever is about to happen, I'd better be ready.

A bunch of the men have surrounded Nine's Chest. One of them is slamming the butt of his rifle over and over on the lock holding it closed, but it doesn't have any effect. He smashes it a few more times anyway, clearly frustrated.

'How about this.' Special Agent Walker pulls out a revolver. She fires at the lock and the bullet ricochets around the room, barely missing another officer's leg.

The broken-nose man grabs Nine by the back of his neck, pulls him to his feet, then shoves him forward. Nine can't maintain the ruse of his handcuffs and braces his fall, landing on his hands and knees. Realizing Nine's hands are now unrestrained, the man yells over his shoulder, 'Somebody get me some more handcuffs! We've got a broken pair over here!'

His chin tucked into his chest, Nine's whole body vibrates with laughter. He pops his legs out and does a pushup. Then he does another one. An officer kicks his right hand out from underneath him, but Nine doesn't miss a beat. He does another pushup with just his left hand. The officer kicks at his left hand, but Nine is too fast to let that knock him over. His right hand is down in a flash and his one-handed pushup shows off his perfect form. Four officers jump on him, each one holding a leg or arm, but Nine just keeps on laughing. Suddenly, I find myself joining him. His bizarre sense of humor is infectious. Man, I have to give him props.

Special Agent Walker turns to me. I slowly pull my arms out from behind me, the broken handcuffs dangling from my wrists. I wiggle my fingers and casually place both hands behind my head and start whistling.

She narrows her eyes and arranges her face in the most intimidating glare she has. 'Do you know what happens to kids like you in prison?' she asks.

'They escape? Like I did last time?' My eyes are wide and innocent.

I hear Nine howling with laugher at my performance from under the pile of officers. I have to admit, Nine does bring a weird kind of fun to the proceedings. My smile breaks wide now. I know these men are just trying to do their jobs. They think they're keeping their country safe. Right now, though, I hate them. I hate them for slowing us down and I hate this woman's tough-guy act. I hate that they have Mog cannons. But most of all I hate them for working with Sarah to capture Sam and me last week. I wonder what they promised her to get her to turn me in. Did they play on her sympathies? Convince her she would save me, by letting them take us? Did they say she could visit me, while I paid the price for my so-called mistakes? I look over at Bernie Kosar, but I don't see the moth anymore. That's when a fat brown and white cockroach scurries up my leg and burrows into my jeans pocket.

Nine will go along with this for a while longer, BK tells me. *But I don't know how much longer. Find out everything you can, quickly.*

The lead guy claps his hands to get the attention of the other men. 'Okay! Let's get these guys out of here before our friends show up.'

'Who are your friends?' I ask him, though I'm already pretty sure that for some reason the U.S. government and the Mogadorians are working together. That's the only explanation for why they'd be using Mog weapons against us. 'Who don't you want to show up?'

'Shut up!' Special Agent Walker yells. She pulls out a cell phone and dials a number. 'We're bringing him in, plus another one,' she says into the phone. 'Two Chests. No, but we'll get them open. See you soon.'

'Who was that?' I ask. She ignores me as she puts her phone away.

'Hey, buddy, I thought you wanted to buy a vacuum,' Nine says to me. 'I really need this sale. My boss is going to kill me if I come home with a full box of Hoovers again.'

They pull Nine to his feet. He stretches his back and smiles, like a cat smug and full of mouse. 'It doesn't matter where

69

you take us, there's no prison that can hold us. If you knew who we are, you wouldn't waste your time with this crap.'

Agent Walker laughs. 'We know who you are, and if you were as smart or as tough as you think you are, we would never have found you in the first place.'

Officers pick up our Chests and walk out the front door. New handcuffs are slapped over our wrists. They use three pairs on Nine.

'You have *no* idea what we're capable of,' Nine says in a sickeningly sweet voice as they lead us through the front yard. 'If I wanted to, I could kill you all in a matter of seconds. You're damn lucky I'm being such a good boy. For now.'

9

We're at a gate. There is a narrow path beyond it and it goes straight up the mountain. Crayton asks me to cover the trail behind us while Six takes the lead with Commander Sharma. I wonder if his soldier's betrayal has had any effect on him. I wonder if he will question the loyalty of his troops when he returns to his command. I can't imagine asking him, not without somehow suggesting he should have known. Of course, maybe he should have.

I'm carrying the small tree branch from my Chest. I need to figure out what it does. The first time I'd held this – the first time I'd ever opened my Chest, back in Santa Teresa at the convent, when Adelina was still alive – I hadn't had time to figure out what it did. But I did remember that when I'd held it out the window, I'd felt some kind of magnetic force. Almost instinctively, I rub its smooth, pared surface with my thumb. After a while, I notice it has an effect on the trees we pass. I aim and concentrate on what I want from the trees, and soon I hear the creaking of their roots and the clattering of their branches. I turn and walk backwards up the path, asking the trees on the edges to keep us safe, and they bend and twist into each other, making it impossible for anyone to follow. I want so much to be of help, I want so much not to be a curse, and to put my Inheritance to use to help us, that every time a tree responds a huge wave of relief washes over me.

We walk mostly in silence. At one point, to break up the boredom of the hike, I tickle Six's face by lowering a branch right in front of her. She swats it away without breaking stride, too completely focused on what may lay ahead. As we walk I think about Six. About how fearless she was back with the soldiers. She's always so calm, cool and collected. She takes command and makes decisions as if it were the most natural thing for her to do. One day I'll be like her. I'm sure of it.

I wonder what Adelina would think of Six – and about me now. I wonder how much further along I'd be if she had trained me. I know all those years in the orphanage without guidance from her means I'm not where I should be. I'm not as strong and confident as Six. I'm not even as knowledgeable as Ella. I try to bury my resentment and focus on Adelina's final act of honor. She charged at the Mog fearlessly, armed with just a kitchen knife. I try to stop the memory before I get to the part where she dies. I almost never do. If only I'd had the courage to fight alongside her, or knew then how to use my telekinesis to unwrap the Mogadorian's hand from Adelina's neck. If I had, she might be walking with us right now.

'We rest here,' the commander says, his voice breaking through my reverie. He points to a couple of flat boulders bathed in the afternoon sun. Just beyond the rocks I can see a small stream of fresh water. 'Not long, however. We need to make a lot more progress up this mountain before nightfall.' He looks up at the midafternoon sky.

'Why? What happens at nightfall?' Six asks.

'Very strange things. Things you are not yet ready to see.' Commander Sharma takes off his shoes and socks, rolls up the cuffs of his pants in a fussy sort of way and wades into the stream.

Crayton removes his shoes and socks too, and follows him. 'You know, Commander, we're already taking a pretty big leap of faith just following you up this mountain. The least you could do is answer our questions when we have them. We have a very important mission. And we deserve your respect.'

'I do respect you, sir,' he says. 'But I follow Vishnu's orders.'

Crayton shakes his head in frustration and walks further upstream. I notice Ella has wandered away and is sitting alone on one of the boulders by the stream. She's been wearing the dark glasses from my Chest the entire hike, and she takes this moment to clean them carefully on her shirt. Seeing my gaze on her, she holds them out to me. 'I'm sorry, Marina. I don't know why I hung on to them. It's just that –'

'It's okay, Ella. They helped you see that attack before any of us could. We may not know their full power, but you seem to be doing just fine with them.'

'I guess so. I wonder if there's anything more I can get them to do.'

'What *have* you seen as we've been walking?' Six asks.

'Trees, trees and more trees,' Ella says. 'I keep waiting for something to happen, or to see something unusual. I wish I knew for sure this meant there is nothing for me *to* see.' I can tell she is frustrated with herself, not the glasses.

With the small branch in my hand, I bend a large tree over to create shade on the boulders. 'Well, keep trying.'

Ella holds the dark glasses up to the light. As she turns

them over it's almost as though I can read her thoughts, thanking me for making her feel like she's part of the team, doing some good.

I look over at Six, who has stretched out on the ground. 'What about you, Six?' I ask. 'You want to check out anything in my Chest?'

She stands, yawns and looks up the path. 'I'm okay, I think. Maybe later.'

'Sure,' I say. I walk down to the stream and splash water on my face and on the back of my neck. Just as I'm about to take a drink, Commander Sharma wades out of the stream and says it's time to go. We all get ready to continue up the mountain. I grab my Chest and balance its weight on my hip.

Immediately, the trail becomes much steeper. It's also surprisingly slick and absent of rocks, as if this path had been recently washed clear by a storm. We're all having difficulty keeping our footing. Crayton tries running to gain some momentum, but he slips and falls in the dirt.

'This is impossible,' he says, standing up and brushing himself off. 'We're going to need to cut through the forest to gain any kind of traction.'

'Out of the question,' the commander says, his arms out like a tightrope walker. 'We will not conquer our obstacles by running away from them. Speed does not matter, just that we do not stop.'

'It doesn't matter how slowly we go? This message brought to you from the guy who says *very strange* things happen at nightfall,' Six snorts. 'I think you need to tell us how much further we have to go, and if it's longer than three hours on foot, then I say we enter the forest and forgo these obstacles,' she says, staring him down.

I look at the small branch in my hand and an idea comes to me. I concentrate on the trees around us, lowering branches in from both sides. Suddenly we have a way to pull ourselves upwards, rope climbing the Lorien way. 'How about this?' I ask.

Six grabs the line of branches and tests their strength, moving up a few feet. Over her shoulder, she yells, 'Brilliant move, Marina! You rock!'

I continue to bend the trees as we climb. Still wearing the dark glasses, Ella watches the woods around us, occasionally glancing over her shoulder. Once the path levels out and it's easier to maintain our footing, Six digs in and starts to run up the trail ahead of us, circling back regularly to report on what she's seen ahead. Every time it's the same: 'It just keeps going.' Finally, she returns to say there's a fork up ahead. Hearing this, Commander Sharma looks confused and picks up the pace.

When we reach the fork in the dirt path, Commander Sharma frowns. 'This is new.'

'How can it be new?' Crayton asks. 'Both paths look exactly the same. Well traveled and equally so.'

The commander paces in front of the fork. 'I promise you the path on the left did not exist before. We are very close to Vishnu. We go this way.' He begins to walk confidently up the path to the right and Crayton follows.

'Wait,' Ella says, 'I see nothing up ahead on the right. The glasses are just showing me dark emptiness.'

'That's all I need to hear,' Six says.

'No. We go right,' the commander says to Six. 'I've traveled this many times, my dear.' Six pauses, then slowly turns to look at him.

'Do *not* call me dear,' Six warns.

As Commander Sharma and Six glare at each other my eyes are drawn to something scratched in the mouth of the path on the left. The figure is shallow and just a few inches long, and I have to look closely, but there is no question. It's the number eight.

'According to *this*, Ella's right. We go left,' I say, pointing at the number.

Six walks over to the markings and drags the toe of her shoe under the number eight. 'Good eye, Marina.' Crayton looks at it too, and smiles.

We fall back into our normal positions, with Six and a reluctant Commander Sharma up front and me taking up the rear. The path ascends slightly, turning rocky. Then, to everyone's surprise, a steady stream of water begins to flow from ahead of us, down the trail. The rocks under our feet soon become tiny islands. I jump from one rock to another, but in a few minutes the rocks are submerged. All of a sudden, we're walking through a river.

Ella is the first one to speak. 'Maybe the glasses were wrong? Maybe this path wasn't the right one after all.'

'No. This is correct,' the commander says, bending down to drag the tips of his fingers along the surface of the water. 'This is a sign I've seen before.' We have no idea what this cryptic comment means but we've gone this far, so we might as well keep going.

The river current becomes faster and it's harder to move against it. We trudge higher up the path until the water is to Ella's waist and I'm having trouble keeping my balance. But just as quickly as it began, the water slows and the land levels out and opens into a large pool of water. A jagged wall of stone stands high behind the pool, and four separate waterfalls descend from its top, crashing into the water.

'What's that?' Ella points.

In the middle of the giant pool, a white boulder juts out of the surface. A gleaming blue statue of a crowned man with four arms rests atop the boulder.

'The Almighty Lord Vishnu,' Commander Sharma whispers.

'Wait. That's supposed to be Eight? A statue?' Six says, turning to Crayton.

'What's he holding?' Ella asks. I follow her gaze and see that there's an object in each of his four hands: a pink flower, a white shell, a gold wand, and on the tip of one of his index fingers, a small blue disc that looks like a CD.

The commander wades further into the pool. He's smiling and his hands are shaking. He turns to us. 'Vishnu is the Supreme God. In his left hands, he holds a conch shell to show he has the power to create and maintain the universe, and under that is a mace to signify his power to destroy materialistic and demoniac tendencies. In his right hands are the chakra, to show he has a purified spiritual mind, below that there is the beautiful lotus flower.'

'Which shows divine perfection and purity,' Crayton adds.

'Among other things, yes! That is right, Mr Crayton. Very good.'

I stare at the statue, at its serene blue face and gold crown and the objects in its hands, and I feel myself forgetting about everything else. About the battle at the base of the mountain and the carnage back in Spain. About

Adelina and John Smith and Héctor. I forget about my Chest and Lorien and the fact that I'm standing in cold water. The energy flowing through me is magnificent. And judging by the peaceful looks on the faces of the others, the energy is contagious. I find myself closing my eyes and feeling blessed to be here.

'Hey! He's gone!' Ella yells. My eyes snap open to see her whipping off the dark glasses. 'Vishnu's gone!'

She's right – the white boulder in the middle of the lake is empty. I look at Six and Crayton and see they're on high alert, ready for danger. I glance around us. What is this, a trap?

'He will now test you,' Commander Sharma says, interrupting my thoughts. He's the only one among us who doesn't look shocked by Vishnu's disappearance. 'That is why I have brought you here.'

We all see it at the same time. Something is blocking the sun on top of the jagged wall above the pool, and a long, oddly shaped shadow is cast along the water. A figure walks slowly along the ridge until it stands directly above the farthest of the four waterfalls on the left.

'Commander?' I ask. 'Who is *that*?'

'*That* is your first test,' the commander says, stepping onto the grassy shore around the lake. We all follow, without taking our eyes off the figure.

A second later it dives gracefully off the cliff. I notice its legs are strangely short and it has a wide, circular torso. It falls slowly, almost floating, as if it can control gravity. When it breaks the surface of the pool, there is no splash. Not even a ripple. Six reaches up and squeezes the large blue pendant that hangs around her neck. Ella takes a few steps back, away from the lake.

78

'This could be a trap,' Crayton says quietly, voicing my fear. 'Prepare to fight.'

Six lets the pendant drop from her hands and rubs her palms together. I set my Chest down and begin to mimick her movements, but I feel ridiculous and glance around as surreptitiously as I can to see if anyone noticed. Good thing they are otherwise occupied. Fact is, Six knows how to fight, has trained for this her entire life. Everything she does has a purpose. I'm just rubbing my hands together. I slowly lower my hands back to my side.

'He'll test you one at a time,' says the commander. Six snorts.

'You don't make the rules. Not for us,' Six says. She turns to Crayton, who nods.

'Commander, this is not what we came here to do,' Crayton adds. 'We came here to find our friend, not to be tested or to fight.'

Commander Sharma ignores him, walks into a patch of short grass and sits. I never would have taken him for a guy who could pretzel himself into the lotus position. 'It must be one at a time,' he says serenely.

The being – or whatever it is – that dived into the lake is still underwater. And I'm the only one with the Legacy to meet it down there. I know what I have to do. Still, I'm surprised to hear the words come out of my mouth. 'I'll go first.'

I look over at Six. She nods at me and I dive into the lake. The cool water becomes darker the deeper I swim. My eyes are open, and at first I can only see a few inches of murky water in front of me. But my eyes soon adjust and my vision penetrates far into the lake, my ability to see

79

in the dark coming in handy. I allow the water to enter my lungs, and a familiar calm sweeps over me. I start breathing normally, letting my Legacy take over.

I reach the muddy bottom and spin around, looking in every direction for the thing that dived from the cliff. Something moves over my right shoulder, and I turn to see a figure coming at me. He's wearing a golden crown over his short, jet-black hair. His eyebrows are perfect semicircles, and his nose is pierced with a gold ring. He is strangely beautiful. I can't take my eyes off him.

I stand perfectly still, waiting to see what he wants. He comes closer. When he gets within a few feet of me and I can see him more clearly, my jaw drops. What I thought was a strangely circular torso is, in fact, the body of a turtle. I'm mesmerized, watching to see what he will do next. So much so, I'm taken by surprise when he lunges towards me and hits me with his two right arms.

I go spiraling backwards, the force propelling me with a speed that stuns me. But I'm not in motion for long. My feet quickly find the muddy bottom and I twist around in a panic, trying to find him in the darkness, my senses on alert and on guard. Something taps my shoulder and I turn to see the blue turtle man. Damn, he moves fast. He winks at me, then swings both of his left arms, but this time I'm ready for him. I raise my forearm and knee in time to block them. Then I plant the bottom of my foot squarely on his chest and kick as hard as I can. I flip over and come at him from the back, wrapping my arms around his neck, and look around for something, anything, I can use as a weapon. I see a large rock sticking out of the mud in front of us, and I use my telekinesis to send it at this alien turtle, using all of my strength to pull it through the water. He sees the rock coming and when it's within inches of hitting him, he just disappears. Poof. The rock smashes me instead and I fall back in the mud.

I lie there dazed, waiting for him to appear again, but he doesn't come. Eventually, I decide to float to the top.

The first thing I see as I break the surface is Six, standing at the edge of the water, looking for me. 'What happened?' she calls.

'She passed.' Commander Sharma nods.

'You okay?' Ella shouts. 'I couldn't see anything through the glasses.'

'I'm good,' I yell back. And I really am.

'What do you mean, she passed?' Crayton demands of the commander. 'That was one of his tests?'

The commander just smiles serenely and ignores Crayton.

'Okay, who's next?' Treading water, my eyes follow the commander's finger high over my head. I turn to see a shadowy figure up on the jagged wall again. This time he's a giant bearded man with an axe in his hand.

Six wades into the water up to her knees as I climb out, wringing water out of my long, dark hair. She is all steely determination and confidence when she says, 'Me.'

The figure walks to the third waterfall and dives. This time he makes a massive splash when he hits the pool. We can see the ripple on the surface of the water as he moves towards Six under water. Then the tip of his axe comes out of the lake, followed by his giant head. Six doesn't flinch, doesn't change expression at all, even when he's fully emerged and stands at least four feet taller than her in the shallow water at the edge of the lake.

With a grunt and a howl, the giant swings the axe. Six leaps out of the way but before he can pull back, she kicks at the wooden handle, breaking it in half.

'Way to go, Six!' Ella yells.

The giant swings a fist at her, which she easily avoids with a bob and a weave. With the next beat, she lands a quick kick to his kneecap. As the giant bends over and howls in pain, Six grabs the end of the broken axe handle as it floats by and swings it at his head. The being disappears before it hits him.

'What the hell was that?' Six asks, whipping her head around wildly, on the alert for any kind of reappearance.

Commander Sharma smiles placidly. This guy is really starting to make me angry. 'That was another test, which you passed. There is one more.'

Before anyone can speak, we hear a roar. I reel back with horror at the creature I see emerging from the water. It's over ten feet tall and has the head of a lion and the body of a man. It has five muscular arms flexed at each of its sides. The creature shakes the water from its mane as it steps onto the shore and marches towards Ella, unleashing a second roar.

'Oh. My. God,' Ella says, mouth open and eyes wide.

'No,' Crayton says, stepping in front of Ella. 'You're not ready for this – it's too much.'

Ella rests a hand on Crayton's arm. A small smile breaks across Ella's face and she seems to transform from a scared kid into a Garde prepared to fight. 'It's okay. I can do this.'

Six comes to my side. We're both ready to fight if Ella needs us. The creature moves towards her; she slides my glasses back onto her face. Then, it attacks.

The creature swings all ten arms at Ella, but she ducks and avoids each one. It's as if Ella sees every punch before it happens. The tree behind her ends up taking the beating. Large chunks of wood fly around her, hitting the creature's face, bouncing off its chest. Not running away but not fighting back either, Ella circles the tree trunk, continuing to dodge the ten fists. The tree is getting pummeled.

Suddenly, Ella screams. 'Oh no! What have I done?'

Before I can figure out what Ella means, there's a loud *crack* and the heavy tree trunk tips forward. It's about to crush the creature when the figure disappears just like all the others. As the tree continues its fall to the ground, a branch swipes the dark glasses off Ella's face and they are crushed by a huge tree branch. 'Marina, I'm so sorry! I knew the glasses were going to be broken, but I couldn't do anything to stop it.'

Crayton, Six, and I run over to Ella, who's staring in horror at the fragments of the glasses by her feet. 'Ella! Don't worry about the glasses. You held your own and that thing disappeared. What's important is that you're okay. I'm so proud of you,' I tell her.

'Ella, that was amazing!' says Six.

'Congratulations,' the commander says, still sitting calmly, Buddha-like. 'You have just defeated three of Vishnu's avatars. You've passed his test. The first was Kurma, a half man, half tortoise who churned the ancient ocean so that other peaceful gods could regain immortality. The man with the axe was Parashurama, the first warrior saint. The last was one of the most powerful incarnations of Vishnu, the man-lion, Narismha. Now, we await Vishnu's arrival.'

'We're done waiting,' says Crayton, turning to the

commander, jaw set and fists clenched by his side. 'He'd better show himself and fast.'

'Chill, chill, chill,' a boy's voice says, emerging from the high grass behind me. 'The commander was just following my orders. I was being cautious.'

From the grass we now see the statue of Vishnu step towards us, alive and smiling.

'I've been waiting a long time to meet you.'

IO

Sitting on a metal chair, I'm in a Plexiglas cage in the back of a small truck. My hands are cuffed to the chair and my ankles are secured with heavy shackles. A strap of leather pulls my forehead back against the Plexiglas wall behind me. I'm facing the side of the truck, but can turn my head just enough to see Nine, also in a Plexiglas cage, a few feet away from mine. In front of me a guard is watching us. I know I could free myself in an instant, but BK, who's still hiding in my pocket, is right. We need to see what they know and how it could help us. Nine must agree because he is even more capable of breaking the binds that hold him, but he, too, does nothing. There are a bunch of locks on our cages and the only way we can talk through the thick Plexiglas is through the eight tiny holes in the cage doors. The truck's engine is running, but we haven't moved an inch.

Special Agent Walker is sitting on a long metal bench near the front of the truck. She has one foot on my Chest, and the other on Nine's. A Mogadorian cannon lies across her lap. The man with the crooked nose is sitting next to her with the other cannon. Walker is whispering into a cell phone. Every so often she glances over at us. I can almost hear what she's saying, catching words like *boyfriend* and *powerless*. I remember Nine saying back in the mountain that he can hear for miles. I hope he's picking up more than I am.

'Hey, John!' Nine yells.

The guard turns towards Nine's cage and aims a rifle at Nine's head. 'You! Shut up!'

Nine ignores him. 'Johnny! When do you want to roll on out of here? I don't know about you, but I'm bored, I could use a change of scenery.' He does enjoy pissing people off. I'm beginning to understand the appeal.

Special Agent Walker closes her phone and pinches the bridge of her nose with her fingers. She looks like an aggravated parent or teacher, her exhaustion wiping away a lot of her authority. Then she takes a deep breath and sits up straight, as if she's made a decision. She knocks on the window, indicating the driver should start moving.

She stands and marches towards us, balancing herself with the cannon over her head. She comes to a stop in front of me. There's something in her eyes that wasn't there before. It's almost as if she's sorry she caught us. Or she's sorry about what she has to do next. Or both.

'How did you find us?' I ask.

'You know how,' she says.

I still have the bracelet around my wrist. It's been quiet for the last few minutes, but as soon as the agent speaks, it begins to buzz again.

Nine shouts, 'Hey, I wasn't kidding about being bored here. I don't feel like playing nice anymore. It's up to you, but you should know that you don't have long before I decide to amuse myself. You can tell us everything you know right now, or I'll kick my way out of here and make you tell me. Guess which one will make my day a little more fun?'

The man with the crooked nose rises slowly from the bench and aims his cannon directly at Nine. 'Who do you think you are, kid? You're in no position to threaten us.'

86

'Whatever you're planning, I promise, I've been through worse,' Nine says.

'I know exactly where you were before. Don't you get that? We *know*.' The man sounds annoyed by Nine's bravado.

'Agent Purdy,' Walker says to him. 'Lower your weapon. Now.'

The agent starts to lower it and I decide to have some fun. I guess Nine is rubbing off on me. Using my telekinesis, I rip the cannon out of his hands and toss it to the back of the truck. It hits the back door before landing on the floor with a clang. Just at that moment we take a sharp corner and Agent Purdy stumbles towards me, his right shoulder slamming against my cage. I use my telekinesis to keep him pinned in place.

'Son of a . . .'

'Don't you know you should always wear a seat belt, Agent Pretty?' Nine laughs. 'Safety first! Here, take one of mine. You just need to come on in here to get it.'

Agent Purdy says, 'However you're doing this, you better stop it.' He tries to sound scary, but it's hard to sound threatening in his position.

I lean forward, easily breaking the strap across my forehead. Play time is over. 'Agent Purdy, do you know where Sam Goode is?'

'We have Sam,' Special Agent Walker says, turning towards me. Her voice is casual but her cannon is pointing right at me.

For a second, I'm so blown away by this new piece of information, my mind goes blank, and I accidentally release Agent Purdy. He crashes into the aisle.

They have Sam? Setrákus Ra isn't torturing him in the

cave like I saw in my vision? He's okay? I'm about to ask where Sam is when I notice the lights swirling in the tube of Special Agent Walker's cannon. Instead of green, these lights are black and red.

She grins at the alarmed look on my face. 'If you're lucky, *John Smith*, or whatever your name is, we'll show you a video of how we use our interrogation techniques on Sam. But if you're *really* lucky, we'll show you some footage of that little blonde girlfriend of yours. What's her name again?'

'Oooooohhhh, shit,' Nine says. I can hear the grin in his voice as he knows what is about to go down. 'Now you've gone and done it.'

It takes me a second to find my voice. 'Sarah,' I whisper. 'I know she's working with you. What did you have to tell her to turn her against me?'

Agent Purdy grabs his cannon and settles back into his seat. 'Are you kidding me? That girl wouldn't tell us a thing, and, believe me, we asked *many* things in *many* different ways. She had nothing to say to *us*. She's *in love*.'

Once again, I'm stunned. I was so sure Sarah was working with the government to bring me in. When I saw her last week in Paradise, she acted so strange. She met me in the park, but then started getting mysterious text messages – at two in the morning. Seconds later we were surrounded by agents and being slammed to the ground. I can't think of anything else that explains it. It had to have been those text messages; they must have been from the police. How else could they have known that Sam and I were there? Damn. Now I don't know what to think. *And* she's still in love with me?

'Where is she?' I demand.

'Far, far away,' Special Agent Walker says. Is she taunting me?

'Who cares, dude?' Nine yells, interrupting. 'Big picture, Johnny, big picture! She's not in it! Neither is Sam!'

I ignore him. Now that I know the U.S. government has Sam *and* Sarah, I'm determined to find them both. I'm thinking of my next move, my next question, when I feel Bernie Kosar crawling out of my jeans pocket.

It's almost time to go, he says. *We'll take the woman to lead us to Sam and Sarah.*

'Nine,' I say. 'You ready to get out of here?'

'God, yes. Been ready forever. I really have to pee.'

Special Agent Walker glances from me to Nine and back again. She doesn't know where to point the cannon, so she moves it back and forth between us. Agent Purdy stands again and does the same. The guard in the back of the truck points his rifle at us.

'If they move, shoot anything but a vital organ!' Agent Purdy says, moving to stand shoulder to shoulder with Special Agent Walker.

Bernie Kosar jumps from my lap and crawls up the glass door. He flitters his tiny cockroach wings at me and he says to count to five.

'Hey, Nine?' I ask.

'I'm already on three, my man,' he says.

Walker shouts at us to shut up. My bracelet vibrates and sends a thousand pinpricks up and down my wrist but I ignore it. Nine breaks all of his restraints as if they were nothing, and stands up. I do the same, though it takes more effort for me. Nine kicks the Plexiglas wall at the front of his cage and the whole thing pops easily out of its frame. As he steps out, the guard fires at him. With a smile he just raises his hand and stops bullets in midair. He lowers his hand, and the bullets fall to the floor one at a time.

He looks over at me, 'Need some help there, buddy?' He kicks in a wall of my cage, and I step out. BK scrambles back into my pocket.

Before the guard can do anything, I use my telekinesis to launch him to the ceiling and twist his weapon into a useless piece of metal. Agent Walker and Purdy both fire their Mog cannons at us, but Nine stops the streams that come out of them. He smiles, and shakes his finger at the two agents. 'No, no, no. You should know better by now.' He looks over at me. 'Get ready, Johnny, 'cause we are going for a spin!'

The truck immediately flies off the road and starts rolling. Without warning, Nine grabs me and links arms, pulling me along until I gain my footing. We run up the left side of the truck, moving like a hamster in a wheel so we can stay horizontal as the truck flips over and over. Metal crunches around us, sparks rain from every corner and the guard and agents look like rag dolls as they're tossed in all directions. The force of the crash causes the back doors to pop open and when the truck stops rolling, we jump out. There were a number of police vehicles trailing us and they've all come to a screeching halt with their sirens blaring.

'Hey, John?' Nine says, unfazed by any of it.

'Yeah?' I say, shaking my head as I try to lose the dizzy feeling from the spinning truck. Neither of us is taking our eyes off the blinking crowd of police cars.

He starts to step back towards the truck and I do the same. 'We gotta get our Chests back, dude, and do what BK said and get that woman agent.'

'Definitely.' I pat my pocket, making sure BK is still there.

'So why don't you take care of that, while I take care of this.' Nine telekinetically lifts two police cruisers off the ground, and the officers inside struggle to get out.

I dash back to the truck, now smoldering in the ditch. I jump inside, avoiding the guard and Agent Purdy, moaning on the floor, and find our Chests. Special Agent Walker sits against what remains of the metal bench, staring at the blood on her hands in a daze. Her red hair falls loosely down her shoulders, and there's a long scrape along the side of her face. The Mog cannon is now a shattered pile of parts under her legs. She watches me arrange the Chests under my arms, and I drop to a knee in front of her.

'You're coming with us.' I am not asking.

She opens her mouth to speak, and a trail of blood trickles out. It's then that I see the piece of metal sticking out of her shoulder. I put down one of the Chests and try picking her up, but she groans and coughs up more blood. I let go, afraid if I move her again she'll bleed out and die before I can find out where Sarah and Sam are.

'Where are they?' I ask. 'Tell me now! You are going to die any second, lady, and I'm trying to save Earth and my friends. Now, tell me! Where are Sam and Sarah?'

Special Agent Walker's head flops in my direction and her green eyes open wide, as if seeing me for the first time. The gunfire outside is getting closer. 'You . . . you're an alien,' she finally whispers.

I punch the side of the truck in frustration. 'Yeah, I am! But I'm here to help, if you would just let me! Now, before you run out of time, out of breath, tell me where they are. In Washington?'

Her breathing turns ragged and it's as if she can't see or hear me. I'm losing her. I'm losing her and I still don't know where Sarah and Sam are. My voice sounds small all of a sudden. 'Just tell me where they are. Please.' Our eyes meet and I can tell I've gotten through to her.

Special Agent Walker's mouth opens to speak and it takes a couple of tries to find her voice. 'Out west. In . . .,' then her voice trails off and her eyes close. Her bloody hands clench and then relax; her whole body goes slack.

'Wait! Hold on!' I frantically grab at my Chest, trying to get it open so I can get my healing stone. All I can think is, if I heal her she'll tell me where they are. I've just placed my hand on the lock of the Chest when a group of officers jump into the open end of the truck, guns drawn.

'Get away from the agent! Move! Or we'll shoot! Down on the ground! Hands behind your back! Now!' They are barking orders at me, but I can't obey. I don't want to obey. I need to get the healing stone. I need to hear what she was going to say. I reach to open the Chest and I hear the officers scream-ing, 'Hands up. HANDS UP. HANDS UP!' I reach into my Chest anyway.

I hear the first gunshot, immediately followed by dozens more. As the hail of bullets fly around me, my wrist starts to tingle more strongly than ever. It doesn't hurt anymore, and the bracelet starts to expand, covering my entire arm with a sheath of red material before spreading and popping open like an umbrella. I have no idea what is going on and I really don't care. I can only think of my healing stone and the limp body of Walker so close and yet so useless. Suddenly, I'm behind a six-foot-high shield that curls up over my head and under my feet. The bullets bounce right off it.

An orchestra of gunfire erupts, and countless bullets ricochet off my shield. After a couple of minutes, they become
less and less frequent, like microwave popcorn that's almost
done. When the gunshots finally stop, the red material com-
presses itself back into the arm sheath, and then shrinks
into the tingling bracelet around my wrist, all of its own vol-
ition. I look down, amazed at how effective it is, how perfect
its timing is.

Walker is still lying unconscious by my feet. The officers
with their guns trained on the back of the truck just a moment
ago are gone, but I hear gunfire outside. I'm torn between
looking for my healing stone to revive Walker and going outside to see if Nine needs help. I want to wake her up, force
her to tell me where Sam and Sarah are, but I can't leave
Nine alone if he's in trouble. I decide that Walker will keep –
she's clearly not going anywhere and I just have to hope she
doesn't die on me. I take the opportunity to stuff a Chest
under each arm and run out. As soon as I emerge I see the
officers running in the opposite direction. I don't know what
Nine did while I was in there getting to know my bracelet a
little better, but they all look terrified.

'Ah, Nine?' I call over. 'What exactly did you do to them?'

He smiles. 'Just used my telekinesis to lift them all about
thirty feet in the air. Then I offered them a choice: go higher or
run away. I applaud the wisdom of their decision, don't you?'

'Looks like they made the right choice,' I say.

'Hey, I thought we were bringing the agent woman with us,'
Nine says.

'She's still inside – she's unconscious and I was going to
use my healing stone on her, but I wanted to check on you
first, make sure you were okay,' I tell him.

'Dude, you were worried about *me*? I *got* this. We need her to tell us where we're going! You're the one who refuses to go anywhere that isn't towards your friends. Remember?' Nine picks up an assault rifle and shoots it into the air. 'Get in there and get her! I'll be out here, playing with the soldier toys.'

Officers continue to retreat on foot, some hiding behind trees on the side of the road. Nine aims the gun above their heads. The rifle rocks against his shoulder and the bullets zip through the high branches. I can hear him cackling, enjoying the spectacle, as I move back to the truck.

I open my Chest and pull out my healing stone and duck into the truck to see how badly Walker is injured.

But she's not there. I look around, as if she might have gotten up and moved to a different part of the truck. I'm completely confused by what I'm seeing. What I am *not* seeing. There is no one there. The bodies that were there minutes ago are all gone. Shit.

I'm furious with myself. I can't believe how badly I've screwed this up. Not only do we still not know where they have Sam and Sarah, but it is likely that Purdy and Walker are still out there.

I I

Number Eight is sitting in the grass. The lake is calm and still behind him. 'I am known by many different names. Some call me Vishnu, while others call me Paramatma or Parameshwara. I am also known by my ten avatars, three of whom you have met and battled. Quite successfully, I might add.'

'If they are your avatars, they are a part of you. Which means, *you* felt it necessary to declare war on three girls who were trying to reach you.' Crayton spits out. 'You're supposed to be impersonating a peaceful god, aren't you?'

'You have a lot of explaining to do,' Marina adds.

He is unmoved by our anger and remains seated. 'I had to be sure you are who you claim to be. I had to be sure you were ready to meet me. My apologies if your feelings, or anything else, were hurt. You all proved yourselves, if that makes you feel any better.'

I'm fed up. I'm tired and hungry. Not to mention I flew across the world *and* fought an army to get here. I want answers. I stand up, fists clenched at my sides. 'I'm going to ask a question, and if you don't answer me directly, we're leaving. This isn't a philosophical discussion; and you had no right to test us. Are you, or are you not, Number Eight?'

He looks up at me and purses his lips. His skin

color changes from blue to a deep copper tone. When he shakes his head, the crown falls off and his black hair grows into a shaggy mop of curls. Two of his arms vanish, and in a matter of seconds, a shirtless teenage guy sits on the grass in front of us. Commander Sharma gasps.

He's kind of thin, but toned. With his full lips and thick black eyebrows, I must say, he's kind of hot. Around his neck hangs a blue Lorien pendant.

He's one of us.

Ella looks over at Crayton, who exhales a long breath. He opens his mouth, about to say something, but the boy speaks first.

'My Cêpan originally named me Joseph, but I have gone by many names. In this region, most people know me by the name Naveen.' He pauses and looks at me, then pulls up the ragged leg of his pants to reveal the scarred Loric symbols of One, Two and Three on his ankle. 'If you want to get all Loric on me, then yes, you can call me Number Eight.'

The anger bubbling inside of me pops and disappears. We have found another member of the Garde. We just got stronger.

Crayton steps forward and offers his hand. 'We've been looking for you, Eight. We've traveled a long distance. I'm Crayton, Ella's Cêpan.'

Eight stands and shakes Crayton's hand. He's tall, and every muscle in his upper body and stomach is *very* well defined. He's clearly been training for years, surviving alone in the mountains.

Ella stands as well. 'I'm Ella,' she says. 'I'm Number Ten.'

'Whoa!' Eight says. He looks into her eyes. 'What do you mean, you're Number Ten? There're only nine of us. Who told you you're Number Ten?'

All of a sudden, Ella shrinks down to become a six-year-old girl. I guess there's nothing quite like having your identity being questioned by a former statue to give you a crisis of confidence. Crayton nudges Ella, and then, just as quickly, she transforms back into her tall, twelve-year-old self.

Eight responds by growing five feet taller to tower over her. 'That all you got, Ten?'

Determination covers Ella's face and it looks as if she's trying to grow another few years, but nothing happens. After a few seconds, she shrugs, 'I guess so.'

Crayton turns to Eight. 'I'll fill you in later, but there was another ship that left Lorien after yours. Ella and I were on that ship. She was just a baby at the time.'

'Is that it, or is there a Number Thirty-Two I should know about?' Eight asks, shrinking back down to his regular height. His voice is husky, but also kind. For the first time, I notice his eyes are the most amazing shade of deep green. By the look on Marina's face, she is noticing all of this too. I can't help but smile as she nervously tucks her hair behind her ears.

'Ella's the last,' Crayton answers. 'This is Six, and this is Marina, Number Seven. You appear to be able to shape shift. Anything else we should know about?' Crayton asks.

In response, Eight expands into a two-headed giraffe, towering twenty feet above us this time. I try to suppress my smile.

'Indeed I do have that Legacy,' the head on the left says.

The head on the right lowers to the water and takes a drink before looking up and adding, 'Among other things.'

'Oh, yeah? Like what?' Marina asks.

Eight turns back into a boy and skips along the surface of the pool as if it were solid ice. When he circles back to us, he begins to sprint before skidding to a stop, sending a wave of water towards Marina.

But Marina is not going to get shown up by the new guy. Without flinching, she lifts her hands and stops the water midair, then pushes it back at Eight with her telekinesis. He in turn blows the wave high into the air like a geyser. Not to be left out of whatever game it is they're playing, I take control of the wind and I use it to push the geyser across the pool until a wall of moving water surrounds Eight on three sides.

'What else ya got?' I shout, my voice daring him to keep things going.

Eight disappears from where I've trapped him behind the water and an instant later reappears on the jagged rocks above the pool. He disappears again and shows up inches from my nose.

Eight's sudden closeness is so jarring I reflexively throw a fist into his ribs. He grunts and stumbles backwards.

'Six! What are you doing?' Marina yells.

'Sorry,' I say. 'It was a reflex.'

'I deserved it,' says Eight, shrugging off Marina's protectiveness.

'So you can teleport?' Marina asks. 'That is *very* cool.'

He suddenly appears at her side and casually leans an arm on her shoulder. 'I'm a fan of it.' Marina giggles and shrugs him off. *Giggles? Is she kidding me?*

Eight smiles, disappears and shows up again standing on Crayton's shoulders, balancing with exaggerated arm circles and wobbly legs. 'Sometimes I pick stupid places to land, though.' Eight is our jester, all of a sudden.

I'm struck by his playfulness, unsure if it's going to be an attribute or a liability. I decide to view it as a positive. I can just see the annoyance and confusion on the Mogadorians' faces moments before this kid turns them to ash. Crayton leans forward and, as if they'd rehearsed the routine in advance, Eight does a flip onto the ground, then claps his hands, obviously pleased with himself.

'Where's your Cêpan?' Marina asks.

Eight's cheerful face turns serious. We all know what this means. Instantly, my mind goes to an image of Katarina gagged and chained to a wall. I think of John and his Cêpan, Henri. I shake away the memories before tears form in my eyes.

99

'How long ago?' Crayton gently asks the question we are all thinking.

Eight spins to look out over the field of high grass beyond us. With his mind, he parts the grass left and right until there's a narrow path. He raises his head at the setting sun. 'Listen, we have to get out of here. The light is going. I'll tell you all about Reynolds and Lola on the way.'

Commander Sharma runs up to Eight and grabs his wrist. 'What about me? What can I do for you? Please tell me.' He startles me. I've been so wrapped up in our little session of getting-to-know-you, and he's been so quiet, I completely forgot his role in all this.

'Commander,' Eight says. 'You have been a loyal friend to me and I want to thank you and your soldiers for all your hard work. Vishnu would be very happy with your devotion. I'm afraid now we must part ways.'

It's clear by the expression on the commander's face that he thought he was in this for the long haul.

'But I don't understand. I have done everything you have asked of me. I brought you your friends. My men have died for you.'

Eight looks Commander Sharma in the eyes. 'I never wished for anyone to die for me. That's why I refused to leave the mountain and walk with you in the streets. I'm sorry lives were lost, more sorry than you will ever know. Believe me, I know what it feels like to lose people. But, this is where we must go our separate ways.' He's firm, but I can see it's hard for him to do this.

'But –'

Eight cuts him off. 'Good-bye, Commander.'

The man turns, a look of despair on his face. Poor guy. But he is a soldier who knows when to take an order, when to accept how things are going to be. 'You're leaving me.'

'No,' Eight says. '*You* are leaving *me*. You are off to something bigger and better. A wise man once told me that only by leaving someone good can you meet someone better. You will be with your Vishnu, and you will only know him once I am gone.'

It's hard to watch. Commander Sharma opens his mouth to say something, but closes it when Eight turns and walks down the path without looking back. At first, I think Eight is being too harsh. Then I realize, this is the kindest way he can do what must be done.

'Hey! Wait!' Crayton calls after Eight. 'The base of the mountain is the other way. We have to get to the airport.'

'First, I need to show you all something,' he calls back. 'And we may not need an airport.'

'Where are you going? There are things you don't know yet. We need to sit down and talk, we need to make a plan!' says Crayton.

'I wish I didn't break those glasses,' Ella says. 'We can't just *follow* him without knowing where he's taking us or if it's a good idea. He thinks he knows everything, but he may *not*.'

We watch Crayton think about what to do. I know what *I* think we should do. We've finally found another member of the Garde, and we have to stick together now. I nod towards Eight's quickly disappearing figure. Crayton looks at me, then nods back. He scoops up Marina's Chest, and begins to walk after Eight. Without saying anything, Marina and Ella hold hands and start to follow him. I get in line behind them. I use my advanced hearing to listen for sounds of the commander moving from the spot where we left him. I hear nothing. I can picture him standing there, still and silent long after we've left. I understand why it had to be done, but I still feel sorry for the guy. Left behind, after all his loyalty. I look at Eight's back, ramrod straight ahead of me, and I feel bad for both of them.

Eight leads on. We follow him down a hill and find ourselves in a wide-open valley. Everywhere I look there are snow-tipped Himalayan Mountains. Closer by, there are patches of forest with fields of yellow and purple flowers in between. It's beautiful. We're all soaking it in as we walk when Crayton breaks the silence.

'So. Who were Reynolds and Lola?'

Eight slows so we can walk together. He reaches down to pick a handful of purple flowers only to crush them in his hand. 'Reynolds was my Cêpan. He laughed a lot. He was always laughing. He laughed when we were on the run and when we slept under a bridge or hid in someone's leaky barn in a monsoon.' He turns to look at us each in turn. 'Does anyone remember him?'

We all shake our heads, even Crayton. I wish I could. But I was only two years old when we made the journey.

Eight continues. 'He was a great Loric and an even better friend. But Lola ... Lola was a human he fell in love with when we first got here. That was eight years ago. They met at the market, and from that moment on they were inseparable. Reynolds was so in love. Lola moved in with us very quickly. She barely left our house.' Eight kicks a patch of flowers. 'I should have *known* she couldn't be trusted by the way she looked at me, how she always wanted to know where I was, what I was doing. I wouldn't let her near my Chest, no matter how many ways she tried. But Reynolds trusted her so much, he eventually told her who we were. He told her *everything.*'

'Not smart,' I say. John told Sarah, and look at where that got them. Trusting humans with our secret is too risky. Love only makes it more risky.

'I can't even describe how angry I was. When I realized what he had done, I lost it. He and I fought for days. We had never argued before. I trusted him completely, and it wasn't that I suddenly didn't trust *him*. It was *her*. That was when Lola started pushing us to come into the mountains with her to hike and camp. She said she knew the perfect place. She convinced Reynolds it would help him make peace with me, for us to *bond*. I thought Lola's plan to get Reynolds and me to kiss and make up was unlikely, but I went anyway.' He stops walking long enough to point at a mountain peak due north. 'We went to that mountain right there. I brought along my Chest. By that point I could teleport and I had telekinesis, plus my strength was off the charts – and I needed to train and figured the mountain air would help me get stronger, faster. But as soon as we arrived, Lola kept trying to separate us. She did everything to get Reynolds to leave me alone. In the end, she had to make do with Plan B.' He turns away and resumes walking. We give him a few steps to pull himself together.

'So what was Plan B?' Marina asks gently, trying to move him along. He needs to tell us all of this, but we don't have to torture him.

'On the third night in the mountains, she left to gather firewood, leaving me and Reynolds alone for the first time the whole trip. I knew something was wrong. I felt it in the pit of my stomach. Lola returned quickly – with a dozen Mogadorian warriors. Reynolds, he was so in love with her, he was heartbroken before he remembered to be scared. He screamed at her, begging her to explain why she would do this to him, to us, to me. Then one of the warriors threw a bag of gold coins in Lola's general direction. She was promised a lot of money by the Mogadorians to provide a *service*.' Eight sneers the word. 'Like a dog jumping on a treat, she dived at it. It all happened so fast. She dived, one of the Mogadorians raised a glowing sword and stabbed her in the back, and the bag of coins exploded at her feet. Reynolds and I just stood there, frozen, watching her die.'

I resist the urge to dash ahead, grab his hand, and squeeze it to show how much I understand how he feels. I look at his straight, proud back, watch the purpose in his long strides, and know what he needs right now is his space. At least, that's what I want when I think about Katarina dying.

His last word, *die*, hangs in the air. Finally, Crayton clears his throat and says, 'We don't need to hear any more right now. You can stop if you want.'

'They couldn't kill me,' Eight's voice gets louder, as if he's trying to drown out the sad memories. I know the trick. It rarely works. 'Even when they managed a direct hit with one of their swords, across my neck or into my stomach, I didn't die. But they did. The deadly cuts meant for me happened to them instead. They couldn't kill me because of the charm, and I did everything I could to protect Reynolds. But we were separated in all the chaos and I teleported too late. Reynolds was . . .' He pauses for a second. 'One of them took my Chest. I tried to stop him. I grabbed one of their swords and I tried to stab him through his stomach, but I missed by *this much*. Pretty sure I took off his hand, though. Anyway, he got away. Right after he ran into the woods, I saw a tiny silver ship shoot up through the trees. I killed the others.' His voice is so cold, so emotionless, I shiver.

'I lost my Cêpan too,' Marina says quietly after a moment.

'Me too,' I add. I glance over at Ella, who has moved closer to Crayton. At least she still has him. Hopefully we won't lose the last Cêpan that any of us knows.

The sky above us grows darker by the second. Marina volunteers to walk in front so that she can lead the way with her Legacy of night vision. I smile when she takes Eight's hand, happy that someone tries to comfort him.

'I've spent so much time in these mountains,' Eight says.

'All alone?' Ella asks.

'I was alone for some of it. I didn't know where to go. And then one day I came across an old man. He was sitting under a tree with his eyes closed, praying. My Legacy to become other shapes had arrived months earlier, and I approached him in the form of a small, black rabbit. He felt my approach. He laughed before he even opened his eyes. There was something about his face that I trusted. I guess he reminded me of Reynolds, before Lola came into our lives. So I hopped into the bushes and teleported behind a line of trees in the opposite direction. When I approached him again, in my regular form, he offered me some lettuce. It was clear that he knew me, would always know me, no matter what form I took.'

'We're coming to another lake,' Marina says, interrupting Eight. Now that the talking has stopped,

I can hear the lapping of water and a quiet water-fall beyond.

'Yes, we're close,' Eight confirms. 'We'll eat and sleep soon.'

'So, then what happened? With the old man?' Crayton asks.

'His name was Devdan and he was a very enlightened, spiritual person. He told me all about Hinduism and Vishnu. I clung to his stories. In my mind, they represented how we're trying to save Lorien. He taught me ancient forms of Indian martial arts, like kalarippayattu, silambam and gatka. I worked with my Legacies, my powers, to see how far I could take what I learned from him.

'One day, I went to meet him in our usual spot and he wasn't there. I went back day after day. But he never returned and I was alone again. It was many months later when I stumbled upon Commander Sharma and his army during a training exercise.' He hesitates before continuing. 'Unfortunately – or fortunately, I'm not sure yet – it was while I was in the shape of Vishnu and they vowed to protect me from any evils. I knew it was because I was in a form they worshipped, and I hated preying on their beliefs, but I couldn't resist. I guess I hated being alone even more.'

Marina starts to lead us around the lake. Eight tells her to head for the waterfall we can hear in the distance.

'Did the Mogs ever come back?' Crayton asks.

'Yes. They still return in the tiny silver ships

every so often, buzzing around the mountains to see if I'm still here. But I just turn into a fly or an ant and they keep going.'

Crayton says, 'That lines up with all of the reports of UFO sightings in this region.'

'Yes, that's them,' Eight says. 'With every visit, they become more careless about detection. I haven't seen one in a few days, but they've been much more frequent in the last six or eight months. I took this to mean the conflict was escalating.'

'It is,' I say. 'We've been finding each other, joining up. Marina, Ella, and I just met up in Spain a few days ago. Number Four is waiting for us back in America. And now we've found you. That just leaves Five and Nine.'

Eight is silent for a moment. 'I want to thank you for traveling all this way for me. It's been so long since I've had anyone to talk to. To talk about my real life.'

The waterfall is now just feet away. 'Now what?' I have to yell to be heard over the noise of the water.

'We climb!' Eight yells back, motioning to a sheer, stone wall in front of us.

I place my hand on the stone's smooth surface and tap my foot around to find a toehold. My foot immediately slips, and when I'm about to try it again, I hear Eight's voice far away, above me. He is already at the top, yelling something down at us. Teleportation is even better than I thought. It may even be better than invisibility. I wonder if we can combine them somehow.

'Just use your telekinesis to float your way up,' Marina says to me. 'You get Ella. I'll get Crayton.'

I follow her advice and we float up. It's actually much easier than I imagined. Up at the top is Eight's campsite. Soon we're sitting around a fire, cooking a vegetable stew in a large pot. The trees overhead form a thick canopy and, with the water below, it's a perfect spot to hide. Eight's mud hut is somehow both depressing and ideal at the same time. The walls are uneven and the door is a lopsided oval; but it's also warm and dry, and it smells of fresh flowers. Inside is a homemade hammock and a small table, and three colorful rugs hanging from the walls.

'Nice place you've got here,' I say, walking back to the fire. 'I've been on the run so long, I forget what it's like to have a home. Even a hut.'

'There is something about this place. There will always be a piece of me that remains here. I'm really going to miss it,' he says, looking around fondly.

'So, does that mean you'll come with us?' Marina asks.

'Of course I will. The time has come for us to be together, to work together. Now that Setrákus Ra is here, I have to go with you.'

'He's here?' Crayton asks, suddenly uneasy.

Eight takes his first bite of stew. 'He arrived a few days ago. He's been visiting me in my dreams.'

12

We jumped a freight train in West Virginia. I've been trying to sleep, but too many thoughts are swirling around in my mind. I squint as my eyes adjust to the morning sun coming through the slatted door. I'm relieved to see we're still headed west. That's all Special Agent Walker said before disappearing: west. So, that's where we're going. I try not to think about the possibility that she may have deliberately misled us, and instead focus on how she thought she was about to die and had nothing left to lose, and therefore no reason to lie to me.

I roll onto my back. The ceiling of the train car is dirty, stained a variety of colors. I stare at a dark blue spot directly above my head for so long, I finally drift off to sleep. I dream, which I often do. But this one is different, more of a nightmare than a vision.

I'm in West Virginia, back in the prison cell. Only this time, it is empty and brightly lit from above. The spherical cage that held Sam is now empty. The only indication he was ever there is a pool of still-wet blood on the floor. I walk into the middle of the cell, look around frantically and try to scream his name, but as soon as I open my mouth the bright lights from above are sucked into my throat, stealing my breath, choking me. I fall to my hands and knees, trying to get some air.

Still gasping, I look up. Now I am in a large arena, with thousands of Mogadorians going wild in the stands. They chant and throw things down at me while fights break out among them. The floor is a shiny black slab of rock. I rise from all fours shakily. When I take one step forward, the ground behind me falls away, leaving only a black abyss. Above me is a giant hole and through this hole I see a group of clouds moving across a blue sky. It takes me a moment to realize where I am – inside the peak of a mountain.

'Four!' It's Nine's voice. Nine! I'm not alone. I look around and try to yell back, but my throat is still clogged. A beam of light escapes my mouth. Instinctively, I twist around and try to aim the light until it finally lands on Nine. He's on the other side of the arena, but something is blocking my view of him. It's Sam. He's hanging between us, his wrists in shackles. Agent Purdy and Special Agent Walker stand below him, their Mogadorian cannons aimed at Sam's chest. I don't hesitate. I run to my best friend, the rock falling away behind me with every step I take. The roar of the crowd escalates until it's absolutely deafening.

When I've almost reached them, the black rock where the agents stand drops away, and they fall with it.

'Help! Help me, please, help me,' Sam yells, his body twisting, trying to break free from the shackles.

I try using my telekinesis to free him, but it doesn't work. I try to use my Lumen, but my palms remain dark. My Legacies are failing me.

'Bring the rest, John,' Sam says to me. 'Bring them all.'

His voice sounds strange, like it's not his. It's almost like someone – or something – evil is speaking through him.

Suddenly the tan, thin boy who appeared in my last vision is next to me. Once again, he's transparent, like a ghost. When I see he's wearing a Loric pendant around his neck, I reach out for him. But he shakes his head at me and places a finger to his lips. The boy leaps onto Sam and climbs up his legs and body until he can get his hands around the chains. I watch him strain, trying to pull apart the shackles, and I can see the surprise on his face when he realizes he doesn't have the strength to do it.

In my last vision, he asked me what number I was, and I feel an enormous pull to speak to him. I cough, clear my throat, and I know my voice has finally returned. I yell, 'I am Number Four!' just as the arena falls silent.

'Have you made your decision?' Sam asks. He continues to twist and turn in his shackles, the other boy still struggling to break his chains above him. Sam looks right at me and I can see his eyes are a deep maroon color. This is not Sam, I tell myself.

All at once, Sam's body begins shaking so violently that the other boy loses his grip on him and I can only watch in horror as he falls and disappears into the same chasm that swallowed the agents. A purple glow then surrounds Sam, and the chains break of their own accord. Instead of falling, like the boy, like the agents, Sam floats, suspended in midair. A spotlight snaps on and I watch, disbelievingly, as Sam grows and transforms – into Setrákus Ra. The three Loric pendants around Setrákus Ra's neck glow brightly, as does the purple scar circling his throat. 'Do you want the human back?' he bellows.

'I will take him back!' I yell at him, furious. I'm rooted to the spot, nothing but abyss around me, nowhere to step on to get closer to him.

Setrákus floats slowly to the ground. He lands and the rocks show no sign of giving way as they have for the rest of us. 'This is your surrender? Fine. I shall accept your pendant now.'

I look down and my pendant is already gone. I look up again to see it hanging from Setrákus Ra's giant fist. His cracked lips open to reveal a sharp, crooked-toothed grin.

'No! I will not surrender!' The moment I say it, I feel a sudden weight around my neck. My pendant is back.

The other boy leaps from the chasm into which he fell and lands near Setrákus Ra, his head held high. The boy joins my cry, 'I will never surrender to you! Let Devdan go, and fight me!'

'Time is running out,' Setrákus Ra says and I now realize he is speaking to both of us — that he has been the whole time. He was trying to get both of us to surrender. Did he think he could convince us both to sacrifice ourselves in the belief that he would allow the others to live? I can only hope none of the others fall for his tricks.

The blue stain on the ceiling of the train car is suddenly all I see, and I sit up abruptly, trying to shake off the dream that has left my brain fuzzy. I touch the bracelet around my wrist. Before I drifted off into my vision, my nightmare, I had discovered that by concentrating on the bracelet's abilities, I was able to remove it. But the moment it left my wrist, I felt unsafe without it and hurriedly popped it back on. I touch it again and wonder if my reliance on it is a good or a bad thing. All of a sudden, something small bumps against my back and I jump up and spin around.

Clearly I'm on edge from my dream. It's just Bernie Kosar, this time as a beagle, my favorite incarnation of him.

'Another nightmare?' Nine yawns from the corner. He sits on his Chest, absentmindedly carving symbols into the wall with a nail, the very picture of someone who is *not* on edge. The soles of his bare feet are black.

114

'They're getting really strange,' I say, and I hope I don't sound as shaken as I feel. Last thing I need is Nine seeing me as some kid, scared by bad dreams. 'And I think others are having them at the same time.'

Nine lifts the nail to examine it more closely. He tilts his head, as if it's a rare specimen and not the most ordinary object in the world. With his tongue sticking out of the corner of his mouth he looks as if he is concentrating all of his energies on this one nail. With a small smile, he bends it between his fingers, snapping it into two perfectly equal pieces. He turns to face me. 'And what does that mean? You think they are all having visions of some kind? Or, they are having the same action-packed nights you are?'

I shrug. 'I don't know. I keep seeing this really skinny kid with curly black hair. He's wearing one of our pendants, so I have to assume he's one of us. We are aware of one another, but things in the dream seem to be tailored for him in some ways and to me in others. I see *you* in these visions too.'

Nine frowns, then opens his Chest and digs around inside. I'm hoping he is going to pull out something that will help me decipher my visions, help me figure out what, if anything, I'm supposed to do with them. 'I'd like to try to contact the others with the red stone, but I guess the government has it tapped somehow. Which is total bullshit.' He sits back looking frustrated.

I walk across the empty car to where he's sitting. He has a yellow cube in his hand that I've never seen before. 'What do you think it means, if the government has your stone tapped? How do you think it happened? I mean, it must have been the Mogs, but how did they convince the government to work with them?'

Nine looks at me incredulously. 'Are you serious? Who cares why they're working together or what the Mogs had to say to get them on their side? The point is, they *are* working together. The U.S. government and the Mogadorians have teamed up! For them, it is official: *we* are the bad guys!'

'But the Mogs will destroy Earth – or worse – once they get rid of us. Doesn't the government know this? Isn't it obvious that we're the *good* guys?'

'Apparently not. Who knows how it happened? Maybe they're just using one another, both trying to double cross the other. Whatever it is, the government *has* to be underestimating the Mogs. If they weren't, they'd be scared out of their freaking minds.' Nine places the yellow cube in his mouth. A look of satisfaction appears on his face.

'What is that?' I ask.

'Sustenance,' he says, his voice garbled. 'It's a food substitute. You suck on it and it fills you up for a little bit. Take a look. You might have one too.'

I unlock my Chest and poke around for a yellow cube. My hands pass over the white tablet we found in Malcolm Goode's hidden office in the well, and I take a second to press its buttons. Still dead. I push it aside. I don't find a yellow cube, but there's a blue one. I hold it out for him to see. 'Do you think this does the same thing?'

He shrugs. 'Dunno. Won't know till you try. Go for it.'

I hesitate for a few seconds, then place it on my tongue, and my mouth is immediately flooded with ice-cold water. I am only able to drink a little before some goes down the wrong way, causing me to cough the stone onto the floor. Nine spits his yellow stone into his hand and offers it to me, but I pass.

'You have to eat sometime,' he says.

Bernie Kosar walks over to Nine and opens his mouth. 'Sure, BK,' Nine says obligingly, placing the yellow cube on the dog's tongue.

'At least we're headed west, where Sam and Sarah are. I'm sick of running and hiding, running and hiding. First things first, we find them.'

'Yeah, well, speak for yourself. I've been locked up and tortured for the past year, man. Being in motion, in control of where I am and when I'm going there, is something I do not plan to give up anytime soon. Just relax, Johnny. I have an idea and you need to remember the plan. We're not wasting time finding your human friends. We contact the others and meet up, and when we're ready, we face Setrákus Ra. In that order.'

I turn and punch a hole in the side of the train car, and the impact causes the wheels on one side to momentarily lose their grip on the tracks below. I'm angry and I feel like I'm spiraling out of control. 'How exactly are we going to meet up with them when our only means of communication might be being monitored? I say we head for California, or whatever government facility is out west, and we demand they give up Sarah, or we'll start blowing stuff up! Or, we threaten to tell the media that the government is working with a bunch of evil aliens. We'll see how that goes over.'

Nine laughs, shaking his head. 'Um, no. That's not going to happen.'

'Well, shit, then I don't know what to suggest. What if we go back to Paradise to see if maybe Sarah's there. If I can just see that she's safe, I promise I'll drop it. We have to be close to Ohio by now, don't we?'

Nine walks over to the hole I've created in the wall and peeks out. His voice is quiet when he speaks. 'It all looks the same to me, man. You know, Earth has *nothing* on Lorien. Sure, Earth looks pretty nice in some places, but Lorien was beautiful everywhere. It was the most beautiful planet in all the galaxies. You've seen how it used to be in your visions, right?' I'm surprised with how impassioned he's suddenly become. Talking about Lorien his face is as happy and relaxed as I've ever seen it. For the first time I see a homesick kid. But it's fleeting. He quickly rearranges his face into its usual mask of snark and dismissal.

'We are *not* going to Ohio to see if another one of your *humans* is all cozy and safe. This is *not* our home, Four. These humans are not our brothers and sisters. Everything we do here on Earth is for our *real* home, for our *real* brothers and sisters; for the Elders who sacrificed their lives to put us on that ship.'

Nine steps back, swings, and punches another hole in the wall of the car, right next to mine. Unlike mine, his punch is so hard and so fast that the wheels underneath us don't shift. Nine sticks his head through the hole and he breathes deeply, his black hair blowing and flapping in the wind, then pulls his head back inside. He clenches his fists and turns to look at me. 'If you don't have Lorien in your heart, then you should say so right now. I won't run around with a traitor. Our *only* goal is doing everything we can to be at full strength so we can defeat Setrákus Ra and his army. That's it. Got it?'

I decide to remain silent. My feelings for Sam and Sarah will never subside. I know this. But Nine is right about what comes first. We are of help to no one if we do not increase our strength, and that only happens if we can find the others.

I need to concentrate on Lorien. When we defeat Setrákus Ra, Sam and Sarah – along with everyone else on Earth – will be okay. I nod.

Nine sits down and closes his eyes, hands clenching his knees so tightly his knuckles are white. 'We just passed a sign I recognize. We're a couple of hundred miles away from the safe house my Cêpan set up. We can go there, order a pizza, maybe watch a little TV. You can sit around and sigh and think sad thoughts about your poor, lost Sarah. I will go out, find some hot chick to make out with for an hour or so, *then* we'll figure out how to communicate with the rest in some other way.'

BK drops the yellow cube out of his mouth and looks up at me. He doesn't even have to ask. I place my blue cube on his tongue and he closes his mouth and sighs happily.

I look over at Nine. He is so sure of himself, so confident. 'And how are we going to do that? The macrocosms are tapped! We have no other way to communicate with them!'

'No, this is perfect,' Nine says, getting excited. 'Wait until you see my place, Four. It's totally badass. Whatever we want, we'll have. Whatever we need, we'll get. We'll rest and train, we'll be in the most amazing shape, ready for whatever comes at us. And we will figure out a way to get in contact with the rest of the Garde.'

13

I lie awake for hours, sitting and watching the fire outside the hut. Inside, Ella sleeps on the hammock; Six and Crayton snore under blankets on the floor. After a while, the fire goes from a raging and crackling blaze to glowing embers. I watch the smoke waft through the air, drifting to hang around beneath the canopy of trees. Eventually, the fire dies out entirely.

I just can't sleep. For so many years, I was alone with my envy and anger, trapped in that orphanage. Now, finally, I can let it go. Now I believe there's nothing we can't do with all of us together. So I don't know why I still feel this pit in my stomach whenever I get a moment to think. I know what the pit is, too; I feel lonely. But I'm not alone, I keep telling myself.

I look over at Eight, sleeping as close as he can to the fire for warmth. In the early morning light, all curled up, he looks small. He sleeps restlessly, under a thin blanket of twisted vines. I watch him toss and turn, running his hands through his already messy hair. I stoke the coals to create as much heat as possible and the crackle is enough to make him stir. I don't know why, but I feel protective of him. At the same time, I think about his muscular arms and I want him to protect me. Must be something about opposites attracting. He is playful and I am, well, not.

Crayton's forehead is creased with worry when he finally

gets up and wakes the others. We all try to shake off the sleep cobwebs as quickly as possible. I know Crayton is wondering how he's going to get us all on a plane.

My thoughts turn to Eight's vision of Setrákus. He poses the greatest threat of all, even more than a bunch of well-armed Mogs. I know Crayton doesn't think we're ready to face Setrákus. We haven't developed our Legacies, we haven't had a chance to learn how to fight together, and we must find Four, Five and Nine before we face a threat like Setrákus Ra. When I said as much last night, Eight shook his head, frustrated by all the skepticism. 'I know we could take him, together,' he said. 'I've seen him in my dreams and felt his power. I know what he's capable of; but I also know what *we* are capable of, and it is far greater than anything he could *ever* be. I believe in us. But it won't happen if we aren't all convinced.'

'I agree, we do need to bring down Setrákus Ra. But first we need to find the others. The chances of beating him are far better if you are all together,' Crayton had argued. I could hear the worry in his words.

Eight stood firm, clearly believing we're enough to take him. 'My dreams have guided me to you all. And they tell me we can do this; we can't run away, even if it is to find the others.'

Now Eight stands and stretches, revealing a bit of his stomach as his shirt lifts. He leans down and picks up a walking stick and twirls it in his hands. I can't take my eyes off him. It's such a new and unusual feeling for me and makes me feel shy and excited at the same time. 'So where do you want to go?' he asks, looking around at all of us.

'East coast, United States,' Six says. She kicks the bottom of his walking stick as it swings by and it flips up and into her hand. These two are quite the comedy duo. Six throws the stick back to him and he makes a big show of diving and missing it on purpose. Their play looks a lot like flirting. I have to admit, it makes me jealous. Even if I wanted to, I could never be this way with Eight, with anyone. This is just how Six is, easy. No wonder they're having so much fun.

'Okay, if that's where you want to go, we have a couple options. A plane? Do we have enough money to buy tickets for all of us?'

Crayton pats his shirt pocket, nodding. 'That shouldn't be a problem.'

'Great. We head back to New Delhi, buy some tickets, and we can be in the United States in a day or so. *Or*, we could be in the state of New Mexico in just a few short hours.'

'We can't *all* teleport,' Six points out, drawing in the dirt with her toe.

'Maybe we can,' Eight says, a sly smile on his face. Six has drawn a circle and Eight reaches his foot over to add two eyes, a nose and a big smiley face. They grin at each other. 'We just need to take a short walk, then it's a simple matter of a giant leap of faith.' He is clearly enjoying keeping us in the dark; I see the others nodding at him, so caught up in his confidence they forget to ask for any details. I don't want to be the one to point out we have no idea what he has in mind.

'Sounds a lot faster than a plane,' Ella says. 'And a whole lot cooler.'

'You've got my attention,' Crayton says, hefting my

Chest up onto his shoulder. 'You need to show us what you're talking about, the quicker, the better. If Setrákus Ra is already here on Earth, we've got to move fast.'

Eight holds up a finger, telling Crayton to be patient. Then, he pulls off his shirt and pants. Wow. 'Not before my morning swim,' he says.

Eight sprints to the edge of the cliff where the waterfall drops off. Without pausing, he dives with his hands out at the side. Like a bird, he seems to float, riding the waves of air. I rush to the edge of the cliff and look over the side, just in time to see him change shape and enter the water as a red swordfish, and then surface as himself. I suddenly get the urge to jump in too, and I follow him.

The water is startlingly cool when I dive in, but when I come up for air I can feel my face is flushed. What is going on with me? I'm not usually this impulsive.

'Nice dive,' Eight says, swimming over and treading water close to me. He shakes his head and his black, glistening curls whip around his head. 'So, do you prefer being called Marina or Seven?'

'I don't care. Whatever,' I say, feeling shy.

'I like Marina,' he says, speaking decisively for both of us. 'Is this your first time in India, Marina?'

'Yes. I was in Spain for a long time. In an orphanage.'

'An orphanage, huh? At least you had lots of kids around you; you could make friends. Not like me.'

I can see how lonely he's been. I decide not to correct him and tell him how all the other girls hated me and I had no friends until Ella showed up. I just shrug. 'I guess. I'm happier now.'

'You know what? I like you, Marina,' he says. It sounds

like he is rolling my name around in his mouth, savoring it. 'You're quiet, but cool. You remind me of –'

Suddenly, there's a huge splash right between Eight and me. The waves rock us away from each other and I watch Six emerge, her wet blond hair falling perfectly down her back. She doesn't say a word then dives back under the water, pulling Eight with her. I dive too, and watch them wrestle underwater until Eight, laughing, begs for mercy and Six lets him go.

'Damn, you're strong,' he says as he breaks the surface, coughing.

'And don't you forget it,' she says, grinning. 'Now, can we please get out of here?'

The sight of Six and Eight all tangled up makes me jealous, but this is not the time for it. I duck my head under water to give myself a minute to pull myself together. I let the water enter my lungs and I sink and sink, until my toes touch the muddy and rocky floor. I sit down in the mush and try to collect my thoughts. I'm angry at myself for feeling so vulnerable. This is a crush! Nothing more. And do I *really* care if Eight prefers Six's perfect, blond hair to my mop? I mean, *she* isn't a threat to me. We have to work as a team, trust each other. I don't want to be angry with Six, especially after everything she has done for me. For a minute I pace around the bottom, hoping to come up with something witty to say when I surface. *I can do this.*

I realize I'm directly under the spot where the waterfall enters the pool, where the water is clear and sparkling. The glint off something catches my eye. It's a long silver object stuck in the muddy floor.

I go to take a closer look. It's maybe fifteen feet long

and, when I circle it, I'm stunned to realize it's some sort of cockpit behind a long windshield. That's when I see a Chest, just sitting there on the seat inside. I can't believe it – is it possible that this is the silver ship that Eight saw fly away the day that the Mogs attacked, the day that his Cêpan was killed? I hear a muffled cry and realize it's mine. I grab a handle on the fuselage, and pull. It doesn't budge. The pressure at the bottom of the lake is so strong, but I keep pulling and soon the cockpit door swings open. A rush of water mixes with water that was trapped inside. The Chest is slimy when I grab it and race for the surface.

The first thing I see is Six and Eight, sitting in the grass and talking. Ella is twirling Eight's walking stick over her head, then out in front of her. Crayton is watching Ella, his chin cupped in his hands. Ella sees me coming out of the water and spikes the stick into the grass.

'Marina!' she calls.

'Hey, there you are! Where'd you go?' Eight yells, coming over to the edge.

'Come on out, Marina,' Six calls. 'We really have to boogie now!'

I lift the Chest up and out of the water, holding it aloft so they can all see it. I don't even care the most revolting, mucky water is pouring off it and onto my head. I'm grinning so wide, my face hurts. I love the looks on their faces, mouths agape and eyes wide. I'm enjoying it so much I use my telekinesis to float the Chest over to Eight and Six and leave it there, in midair.

'Look what I found, Eight!'

Eight disappears from the grass and reappears up in the air next to the Chest. He wraps his arms around it and hugs it. Slime and all. Then he teleports back to the edge of the lake, the Chest still in his hands. 'I can't believe it,' Eight finally says. 'All this time, it was right here.' He looks stunned.

'It was inside a Mog ship at the bottom of the lake,' I say, walking out of the water.

Eight disappears again and teleports directly in front of me, our noses practically touching. Before I can register how nice his warm breath feels on my face, he picks me up and kisses me hard on the mouth as he twirls me around. My body stiffens and I suddenly have no idea what to do with my hands. I don't know what to do at all, so I just let it happen. He tastes salty and sweet at the same time. The whole world disappears and I feel as if I'm floating in darkness.

When he sets me down, I pull back and look into his eyes. One glance and I know this huge, romantic moment was a spontaneous and grateful gesture for him. No more, no less. I'm an idiot. I really need to let this crush go.

'I never swim over here. From the start, I always dived off on the other side there,' Eight says. 'Stuck in the same area.' He shakes his head. 'Thank you, Marina.'

'Um, you're welcome,' I whisper, still dazed by the first part of his thank-you.

'Now that you've hugged it hello, don't you want to open it?' Crayton asks. 'Come on, already!'

'Oh! Right, of course!' Eight yells, and he teleports back to the Chest.

Six walks towards me. 'Marina! That was so awesome!' She hugs me, then pulls away to shake me by the shoulders, smiling at me meaningfully. In a low voice, she whispers, 'And am I seeing things, or did you just get kissed?'

'Kind of weird, right?' I whisper, watching her for any signs of jealousy. 'But I don't think it means anything.'

'Not weird at all. I think it's kind of *great*,' she says, clearly thrilled for me, like a friend, or a sister. I'm ashamed of myself, for feeling jealous of her earlier. We both look over at Eight as Ella begins to make a drumroll noise to announce the Chest's opening.

Eight has his palms on the lock. Almost immediately, it shakes and the Chest falls open. He quickly dives in elbow-deep, trying to touch everything all at once. He's like a kid in a toy chest; he's so excited. We all crowd around and watch. I can see some of the stones look like mine, but other items are completely different. There's a glass ring, a curved antler, a black piece of cloth that shimmers blue and red when Eight touches it. He grabs a thin piece of gold the length of a pencil and holds it up. 'Ahh, good to see *you* again.'

'What is that?' Six asks.

'I don't know its real name, but I call it "the Duplicator."' Eight holds it above his head, like a wand. Then he snaps his wrist and it expands out, and down, like a scroll. Soon, it's the size a doorframe. He lets go and the frame hovers in front of him. Eight steps behind and we can see the occasional pair of hands and feet when he starts doing jumping jacks.

'Okay,' Six says. 'That is the weirdest thing I've ever seen.'

Eight teleports to her side and stands there, head cocked to the side as he scratches his chin, like he's judging a show.

Our heads snap back to the golden doorframe. The hands and feet are continuing their steady pace. Wait. There are *two* of him now! The one standing next to Six claps, opens his palm, and the piece of gold contracts and zips back into his hand. Immediately, the second Eight disappears.

'Impressive,' Crayton says, clapping his hands slowly and loudly. '*That* will come in very handy sometime soon. At the very least, you will make an excellent distraction.'

'I used it to sneak out of our house a few times,' Eight admits. 'Reynolds never figured out what I could do. Even before he died, I was *always* trying to figure out how to do the most with my Legacies.'

Crayton throws Eight's clothes to him, and picks up my Chest. 'Now, we *really* need to get going.'

'Aw, come on,' Eight says, pulling on his pants. As he hops about, he bats his eyes at Crayton and says in a wheedling voice, 'I just got my Chest back. Can't I get reacquainted with it? I've missed it so much.'

'Later,' Crayton says curtly. When he turns towards us, though, I can see he is smiling.

Eight drops the piece of gold inside the Chest and pulls out a green crystal, stuffing it into his pocket. He closes the Chest and picks it up with a dramatic sigh. In his most pathetic voice he says, 'Oh, all right. Our reunion will just have to wait. Follow me, everybody.'

'How often has Setrákus visited you in your dreams?' Crayton asks. We've been walking more than five hours and we're making slow progress up the mountain. Eight is leading us up a winding path that is more ledge than road. There's a thin blanket of snow everywhere, and the wind is brutally strong. We're all freezing, but Six protects us with her Legacy, pushing the wind and snow out of our way. Weather control is one of the more useful Legacies, that's for sure.

'He's been talking to me for a while now, trying to trick me and get me to lose my temper,' Eight says. 'But now that he's on Earth, it's a lot more frequent. He taunts me, lies, and now he's trying to get me to sacrifice myself so that you can all go back to Lorien. He's been getting to me more than usual lately.'

'What does that mean, exactly? "Getting to you"?' Crayton asks.

'Last night in a vision he showed me my friend Devdan hanging from chains. I don't know if it's a vision of something that's actually happening or just a trick, but it's really messing with my head.'

'Four sees him, too,' Six chimes in.

Eight spins around with a surprised look on his face and walks backwards, his mind clearly putting the pieces together. His foot comes dangerously close to slipping off the ledge, making me gasp and reach out nervously. But he never wavers as he continues. 'You know, I think I saw him last night. I forgot about it until now. He has blond hair? Tall guy?'

'And better looking than you? Yup, that's him,' Six says with a smile.

Eight stops backpedalling and looks thoughtful. The drop off to our left is almost two thousand feet. 'You know, I always assumed it was me, but guess I was wrong,' he says thoughtfully.

'Assumed you were what?' I ask, willing him away from the edge.

'Pittacus Lore.'

'Why would you think that?' Crayton asks.

'Because Reynolds told me that Pittacus and Setrákus were always able to communicate with each other. But now that I know Four can, too, I'm confused.'

Eight starts walking forwards again when Ella asks, 'How can *anyone* be Pittacus?'

'Each of us is supposed to take on the roles of the original ten Elders, so I guess that means one of us will take on Pittacus's role,' Six explains. 'Four's Cêpan told him so, in a letter. I read it myself. Eventually, we're supposed to become even stronger than them. That's why the Mogs are moving so quickly now, before we become more dangerous, better able to protect ourselves and attack them.' She looks over at Crayton, who is nodding as she speaks.

I feel like I'm the only one who knows so little – nothing, really – of my history. Adelina refused to tell me anything, to answer a single one of my questions, or even hint at what I would one day be capable of. Now, I'm so far behind everyone else. The only Elder I even know of *is* Pittacus, never mind knowing which one I might become. I just have to believe I'll figure out who I am when the time is right. Sometimes, I get sad when I think about everything I wish I already knew and when I think about what my childhood should have been. But there's no time for me to mourn what can't be changed.

Ella comes to walk with me, brushing her hand against mine. 'You look sad. You okay?'

I smile at her. 'I'm not sad. But I am mad at myself. I've always blamed Adelina for why I haven't developed my Legacies the way that I might have. But look at Eight. He lost his Cêpan, but took what he had and just kept working at it.'

We walk together in silence for a few more minutes, until Eight speaks. 'Do you ever wish the Elders had given us our Inheritance in locked backpacks instead?' He switches his Chest to the other arm.

I look guiltily at Crayton. I move to take my Chest from him, but he just pushes me away gently.

'I have it for now, Marina. Soon enough I'm sure you'll need to bear its burden alone, but I'll help while I can.'

We walk for another few minutes until the path along the ridge suddenly ends at a steep cliff. We're a few hundred feet from the peak, and I stare over the Himalayas spread out on my left. The mountains are vast and seem endless. It's a breathtaking sight, one I hope I'll remember forever.

'So, now where?' Six asks, looking skeptically up at the mountain. 'There is no way we can go straight up the peak. There don't seem to be a lot of other options, though.'

Eight points at two tall, hulking boulders leaning against the mountainside, and then clenches his hand. The boulders separate, revealing a curved stone staircase that winds around and leads inside the rock face. We follow Eight up to the stairs. I feel both claustrophobic and vulnerable. If someone follows us, there's no way out.

'Almost there,' Eight says over his shoulder.

The stairs are so cold; their iciness seeps up through my feet and body. They finally lead us to a huge rock cavern that has been carved out of the mountain.

We pour into it, gazing around in awe. The ceiling is a couple of hundred feet high, and the walls are smooth and polished. Carved deep into one of the walls are two sets of vertical lines several feet high and spaced five feet apart. A small blue triangle sits between the two lines, with three more curved lines carved horizontally above it.

'Is that supposed to be a door?' I ask, following the lines with my eyes.

Eight steps aside, to let all of us see better. 'It's not supposed to be; it *is* a door. It's a door to the far corners of the Earth.'

14

I pull my hoodie up over my head and hunch my shoulders. Nine's wearing a dirty Cubs cap and cracked sunglasses, items he found in the train yard where we jumped off. After an hour's walk south, we're standing against the wall of a platform, waiting for another train. This one is elevated. The el, as Chicagoans call it. The Chests in our arms stand out against the other passengers' briefcases and backpacks, and I do my best to act casual. Bernie Kosar sleeps comfortably inside my shirt, now a chameleon. Nine is still kind of pissed that I was skeptical that anyone would put a *safe* house in such a densely populated area. I know Henri would never have chosen such an exposed place.

We don't speak as the train rumbles into the station. Bells chime, the doors slide open, and Nine leads me into the last car. When the train pulls away, we watch the city of Chicago slowly grow closer.

'Just enjoy the view for now,' Nine says. He looks more and more at peace the closer we get to the city. 'I'll tell you more when we get off.'

I've never been to Chicago before. We pass what feels like a million apartment buildings and houses as we clatter through the different neighborhoods. The streets below are full of cars, trucks, people, dogs being walked, babies being pushed in strollers. Everyone looks so happy, and safe. I can't help but wish I were one of them. Just going to work or school, maybe for a walk with Sarah to get a cup of coffee. A normal life. Such a simple idea, but it's almost impossible for me to picture. The train stops, people stream off and others push to get on. The train gets so crowded that two girls, a blonde and a brunette, are forced to stand practically leaning over us.

'Like I said,' Nine says, smiling happily, 'just enjoy the view.'

After a few minutes, the blonde kicks the Chest under my feet. 'Ow! Jeez, guys. What's with the ginormous boxes?'

'Vacuum cleaners.' I'm nervous and Nine's story from the other night is the first thing that pops into my mind. 'We're, uh, salesmen.'

'Really?' The brunette asks. She looks disappointed. I sag a bit; even I'm a bit disappointed in my fictional life.

Nine takes off his cracked sunglasses and elbows me in the ribs. 'That was a joke. My friend here, he thinks he's so funny. Actually, we work for an art collector and we're taking these artifacts down to the Art Institute of Chicago.'

'Oh, yeah?' the blonde asks. The two girls glance at each other and look pleased. As she turns back to us, she tucks her hair behind her ear. 'I'm a student there.'

'Seriously?' Nine says with a pleased smile.

The brunette bends down, looking curiously at the intricate carvings on the lid of my Chest. I hate that she's so close to it. 'So, what's inside? Pirate treasure?'

We should *not* be talking to them. We shouldn't be talking to anyone. We're no longer just teenagers trying to blend in with the humans around us. We are *alien fugitives* who just destroyed a fleet of government vehicles. There's a bounty on my head and I bet they're putting one together for Nine right now. We should be hiding in the middle of nowhere, back in Ohio, or even out west. Anywhere but sitting on a packed train in the middle of Chicago, flirting with girls! I open my mouth to say that the Chests are empty, to make them stop asking questions and leave us alone, but Nine talks first. 'Maybe my friend and I could swing by your place later this evening. We'd love to show you what's inside then.'

'Why don't you just show us now?' the brunette asks with a pout.

Nine looks left and then right. He's really hamming it up. 'Because I don't trust you yet. You two are kind of, ah, suspicious. You know that, right? Two beautiful girls like you, you're right out of a spy movie.' He winks at me. It suddenly dawns on me; he's just as bad around girls as I am. He overcompensates and looks kind of ridiculous doing it. It makes me like him more, even if he is totally embarrassing us both.

The girls look at each other and smile. The blonde digs into her purse, scrawls something on a scrap of paper and hands it to him. 'The next stop is ours. Give me a call after seven and we'll think about hooking up with you guys somewhere later. I'm Nora.' I'm stunned his stunt worked.

'I'm Sarah,' the brunette says. Of course that's her name. I shake my head. If that isn't a blinking sign that we must end this conversation now, I don't know what is.

Nine reaches his hand out to shake theirs. 'I'm Tony, and this handsome stud next to me is Donald.' I clench my teeth and give them a polite wave. *Donald*?

'Cool,' Nora says. 'Well, talk to you later.' The train stops and they get off. Nine leans over and waves to them through the window. After the train pulls out of the station, Nine chuckles to himself. He is looking very smug.

I elbow him in the ribs. 'Are you nuts? Why would you

deliberately draw that kind of attention to yourself – to us? You had no right to drag me into your stupidity. And, why *in the world* would you do anything to encourage them to look at our Chests? Let's hope any girl stupid enough to buy your crap is too stupid to think too hard about any of it!' I liked him a whole lot better when he just looked like a loser.

'Calm down, *Donald.* You think you could keep your voice from squeaking so loud? It's no big deal. Nothing is going to happen to us here.' He leans back, hands folded behind his head. When he speaks again, though, he doesn't sound so puffed up. 'Sandor would have been so damn proud of me just now, you know? I bet you'd never know it, but normally, I'm crazy nervous around girls. And the more I like them, the worse it is. No more. After what I've been through this past year, nothing really scares me anymore.'

I don't respond. I slump down in my seat and watch the city get taller and taller, the architecture more interesting. There are playhouses, shops and beautiful restaurants all wrapped in glass. Some of the buildings shine so bright in the sun I have to shield my eyes. Cars clog the roads below us, their honks reaching us up on the track. No place could be more different from Paradise, Ohio. Our train stops and starts up again through two more stations, then Nine tells me to stand up. We're next. A minute later we're walking east on Chicago Avenue, each of us carrying our Chest under an arm. Lake Michigan is straight ahead.

When the crowd around us thins, Nine says, 'Sandor loved Chicago. And he thought it was smart to hide in plain sight in a city like this. No chance of sticking out, always a crowd to disappear into, that kind of thing. I mean, think about it, where are you more anonymous than in a busy city?'

'Henri would never have allowed it. Being in a city like this would have freaked him out. He hated being anywhere he couldn't keep an eye on anyone who might have an eye on us. On me.'

'And that's why Sandor was the best Cêpan that ever lived. He had rules, of course. First and most important, "don't be stupid."' Nine sighs. Amazingly, he has no idea how infuriating, how insulting this talk about Sandor is.

I'm pissed and I don't care who knows it. 'Oh, yeah, if Sandor was so great, why did I find you in a Mogadorian prison cell?' I feel horrible the minute I say it. Nine misses Sandor, and we're in the last place they spent real time together, where Sandor told Nine he was safe. I know how powerful that kind of assurance is.

Nine stops dead, right in the middle of a busy corner with people streaming past us. He steps up to me until our noses are inches apart. His fists are clenched, not to mention his teeth. 'You found me in that cell because *I* made a mistake. It was *my* mistake, not Sandor's. And you know what? Where's your Cêpan? You think yours was so much better than mine? Wake up, idiot! They're both *dead*, so I really doubt one was so much better than the other.'

I feel bad for what I said but I'm sick of Nine trying to bully me. I push him away. 'Back off, Nine. I mean it. Just. Back. Off. And stop talking to me like I'm your little brother.'

The light changes and we cross the street, both of us fuming. I follow him onto Michigan Avenue and we walk in silence. At first I'm too angry to pay attention to my surroundings, but slowly I become aware of the skyscrapers above me. I can't help it. This city is awesome. I look around. Nine sees me admiring the city, *his* city, and I can feel his mood softening.

139

'You see that big black one with the white spires on top?' Nine asks. He looks so happy to see this building I forget I'm pissed at him. I look straight up. 'That's the John Hancock Center. It's the sixth tallest building in the country. And that, *little brother*, is where we're headed.'

I snatch him by the arm and pull him to the side of the sidewalk. 'Wait a minute. *That's* your safe house? One of the tallest buildings in the city is where you think we're going to *hide*? You've got to be kidding me. That's *nuts*.'

Nine laughs at the incredulous look on my face. 'I know, I know. It was Sandor's idea. The more I think about it, the more brilliant I realize he was. We stayed here for over five years, no problems. Hiding in plain sight, baby, hiding in plain sight.'

'Right. Are you forgetting about the part where you got caught? We are *not* staying there, Nine. Not a chance in hell. We need to go back to the train, figure out a new plan.'

Nine rips his arm out of my grip. 'We got caught, *Donald*, because of someone I thought was my friend. She'd been working with the Mogs and I was too stupid to notice. She betrayed me and I couldn't see beyond her nice ass, so Sandor was captured. I watched him being tortured, and there was nothing I could do to stop it. The one person I loved more than anyone in the world. In the end, the only thing I could do for Sandor was put him out of his agony. Death. The gift that keeps on giving.' His sneer can't hide the pain in his voice. 'Fast-forward one year and I see your ugly face outside my prison cell.' He points up at the John Hancock Center. 'Up there, we were safe. It's the safest place you'll ever be.'

'We'll be trapped,' I say. 'If the Mogs find us up there, there's nowhere to run.'

'Oh, you'd be surprised.' He winks and then walks towards the building.

All of a sudden I am very conscious of just how many people are going by us. I'm nervous as hell, without a single clue where else I should be or go. One thing I know for sure, the Mogadorians keep getting better at blending in, so I have zero confidence we'd even know it if one just brushed by. This thought terrifies me so much I literally twitch as it occurs to me. And I have to assume there are thousands of cameras all over Chicago, and with the Mogs and the government working together, the Mogs probably have access to them. Great. We're on some predatory Candid Camera and there is nothing we can do about it. Inside, anywhere inside, is going to be safer than standing around out here. I put my head down and follow Nine.

The lobby is amazingly luxurious. There's a grand piano, leather furniture, and sparkly chandeliers. At the far end I see two security desks. Nine hands me his Chest and takes off his cap. One of the security guards is a large bald guy who is seated behind the desk, until, that is, he sees Nine. Then, he lets out a howl and leaps to his feet.

'Hey! Will you *look* at who the cat dragged in! You don't write, you don't call, where the *heck* have you been?' the man asks, shaking Nine's hand, his other hand clutching his arm. He just stands there, beaming at Nine. The long-lost son returns, and all that, I guess.

Nine is grinning at him with real affection and puts his other hand on the man's shoulder, 'Oh, I think a better question is, where haven't I been?'

'Next time, tell us when you're taking off. I worry! Now, where's that uncle of yours?' He looks over Nine's shoulder, as if expecting Sandor to come up behind him.

141

Nine doesn't miss a beat. 'Europe. France, actually.' No flinch, nothing. He's good. I know how hard this must be for him.

'He got some kind of visiting teaching gig?'

'Yup,' Nine says. He nods at me. 'It's a long gig, he's thinking about maybe even taking a permanent spot, so I've been staying with my friend Donald on the south side. We need to hang upstairs for a while so we can work on a history project. Check out these boxes, man, we have work to last us months!'

I look down at the Chests in my arms and the security guard stands aside and lets us walk past. 'Sounds like you guys have yourselves a plan. Hey, nice to meet you, Donald. Good luck with your project!'

'Same here,' I say. 'And, thanks!' I'm trying to sound friendly, but it's hard. Nine is clearly fine with this guy knowing his comings and goings, noticing his absence, setting up a lie it might be hard to back up later on. But I hear Henri's voice in my head, warning me this is the exact *opposite* of what we should be doing. I try to shake off the nerves making my stomach do flips. Second-guessing things won't help.

We make our way to a small elevator bank and Nine presses a number. The light above one of the sets of elevator doors brightens with a big arrow pointing up.

'Oh, hey, Stanley?' The security officer jogs over just as we are about to step through the elevator doors, his keys jingling on his belt.

I look at Nine with a smirk. 'Stanley?' I mouth. That's worse than Donald!

'Not now,' he mumbles back.

'I've got a bunch of packages for you. We've been holding them in storage. We didn't know where you were and you didn't leave a forwarding address. You want me to send them up?'

'Give us an hour to settle in first, okay?' Nine asks.

'Absolutely, boss.' The guard salutes as we step into the elevator.

Once the doors are closed, I feel Bernie Kosar crawl from one of my shoulders to the other, and back again. He tells me he's tired of hiding. 'Just a few more minutes,' I say.

'Yeah, BK,' Nine says. 'We are just about home. Finally.'

'How could you be so confident this place would be yours to come back to? I mean, you've been gone a really long time.' There seems to be no situation, no idea that makes Nine second-guess what he believes. I wish I could be like that. Even if he isn't always right, it makes for a great team member and an even better warrior.

'Sandor set everything up. Payments for this place are made automatically from his account. We always kept things pretty vague about what he did. And we referred to his "teaching gigs" the other times when we went away for months. Clearly, people bought it.'

Nine presses a series of numbers into a small keypad below the floor numbers and the elevator rockets upwards. The numbers increase so fast I barely have time to think about how high we're going. We pass the eightieth floor and then start to slow down. We come to a stop and the doors open silently, and we step directly into an apartment. I look up at the huge crystal chandelier hanging above two couches in the living room. Everything seems to be bright white with gold trim.

'This is your apartment? You can't be serious,' I say.

'Yup, we've got our own private entrance,' he says in response to my amazed look.

I thought only people on TV lived like this. It's completely boggling my mind that this place belongs to a Garde member.

I see a camera in the upper right-hand corner of the room, pointed our way, and instantly shield my face. But Nine explains it's a closed-circuit camera that can be monitored only from inside the apartment.

'After you,' he says, bowing low and sweeping his arm in welcome with an exaggerated flourish.

'I can't believe you guys have the whole floor,' I say, looking around with my mouth agape.

I hear Nine's hand slide along the wall as he says, '*Two* whole floors, as a matter of fact.' Nine hits another switch and dozens of dark shades rise to reveal floor-to-ceiling windows. The room is bathed in sunlight. Bernie Kosar leaps out of my jacket and turns into a beagle. I walk over to the window and look out at the view. It's incredible. The whole city of Chicago is spread out below. Lake Michigan is a sheet of bright blue on the left. I set my Chest on a plush recliner and place my forehead against the window. As I look down on the roofs of other buildings, I hear something start to whir in the apartment behind me, then feel a whoosh of fresh air from the vents near my feet.

'Hey, you hungry?' Nine asks.

'Sure,' I say. It's weird, but from this height, everything looks fake: the cars, the boats on the water, the trains snaking around on the elevated tracks. To my surprise, I do feel *safe*; I mean, *really* safe. I actually feel as if nothing can touch me, get me, up here. It's been a long time since I felt this way. It's almost strange.

I hear the door to a refrigerator open. 'I am so psyched to finally *relax*,' Nine calls from the kitchen. 'Hey, make yourself at home; take a shower, eat some frozen pizza. We even have time to chill, sleep, before it's time to call those girls. When was the last time you could say any of that? Man, it is good to be home.'

It's hard to turn away from the view; it's kind of mesmerizing. I want to just stand here, right here in this spot, and enjoy feeling safe. The only thing better would be if Henri and Sarah and Sam and Six were here with me.

Something soft and crinkly hits the back of my head. An energy bar.

'Let me show you around.' Nine's giddy, like he's psyched to show off his toys.

I munch on the bar as we walk through a living room filled with plush couches and leather recliners. A giant flat-screen television hangs above a marble fireplace, and on the glass coffee table stands a vase of fake orchids. There is a layer of dust on every surface. Nine says he'll get a cleaning service up to deal with it as he runs a finger over one particularly well-coated table. In the hallway, he opens the first door on the right.

My jaw drops. Standing there are two huge Mogadorian soldiers with alabaster skin and long black hair, wearing black trench coats. They stand just inside, guns poised and ready to shoot. The weeks of training with Six and Sam surge through my brain and I rush the closest one and duck under his cannon, then I deliver an uppercut to his chin and follow that with a thrust kick to his abdomen. The Mog is stunned and falls straight backwards. I look around for something to stab him with, but all I see are free weights and punching gloves. That's when Nine runs in and playfully kicks the other Mogadorian in the groin before flicking its nose. His Mog wobbles on its heels before tipping sideways. It takes one more second before I realize these are just dummies. Nine doubles over and when he finally catches his breath, he slaps my back.

'My, my, those are some *fine* reflexes!' he howls.

My cheeks are blazing hot. 'You could have warned me.'

'Are you kidding? I've been thinking about doing that to you since we got on the el. Man, that was great!'

Bernie Kosar enters the room and sniffs at the rubber feet of the Mogadorian I leveled. He looks up at me.

'They're for training, BK,' Nine says, chest puffed proudly, sweeping an arm out wide. 'We call it the Lecture Hall.'

I take my first real look around. It's a huge, empty room. On the far end, there's a control panel, like a cockpit. Nine walks over and sits at the console and starts flicking switches and typing in commands. From the walls, the ceiling and the floor, combat situations and weapons. He spins the chair around to face me, eager to see how impressed I am. I'm immediately jealous of the time he must have spent here. And it shows.

'This is . . .' I raise my eyes to the ceiling. I can't even find the words. It makes me embarrassed about what I've been doing all this time. My so-called training space was the snow in my backyard, or with Six and Sam at the pool. Suddenly, I'm resentful about Henri moving us around so often, not giving me the kind of training I clearly needed to do my part. If we had made a place like this, then maybe I would be as confident and strong as Nine. Maybe Sandor really was the better Cêpan.

146

'You haven't seen the best part yet,' Nine says.

We move through the training room and he spins opens a vaultlike door in the back. There are shelves and shelves of weapons: guns, swords, knives, explosives and more. There's a whole wall just for ammunition.

Nine pulls a large automatic rifle topped with a scope off a shelf and aims it at me. 'You'd be surprised how easy it was to buy all this stuff. Gotta *love* the Internet.'

He walks towards me with the gun and pushes a button over my shoulder. The far end of the room separates to uncover a firing range longer than a bowling alley. Nine grabs a box of bullets and loads the rifle. Then I watch as he blows to bits a paper target ninety feet away. 'Don't worry. These rooms are pretty well sound-proofed, but we're so high up that no one could hear us anyway.'

A door down the hall leads to a surveillance room. He walks up to a light switch near the front door and flicks the switch while leaning down and placing his face close to it. A faint blue light scrolls over his eyes and the computers come to life. Retinal scan. Cool, very cool. Clearly, Sandor was able to set up a high-tech security system. There are a dozen computers and even more monitors. We're tapped into every camera in the John Hancock Center, all one hundred floors of it, plus what seems to be every camera around the city that's controlled by the Chicago Police Department. Nine touches something on a keyboard and the largest screen in the room comes to life, showing a photo of a muscular man in a black Italian suit, its beautiful cloth and perfect cut apparent even in the grainy picture. He has black hair and a thick beard, and he's holding two laptops. I look at Nine, wondering why he's showing me this.

147

'That's Sandor,' Nine says after a minute. His voice is different. I hear less bravado. He turns to me. I hear vulnerability. 'Come on. You have a decision to make, an important one.' He pauses for dramatic effect. 'Which room will you choose to stay in? There are a few of them to check out. Take your time. The pizzas won't take long.'

15

Crayton steps between Marina and Ella to get a closer view of the lines carved into the mountainside. He presses his palm in the center of the outlined door, then pulls his hand away. 'That's interesting. It's warm. And what, exactly, do you mean when you say it's a door to the far corners of the Earth?'

'Here's the deal,' Eight explains. 'At best, I can teleport two hundred feet. Maybe two-fifty. And the farther I go, the worse my accuracy is. One time I was aiming for a treetop a couple of hundred feet away and I landed in between a mountain lion and her cubs. That got ugly, fast. This teleporting Legacy is truly brilliant and has been incredibly useful so many times, but it's not as easy as it looks. *From inside this cave*, though, I can teleport around the *world.*'

I place my hands on the mountainside and I can feel the warmth move through me. 'How?'

Eight moves out of the way so Ella and Marina can touch the door. 'My best guess is that this is an ancient Loric cave, or maybe one of the Loric headquarters, and I was just lucky enough to find it, and I was even luckier to figure out what I could do here. Whatever it was, I am definitely not the first Loric to visit this place.'

His words are barely out of his mouth when I feel

a surge of adrenaline and fear shoot through me. I know Crayton has the same thoughts when he whips his head back to look in the direction we came from, and then over at me. I do what he's about to ask, and move quickly down the passage, listening for movement. If this is an ancient Loric cave it would've been under surveillance by the Mogadorians. There could be soldiers waiting for us, or devices set to alert them about our arrival.

I turn to Eight. 'Are you out of your mind? Have you completely *lost* it? Actually, maybe we're the ones who've lost *our* minds. We're the idiots who blindly followed you to a known Loric hideout! This place could be crawling with traps!' As what I've just said sinks in, Marina and Ella move closer to us.

'Hey, hey! Look, I'm sorry,' Eight says, dropping his Chest. 'I've been here so many times without anything happening that I didn't think there was any risk.'

'Let's not waste time apologizing or criticizing,' Marina says, stepping forward. 'Just show us how to open it up, so we can get to the rest of the world. Or, at least, someplace else!'

Crayton nods, still glancing around suspiciously. 'Yes. Let's get in there, where we're less vulnerable.'

Eight pulls his pendant over his head. He reaches up to the blue triangle. 'Wait till you see what's next,' he says, smiling. Then he holds his pendant to the blue triangle.

Nothing happens at first, but after a tense moment the carved lines begin to deepen and spread towards each other. Eight lets the pendant drop down to his chest. Dust shoots into the passage and we move back a few feet. When all the lines touch and there is a perfect outline of a door, the right edge separates from the face of the cavern, and swings open. A blast of warm air hits us, and we all stand still, mesmerized by a blue glow coming from inside.

The energy I feel coursing through me is overwhelming and I become completely and utterly calm. 'What's the blue light?' I finally ask.

'That's what makes me able to teleport around the world,' Eight responds, as if this were the simplest concept to grasp.

Ella walks towards the opening. 'I feel weird inside.'

Marina says, 'Me too.'

With a smile, Eight ducks through the doorway; Crayton and Ella are quick to follow. I bring up the rear. As we climb up another staircase Eight talks.

'A couple of years ago, as my Legacies grew, I started having these very vivid dreams, like the ones I'm having now with Setrákus and Four. I learned more about Lorien, and about the Elders. Learned about our history here on Earth, how we helped the Egyptians build the pyramids, how the Greek gods were actually Loric, how we taught the Romans military strategy, and so on. In one of the dreams, there was all this stuff about moving around on earth, and how the Loric used to do it. *This* mountain was in my dream. We'd already moved to India and I recognized it. After the dream, I came up here and started looking around. That's when I found all of this.'

'That's amazing,' says Marina.

The stairs end in another room. The ceiling is domed and several jagged columns hold it up. I realize we're inside the peak of the mountain. The room is empty except at its very center, where an intricate set of rocks form a whirlpool-like pattern, radiating out from one central blue stone that's the size of a basketball.

'Loralite,' Crayton whispers. He walks towards the center of the cave and sets Marina's Chest down. 'That is the biggest Loralite stone I have ever seen.'

'Is the Loralite the reason you can go anywhere you want?' Marina asks, turning to Eight.

'Well, that's the thing,' Eight sighs. 'I can't go *anywhere* I want. More like six or seven far-off places. It took a lot of messing around and landing in places I didn't mean to before I figured out I can only teleport where there's another one of these big Loralite rocks around.'

'So where *can* we go?' I ask.

'Well, so far I've gone to Peru, to Easter Island, to Stonehenge, the Gulf of Aden near Somalia – but I really don't recommend that one for a lot of reasons – and I've ended up in the desert in New Mexico.'

'New Mexico,' I say immediately, turning to Crayton. 'If we go there we could be across the country and with John in less than a day. We know we can move around easily once we are in the U.S.'

Crayton walks over to the wall, looking around at

some markings on it. 'Wait. You're saying you can't control where you go? That's not as promising as I had hoped.'

'No, but if we end up somewhere besides New Mexico – if that's where we want to go – we just teleport again until we get there. It's not so bad,' Eight says.

'And do you know if you can take all of us with you?' I ask. 'If it's anything like my Legacy of invisibility, we may have a problem. I can only turn other people invisible if they're holding my hands.'

'I don't know, to be honest. I've never tried to bring anyone else,' Eight admits.

'Maybe you can take two trips,' Marina suggests.

'These drawings are amazing,' Crayton interrupts, motioning us over to the cave walls. 'Maybe there are some clues for us here.'

He's right. The orange walls are covered with hundreds of symbols, paintings and carvings, reaching as high as the very tip of the dome.

I walk over and my eyes are drawn to a faint green painting of a planet. Instantly, I know it's Lorien, and a lump catches in my throat. Below it, scratched in blue, is a female figure standing over a male, and both are holding sleeping babies. Rays of interrupted white lines come off the bottom of Lorien, ending just above the four figures. Carved next to the female's head, in a different drawing style, are three columns of alien symbols. 'What the hell?' I whisper, confused.

A few feet to my left is a simple black sketch of

a triangular spaceship. There are intricate spirals and symbols on its wings, and a tiny, swirling constellation of stars on the blunt nose. Eight walks up next to me and points to the constellation. 'Do you see? It's the same pattern as the stones in here.'

I turn around to compare – he's right. Immediately, I wish Katarina were here to see all this. I wonder if she even knew about it. I turn to Crayton, who is examining drawings on the ceiling. 'Did you know about any of this?' I ask.

'We left Lorien in a very big hurry. The planet was under attack from the Mogadorians. We didn't have time to gather as much information as we should have. We knew places like this existed, but no one knew exactly *where* they were, or what they did. Clearly, for all the information we did manage to gather before we left, there were important things that we didn't get,' he explains.

'Follow me, everybody,' Eight calls out, gesturing for us to follow his lead towards a dark corner of the room. 'It just gets weirder and weirder.'

He stops in front of a huge carving. It is ten feet high and twenty feet long, split into different scenes. Kind of like a comic book. The first panel shows a spaceship with nine children standing in front of it. Their faces are drawn with detail, and I'm able to pick myself out immediately. The sight of me as a toddler rocks me back on my heels.

'Was this here when you first saw the cave?' Crayton turns away from the wall to ask Eight.

'Yes,' he responds. 'All of this was here, just as you see it now.'

'Who could have done it?' Marina asks, looking up and down the wall, her voice filled with awe.

'I don't know.' Crayton stands with his hands on hips, examining the wall. It's disconcerting to see him look so confused.

The next panel shows a dozen dark figures that I can only assume are Mogadorians. They hold swords and guns, and the figure in the middle is twice the size of the others. Setrákus Ra. The Mogs' tiny eyes and straight mouths are so accurate, so lifelike, I feel shivers run down my back. My eyes move right, and the next scene shows a girl lying in a pool of blood. I compare her face to those in the first panel, and it's obviously Number One. Number Two, also a girl but younger than One, is also down, under the foot of a Mogadorian. Dead. My stomach turns when I see Number Three, a boy, impaled by a sword in a jungle. The last panel in the top row shows Number Four running from two Mogadorian soldiers, jumping over a ray that's been shot from one of their guns. I gasp involuntarily. In the background is a large building on fire.

'Holy shit. That's John's school,' I say, pointing to the last panel.

'What is?' Marina asks.

I stab at the wall. 'That fire at John's school after we fought the Mogadorians. I was there! This is John's school!'

'Is that you in the sky, then?'

I look closer and see a small figure with long hair hovering over the school. 'Okay, that is really freaky. Yes. I don't understand. How did anyone –'

'Look, is this Number Five?' Ella interrupts, pointing at the first box of the bottom row. Standing on the top of a pine tree is a figure throwing something down at three Mogadorians on the ground.

'This is incredible. Everything is here. It's all laid out,' Crayton says. 'Someone foresaw it all!'

'But who?' I ask.

'Oh, no,' I hear Marina whisper. 'Who's that? Who else dies?'

I skim quickly over the next two panels, where we start to come together, to one that shows Marina and me standing next to a lake. And I see John running out of the mouth of a cave with another person. I don't know who it is, maybe Sam. I can't tell because the boy's head is turned away. Then my eyes reach the panel Marina's looking at. With his or her arms out, a Garde is standing with a sword plunged all the way through its body. It's impossible to identify who it is because the face has been chipped away from the wall. Right below it, on the floor, are pieces of stone.

'What the hell is going on here?' I ask. 'Why is only *that* face missing?' Eight is silent, head down. 'Did you do that?'

'Nobody can dictate what's going to happen,' he says.

'So you thought you'd just destroy it? To do what, exactly? Make it less true?' Crayton asks.

'I didn't know what any of this was. I didn't know any of you. I thought it was a story, at least until –'

'Is it me?' Marina interrupts. 'Am I the one who dies?'

I have the same question. Am I the one with a sword through me? It's a chilling thought.

'We're all going to die someday, Marina,' Eight says in a strange voice.

Ella scoops up the pieces of rock and studies them, turning them over.

Crayton steps in front of Eight. 'Just because you destroyed it doesn't mean it's not going to happen. Withholding the information from us does not make it more or less true or destined to happen. Are you going to tell us who it is?'

'I didn't bring you all the way in here to examine a chipped section of the wall,' Eight says. 'You guys need to keep going – look at the last two panels.'

He has our attention again. We are not going to do anyone any good getting caught up on which of us gets killed with the sword. We turn our attention back to the wall. In the panel Eight is now pointing at, Setrákus Ra is lying on the ground with a sword held to his throat. The figure holding the sword is impossible to make out. On both sides of him, Mogadorians lie dead. In the last panel, there's an odd-looking planet cut in half. The top part looks like Earth, and I can see Europe and Russia, but the bottom half of the planet is covered in long, bumpy stripes. It looks dead and barren. A small ship approaches the top half of the planet from the left, and another small ship is approaching the bottom half from the right.

I'm trying to figure out what this means when I hear Ella gasp.

'It's Eight.'

We all twist around to see her holding the pieces of stone from the floor up to the Garde member's missing face. She managed to put the puzzle pieces back together. Number Eight dies in the picture.

'It doesn't mean anything,' he says firmly.

Marina gently places her hand on his arm. 'Hey, it's just a drawing.'

'You're right,' Crayton responds, softly. 'It is just a drawing.'

Eight pulls away from Marina, circling back to the center of the cave; the rest of us are still rooted to our spots in front of the massive wall that tells stories no one should or could possibly know. Someone has predicted Eight's death. Given the accuracy of the other panels, it's hard to come up with a convincing argument for only this one being wrong. No *wonder* he's always joking around; why he acts as if he has reason not to be quite as careful as the rest of us. He's trying to hide from fate, maybe fly in the face of it. I look back over the last two panels. At first I'm relieved to see Setrákus Ra with a sword to his throat. But the fact that he's still *alive* in the picture pisses me off. And what does the last panel even *mean*? It's showing a confrontation so clearly still in progress, the outcome unclear. And, why is the planet cut in half? What is it saying will happen?

Crayton picks up Marina's Chest, walks towards Eight and puts his arm around him. He starts speaking quietly.

'What do you think he's telling him? What can he tell him that would make him feel better?' Marina whispers, turning to me.

Just as I'm about to go join Crayton in comforting Eight, an explosion rocks the cave, and a wave of fire enters the door. Marina grabs my arm as I hear Ella scream across the room. The jagged columns holding the ceiling up crack and begin to sway and break. A large section falls towards Ella, and I use my mind to shield her, propelling the crumbling stone away from her. I look over at Crayton and Eight just as Eight disappears.

'What's happening?' Marina screams, using her telekinesis to shield the two of us from the falling debris while I protect Ella.

'I don't know,' I say frantically, trying to see through the smoke and dust. Suddenly, Eight reappears in the middle of the room. Blood flows from a wound in his side, his face ashen. 'The Mogadorians!' he shouts. 'They're here.'

16

I'm lying in bed, enjoying my choice of room and the amazingly comfortable pillows I found there. I'm just drifting off when I hear the front door open and then Nine speaking to someone in a low tone. I sit up in alarm, my heart pounding in my ears. Then I realize – it must be the doorman bringing the boxes up. I lie back down. Bernie Kosar licks the bottoms of my feet and says he's going to get something to eat.

'I'll be there in a minute,' I tell him. I stare at the ceiling, hands folded behind my head.

The ceiling has a faint texture to it. My eyelids grow heavy again. The next thing I'm aware of I'm no longer looking at the ceiling. I'm outside and it's snowing.

'Concentrate, John!' I hear someone say from behind me. I turn to see Henri holding an armful of kitchen knives. He has one cocked above his shoulder.

'Henri! Where are we?' I call out to him.

'Did you hit your head?' Henri asks. He's wearing jeans and a white sweater, and both are torn and tinged with blood. There's a blue light somewhere behind him, but when I try to see what it is, craning my neck to peer around him, Henri gets angry. 'Come on, John! It's like you're not even here with me. I need you to start concentrating! Now!'

Before I can argue, Henri whips a knife at me and I'm able to slap it away from my face at the last second. He throws a second one at me, then a third, and a fourth. I block each one, but Henri seems to have an endless supply. I am keeping up, but it's getting harder. The knives are coming faster and faster; too fast.

'We didn't have to keep running!' I yell at him, dodging two knives at once.

Henri throws the next knife with such velocity that, when I slap it away, my hand starts to bleed. He yells, 'We can't all live in Chicago in the clouds, John!'

When the next knife comes, I snatch it by its handle and whip it into the snowy ground. The snow around it turns black. I catch another knife and slam it down, too. 'If we had found the right place, we could have had a real home! We never even tried! And you picked Paradise? Of all places?'

'I did my best! And that's where Malcolm Goode was! You found the tablet, John! You haven't even used it yet!' Henri shouts. The blue light behind him disappears, and the darkness in the snow starts to seep outward and spreads, until it's like we're wading in a black sea. Henri pulls a large knife over his head and wings it at me. When I try to defend myself, my hands feel stuck to my sides. I'm watching the knife fly through the air, flipping, end over end, and I know it's about to hit me right between the eyes. Once it's a couple of feet away, a huge hand reaches out and snatches it out of the air. It's Setrákus Ra. In one fluid motion he has the knife firmly in his grip and whips it over his shoulder and back down again, swinging it at me.

As the tip of the knife plunges into my skull, Setrákus Ra yells, 'Your pizza's getting cold!'

I sit up and I'm back in bed, in the Hancock tower. I'm drenched in sweat and gasping for air. Nine stands in the doorway with a whole pizza on a platter. His mouth is full and he continues to chew while he says, 'Seriously, man, you got to eat it while it's still hot. And I still want to get some training in before our double date.'

'I saw Setrákus Ra again,' I say. I know my voice sounds flat. My tongue feels sticky. 'And Henri.'

Nine swallows and waves his hand in the air, still holding half a slice. 'Oh, yeah? Forget about it, they're just dreams. That's what I tell myself, and it usually works out just fine.'

'And how, exactly, do you make that work?' I ask, but he's already gone. I slide off the bed and stumble down the hallway. I see Bernie Kosar attacking a defrosted steak on the kitchen floor. My pizza sits steaming on the table. I haven't dreamed about Henri in so long, I'm having a hard time shaking the vision off. While I eat my pizza, I think about the flying knives, the snow, how we were yelling at each other – when it hits me. Henri mentioned the tablet. I haven't done anything much but look at it. What little time I've spent with it, I've been annoyed by the fact that it doesn't seem to work. I grab my Chest off the chair and open it, taking the tablet out.

It looks as frustratingly blank as every other time I've looked at it. It's nothing but a white metal square with a screen; blank, dead, useless. Nothing I do brings it to life. I turn it over and examine its few ports. They're triangular, unlike any I've seen before.

'Nine?' I yell.

From the direction of the surveillance room, he shouts, 'In here!'

I stuff a slice of pizza in my mouth and chew as I walk, bringing the tablet with me. Nine sits on a rolling chair with his feet up on the long table between monitors. Most of the screens are divided into quarters. Nine hits the keyboard in his lap and the screens rotate. None of them show us anything interesting.

Nine grins. 'Anything you want me to check on first?'

'Yeah. Enter a name, "Sarah Hart."'

Nine grabs his long black hair in his fists. 'Aaargh! Seriously, dude? You have the most incredibly one-track mind. With all this crazy shit going on, *that's* the first thing that comes to you?'

'It's the only thing that comes to me,' I say. 'Just do it.'

Nine types in her name, and to my disappointment, nothing comes up other than a list of school activities. I make him search for 'Paradise, Ohio,' 'Sam Goode,' 'John Smith,' and 'Henri Smith.' Everything that pops up are things I've seen before: the destroyed high school; the domestic terrorism charge; the reward offered for information leading to our arrest or capture. I slide the white tablet onto the desk in front of me and push it in his direction. 'Listen, Nine. I need your help with this.' I tell him about my vision, and about Henri talking to me about the tablet.

'Dude, you've *got* to *chill*,' Nine says. 'I forgot how personally you take these dreams. I'm going to try something with this tablet thing.'

'Be my guest,' I say with a sigh.

He turns it over a few times in his hands, touching every inch of the screen. Then he examines the ports on the back and clicks his tongue. 'I think . . .' he says, trailing off to spin in his chair. He walks over to the corner of the room where there's a stack of opened brown boxes. Nine digs through the top two, saying, 'I asked them to bring these up from storage when they delivered the stuff that arrived for Sandor. I wanted to see if there was something in one of them that could give me an idea for a new way to communicate with the others . . .' He puts aside the first two boxes and then yanks the third off the stack. He opens the top of it, pulls out the two new laptops inside and shouts, 'Bingo!' Nine stands, looking victorious, and holds up a thick black cord. One end of the cable is, amazingly, shaped like a triangle – the same as the triangle-shaped port on my tablet.

'Where did *that* come from?'

'I don't know. Sandor had all this stuff with him on the ship that brought us here. I never even had a chance to see most of it, never mind learn how to use it. I tried to figure out what this stuff does a couple of times, but Sandor was always protective of it, and I never got anywhere. I mean, most of the time, I can't tell the difference between the Earth stuff and ours, which really doesn't help.'

He takes the cord he's found and brings its triangle-shaped end to the triangle-shaped port on my tablet. We hold our breaths as Nine slides the end into the port. It fits and we both sigh in relief. Slowly, he puts the other end into the closest computer's USB slot. A black horizontal line appears on the tablet's screen, and seconds later we're looking at a map of Earth. One by one, seven pulsing blue dots appear: two in Chicago, four in India or China, and one in what looks like Jamaica.

'Um, bro,' Nine says, his voice hushed. 'I think that's us. As in, *all of us.*'

'Damn, you're right. There we are, there we *all* are,' I whisper. 'We don't even need the macrocosm with this thing.'

'Wait a sec, there are seven dots, but only six of us left,' Nine says, furrowing his brow.

I lean back. 'I told you there was another ship, right? '

'Right, right,' he says, suddenly the eager pupil paying close attention to me.

'Well, we know there was an infant inside. This might mean it made it to Earth, after all! And *that* means –'

'Setrákus Ra has seven of us to deal with, not six,' Nine interrupts. 'The more the merrier.'

While we're both taking this new information in, a small box appears in the upper-right corner of the tablet screen with a green triangle inside. I press the triangle and two small green dots show up on the map. One is in the American Southwest, and the other is in northern Africa, possibly Egypt.

'What do you think these are?' I ask. 'Do you think they're nuclear bombs? Mog bombs? Shit, you don't think they're going to blow up Earth, do you?'

Nine slaps my back. 'No. Think about it. A map that shows us is clearly geared for, well, us. Mog bombs are, like, a different category. I think these are our *ships*, dude!'

I'm speechless. It does kind of make sense. If that's true then something almost too wonderful to let myself think about might also be true. After Setrákus Ra has been killed and Earth has been saved, we could actually fly back to Lorien. We could help bring it out of hibernation. *We can go home*. All of a sudden, I'm desperate to know the exact location of the dot in the Southwest, the one closest to us. 'Where is this?' I ask, pointing to it.

Nine pulls up a map on a screen and says, 'The one out west is in New Mexico, the other one is in Egypt.'

Hearing him say 'out west' reminds me of Special Agent Walker's last words to me. My decision is instantaneous and final. 'That's where we need to go. New Mexico.'

17

The minute Eight appears in the middle of the room, gushing blood, I rush over and place my hands on his wound. His blood runs over my fingers and down my wrists, and when another explosion rocks the cave, we both fall to the ground. 'I'm sorry,' he whispers. 'This is my fault.'

'Shh. I can heal you. It's my Legacy. You just have to relax for a second.' The iciness flows from my fingertips to his ribs, and Eight immediately goes rigid with pain. The explosions keep coming and Eight winces with each one, but I stare deep into his eyes, willing him to stay with me. 'It's okay. Six is here. She can deal with this. We *will* be okay.' I sound absolutely certain, trying to convince both of us.

'Maybe this is when I die, maybe the drawing was just off,' he says.

I press down harder, finally feeling his wound start to shrink in response to my touch. I shake my head firmly. 'No, it isn't.'

Through the chaos, I see Six push Ella and Crayton behind a large pile of fallen rock. She looks over at Eight and me, and the next thing I know we're lifted off the ground and floated over to the rest of the group. When Six sets us down, she says, 'All of you, just stay here while I turn invisible and check things out. Fix him up, Marina.'

She winks at me. Her voice tells me we'll be okay if we all remember what we can do. The only way we'll survive is if we pull together.

'I'm trying,' I say, but she's already invisible. Below my hands, Eight's lungs struggle to keep up with my Legacy, and his face drains of color. I can feel his insides shifting, almost as if resisting my powers. That's not it, though. It can't be. He's just more wounded than I thought. Or, my Legacy is fading. But that is not an option. I begin to panic and I fight the sick feeling in my stomach. I need to focus on him, and not let myself get distracted by what is happening around us.

I hear gunfire and the distant screams of Mogadorian soldiers. I can only imagine what Six is doing out there. She is a merciless warrior when she needs to be, incredibly dangerous to any who threaten her – or us.

'How is he?' Crayton asks, hovering over Eight and glancing back and forth between the pain on Eight's face and the panic in mine.

Ella grabs Eight's hand and gets him to focus on her. 'It's okay. It's going to hurt, Eight, but then it will feel better. Trust me.' I watch her calming words wash over him and he begins to nod through his grimaces.

We hear a deafening crash overhead, and the cave's ceiling comes alive with cracks that spread fast and wide. The dome is a jigsaw puzzle of pieces that threaten to break free at any moment, and suddenly the first one falls, a stone the size of a car plunging down towards us. I don't want to withdraw my healing touch, but I have to remove my hands from Eight's side in order to focus all of my energy on deflecting the stone away with my mind. When

I lay my hands back on Eight's wound, it feels like I'm starting all over again. I take whatever solace I can from the cave drawing. It may show him dying, but it does not show him dying here, this way.

'Where's Marina's Chest?' Ella asks. 'Maybe there's something in there that can help.'

Crayton stands. 'Both Chests are on the other side of the cave. I'll get them.'

'No!' Ella grabs the cuff of his sleeve, but Crayton races off. I watch, helpless. Pieces of the ceiling continue to fall and Ella yells for Crayton to come back, to wait for Six. My mind is racing. Six is out there battling single-handedly with a Mog army, and I know I need to forget all of it, and focus my energy on Eight. I can feel his body giving in to the pain and damage that I can't seem to heal quickly enough to save him. I squeeze my eyes shut, willing him to respond to my Legacy, when I see his wound has returned to its original size, as if I've not even touched him.

'Ella.' I look at her, my eyes filling with tears. 'It's not working. I don't know what to do!'

Ella's voice is determined. 'We need him, Marina. Just concentrate. You can do this.'

I try to catch my breath and see Crayton barely dodge a jagged boulder. 'Eight. Hold on. I *will* do this, you *will* be better soon,' I say as he closes his eyes. I shut out the noise of the attack, I shut out the hysteria surging inside of me, and I tell myself, *I can heal Eight. I will heal him and Six will take care of the Mogs. We have a mission and this is not the end.* I sit up straight, my breath slows to a normal rhythm, and a ball of ice seems to form between my shoulder blades. It races down my spine and out to my fingers. The force of it nearly pushes me over, but my fingers stay firmly on Eight's wound. I can feel something happening inside of Eight and my breath quickens. My heart beats so fast I think it's going to explode, and then Eight opens his eyes.

'It's working!' Ella shouts.

Vertigo sweeps through me. I wobble but remain upright as Eight's wound closes. I can feel his broken ribs move back into place beneath my hands. After a few seconds I allow myself to sit back. I'm so exhausted I can barely keep my eyes open. I take a deep breath and Eight sits up. He touches where the wound was, feels his ribs, and then reaches out to take my hand.

'I have never felt *anything* like that,' Eight says to me, looking incredulous. 'I don't know how to thank you.' I open my mouth to respond when Six suddenly appears.

She has a Mogadorian cannon in her hand. Her face is covered in black ash. She's out of breath but in control. 'I've pushed them back, but I could use some help out there.'

Eight staggers to his feet. 'Right.'

'I was thinking of Marina,' Six says, surveying the scene and seeing immediately that Eight is in no condition to be of help to anyone. I'm honored she wants me to fight alongside her, but I know I'm too weak to stand. 'Where's Crayton?' she asks, looking around.

I've been so focused on healing Eight I'd forgotten about him. I whip around just in time to see him digging the Chests out from under some rubble. Then he picks up both Chests and starts to make his way back over to us. Just as Six moves to help, an explosion blows apart whatever was left of the ceiling. Huge chunks of snowy rock fall into the cave, followed by hundreds of bullets. Eight stands over Ella, using his telekinesis to deflect the debris and gunfire. Six starts firing into the exposed sky with the Mog cannon. There's another explosion high overhead, and a few seconds later a silver ship like the one I saw at the bottom of the pool crashes into the crumbling mountain just above us. A bleeding Mogadorian soldier tries frantically to extricate himself from the cockpit. I struggle to my feet as he punches a hole through the windshield, and before he can pull himself out, I use my telekinesis to bring two boulders up and smash him between them. A cloud of ash floats to the ground.

A rocket enters the cave, blasting the wall nearest Crayton. The panel carving we were all entranced by just moments ago is decimated. Crayton is thrown by the blast and he flies into the middle of the cave, landing next to the blue Loralite stone as the Chests skid across the floor. He isn't moving. I'm stunned – it all happened so fast.

'Papa!' Ella screams.

Even though the walls are crumbling around us, I race with Ella to Crayton's side. She takes one of his hands. I put mine on his body and close my eyes, trying to find a sign of life. I search for anything to work with, to heal, but there's nothing.

'Save him!' Ella yells at me, her small face twisted in anguish. 'Marina, please, you can do this! You can fix him!'

'I'm trying,' I say, but it comes out as a sob. He's dead. Her Cêpan is gone.

'Just concentrate like you did with Eight! You can do it again!' Ella is frantic, stroking Crayton's head and petting his hand.

Out of the corner of my eye I see Six charge towards us with her cannon firing into the sky. Eight teleports next to me. He leans over and says, 'You can fix him. Come on, Marina.'

I start to cry. I can't do it. I know there is nothing for me to heal, but I try and try to summon my Legacy, pleading for it to work. But Crayton is dead; there's nothing for my Legacy to connect with. I move my hands to his crushed chest and stomach. I can feel all of his broken bones beneath my hands. Ella gets behind me and pushes on my shoulders, pressing my hands harder onto Crayton.

Six stops shooting and grabs my arm. She looks me in the eye. I shake my head.

Ella falls to her knees, sobbing. She crawls over to Crayton and whispers into his ear, 'Let Marina fix you. Please don't go. Please, Papa.' She looks up at me, tears streaming down her cheeks. Her voice is angry. 'You didn't even try, Marina! Why won't you try?'

I wipe my tears on my shoulders. 'I tried, Ella. I tried, and there was nothing I could do. He was already gone. I'm sorry.' I sit back on my heels, but keep my hands on Crayton's body.

A rocket hits the far wall, separating it completely from the mountain. We know from our walk up that behind the hole is a straight two-thousand-foot drop. Cold wind sweeps in and over us. Eight turns to Six. 'Give me the cannon. I'll be right back.' Six hesitates for a second before handing it to him. Eight disappears, and I look up to see him sprinting along the crumbling lip of the hole, leaping from spot to spot as the rocks crumble away. Even in flight, he never stops shooting. Soon, two silver Mog ships explode into balls of flame.

I keep moving my hands across Crayton, but Six yanks me onto my feet. 'Stop. He's gone.' I look down at Crayton, his rugged face, his bushy eyebrows, and remember the first time I saw him at that café in Spain. I thought he was my worst enemy. Instead, he saved my life. I stretch out my hands to try one more time, but Six hugs me close to her. I feel her tears on my neck. Her lips touch my ear as she whispers, 'There's nothing we can do.'

Sobbing, Ella reaches over and grabs Crayton's left hand. She kisses it and places it against her cheek. 'I love you, Papa.'

'I'm so sorry,' I say again.

She looks up at me and tries to speak, but she can't. Gently, she lays Crayton's hand on his chest and strokes it once more before standing. Eight teleports next to us and returns the cannon to Six. Another strong gust of freezing wind blasts over us and flips open one side of Crayton's jacket. We all see it at the same time – a white envelope in his inner jacket pocket. FOR ELLA is written on the outside.

Six grabs it and shoves it into Ella's hands. 'Ella. Listen to me. I know you don't want to leave him. None of us do. But if we don't leave right now we will die too. You know Crayton would want us to do what is necessary to survive, right?' Ella nods. Six turns to Eight. 'Right. Now, how do we teleport the hell out of here? Has too much of the mountain been destroyed for it to work?'

'Ella, you hold my Chest! Marina, get yours,' Eight says, ushering us towards the glowing blue Loralite. 'Six, you're going to have to hold on to someone's arm so we can all go at once.' He looks around grimly at the wreckage. 'I really hope this works.'

He grabs Ella's hand and mine. Six hooks her arm through my other elbow. I look around at the pieces of the walls that spoke to us about our future and our past. I think about the many Loric who were here before us. I'm sad we'll be the last ones to see it. But I also think about the responsibility that being the last Loric puts on all of us. I take one last look at Crayton, thanking him for everything he did.

'Okay. Here we go,' Eight says. Then, everything goes black.

18

All of a sudden, Nine's at the edge of his seat. 'Holy shit! Four! Check it out. They've moved.'

'Who moved?' I take the tablet out of his hand. The blue dots that identify us have changed position. At least, some of them have. There is still one blue dot in Jamaica and two in Chicago. But there are now three off the coast of Africa, and one in New Mexico. My chest relaxes when I see there are still seven dots, but I'm confused by how they moved to these other places so quickly. 'How did they do *that*?'

'I have *no* idea,' Nine says. 'It's like they teleported or jumped through space. Maybe they found a stargate, or something?'

'Henri said stargates don't exist,' I said, shaking my head.

'Yeah, well, neither do aliens from another planet, according to *some* people. In fact, *many* people.'

He's right. Maybe Henri was wrong. 'One Garde is in New Mexico, Nine. Near what you think might be our ship. That can't be a coincidence. Do you think they're going after it?'

'Man, I hope not. It is *so* not time for that yet. We have a lot of shit to take care of before we leave Earth.'

I stare at the blue dot pulsing in New Mexico, and press the green triangle, revealing where the Lorien ships are hidden again. There is no way this one has accidentally landed so close to it. Add that to the fact I've been told Sarah is out west, possibly with Sam, and I'm convinced.

'I'm serious, Nine. That's where we are going. New Mexico. Now. Everything we've seen and learned points to it, tells us we need to go there right now.' I rush out of the room, slam my Chest shut and put it next to the front door. 'BK?' I call out. Bernie Kosar trots over with the steak bone in his mouth.

Nine follows me. 'Dude. Slow. Down. We are *not* going to up and fly off to New Mexico! *Especially* after what we just saw! These guys are teleporting around. By the time we get in the elevator, they could be in Antarctica! Or, Australia! There's too much we don't know yet. We don't even know for sure that's our ship. What if it's a trap?' Nine moves in front of the door and crosses his arms. I know I must look like a crazed lunatic, punching at the elevator button, trying to pretend Nine is not there blocking my efforts.

The words tumble out of my mouth. 'We have to go there anyway. Even if the Garde member we see now disappears before we get there. New Mexico is *still* the obvious and only place for us to go.' I'm desperate for him to get on board with this. 'We can take some of your guns.' My head is spinning. I sprint into the training room and head for the munitions cabinet. I'm leaping over the mats in the direction of the cabinet when I hear the metal rings clang overhead. Nine drops from above me, into my path, and puts his hand up.

'Whoa. Hold on there, bud. Take a breath,' he says with his hands up, palms out towards me. '*I* think we should go to Paradise.'

'Are you freaking kidding me? *Now* you want to go to Paradise?' I am going to kill this guy.

'I got to thinking while you were asleep. We need to go back to where you found the tablet. You said before there were a bunch of papers down there, not to mention that skeleton and some maps. I think we're missing something, something that is the key to beating Setrákus Ra.'

'You don't get it,' I say, pushing past him. 'Things are happening out west *this second*. Do you have a car?'

He shoves me hard in the back. I almost fall, but I catch myself. I stand there, back to him, fuming. 'I do have a car, *but* we're going to Paradise first. We need to find anything we can to help us fight.'

'Not a chance.' I turn and shove him back, and before I know it, our arms are locked over each other's heads. Nine kicks my feet out from underneath me and I fall to the ground.

Bernie Kosar barks, telling us to stop.

'Relax, BK,' Nine says, waving at him. 'Consider this a little light training before we head to Ohio.'

'Right. We're training now,' I spit, pulling myself to my feet. 'With everything we just learned.'

Nine throws a jab and I deflect it. But I can't do the same for his right hook. My ribs feel like they just got hit with a battering ram. I fall to my knees, clutching my middle, and he side-kicks my sternum, knocking me flat on my back.

'Come on, man!' he yells down at me. 'Step it up, why don't you? You think you can charge into the desert, take on whatever enemy comes your way, but you can't take me?'

I spring to my feet and surprise him with a clean punch to the gut. As he doubles over, I knee him in the mouth.

'*That's* what I'm talking about, Four!' Blood spills from his split lips, but he's beaming at me. We circle each other. 'Tell you what. Since you're showing signs of giving me a decent run, I'll make you a deal. You beat me, we go to New Mexico. Immediately. I'll even let you drive. But if I win, we spend a couple more hours here, figure some shit out, and come up with a *real* plan. *Then*, we go back to Paradise and head down that well.'

'And you call *me* a coward,' I say.

We continue to circle each other and we each land some devastating blows. I hear one of Nine's ribs snap when I connect with my right elbow. I swing around with my other elbow, but he delivers a hard kick to my left knee. Cartilage rips and pain sears through my leg. Limping, I'm able to throw a few more punches, but I can't move, giving Nine a huge advantage. He leaps behind me and kicks my other leg out from under me. My head hits the floor and the world goes white. When I get my bearings, Nine has my arms pinned to with his knees. The fight is over. And with it goes our chances for finding the Garde out west.

'I'll get a healing stone,' Nine says, slowly standing. With blurred vision, I watch him hold his side as he leaves the room. Bernie Kosar whimpers.

'This is bullshit, you know that?' I yell after him. 'You can't just decide things like this! That Garde in New Mexico could die on their own and you don't even care!'

Nine's voice booms through the apartment. 'We're soldiers, Johnny! And soldiers die. We were sent here to train and fight and some of us aren't going to make it. That's the nature of war.'

I slowly hop into the living room on my one good leg. I can see through the windows the sun is setting. BK sits on the floor, in the last patch of light, looking at me. He begs us to sit down and talk and plan our next move with level heads.

Nine walks in with a healing stone held to his ribs. He tosses it to me and I immediately place it to my left knee. Through the pain, I feel the cartilage slowly reconnecting. It doesn't take long for it to do its thing and soon the pain has disappeared completely. I plant a hand on the window frame and say, 'If we're not going to New Mexico, then let's deal with Setrákus Ra. Right now. You and me. Maybe if we take him out, the rest of the Mogs will die, and we'll save *two* worlds.'

Nine sits down on a leather couch and puts his feet up on the glass coffee table. He sighs and closes his eyes. 'Sorry, Johnny, but even if Setrákus Ra dies, the Mogs will still fight. Just like Pittacus Lore died and we still fight. Stop looking for an easy way out and face it. We're all going to fight until the last one is killed.'

I look out the window and gather the strength to say what I've wanted to say for weeks, ever since I read Henri's letter: 'Pittacus isn't dead. I'm Pittacus.'

'*What* did you say?'

I turn to face him. 'I said, I'm Pittacus Lore.'

Nine leans back laughing so hard he nearly flips over the couch. '*You're* Pittacus? Why on Earth would you think *you're* Pittacus Lore?'

'I feel it,' I say. 'It's why Lorien hibernates. Pittacus lives on through me.'

'Oh, yeah? You know what? I think I can I feel it, too,' he mocks, feeling his torso. He stands and marches over to me. 'But, hey, if you *are* Pittacus, the strongest, *wisest* Elder of Lorien, then I just kicked Pittacus's *ass*. I wonder what that makes me?'

'Lucky,' I say, regretting I said anything.

'Really? Sounds like *somebody* wants a rematch.'

Enough, Bernie Kosar says. *No more fighting. Save your strength.*

179

I ignore him. 'Fine. A rematch it is, then.'

'If you want to take me on again, then there's going to be a change of venue. And to make it even more interesting, *Pittacus*, I say we each get to use one item from our Chests.'

'Fine.'

I open my Chest, reaching immediately for the four-inch dagger. The handle vibrates the moment I touch it and quickly wraps itself around my fist. I see Mog ash still stuck in its grooves; the smell of it makes me hungry for another fight.

Nine grabs the short silver staff with his right hand. Okay, *that* makes me nervous; I saw how he decimated all those pikens in West Virginia with that thing. He waves his finger at me when he sees my dagger. 'Ah, ah, ah. I said only *one* item.'

'I have my dagger. That's it. And that's all I'll need.'

'And what about your cute little bracelet?'

'Uh, I forgot about it. It's probably the better choice for me. Thank you.' I toss the dagger back into my Chest.

'Follow me,' Nine says. Ignoring Bernie Kosar and his pleas to stop, I follow Nine through the apartment and into the elevator, both of us silent. I assume the fight will be in the building's dark basement among columns and cement walls, our powers hidden from the world. Instead, we ascend. The elevator doors open and Nine punches a keypad by the door in front of us, and it clicks open. We're on the roof of the John Hancock Center.

'No way, no *freaking* way. Too many people can see us up here!' I say, shaking my head, turning back towards the door inside.

Nine walks out onto the roof. '*Nobody* can see us up here. That's what's so great about being at the top of one of the tallest buildings in the city.'

I don't want to look like I'm chickening out, so I follow, showing a lot more confidence than I feel. But I'm not prepared for the fierce wind that hits me hard, almost pushing me back into the doorway. Nine keeps walking, his black hair whipping around his head, seemingly impervious to the force of the wind. His white T-shirt balloons around his torso until he strips it off and lets it fly over the ledge. When he gets to the center of the roof, he snaps his wrist, expanding the silver staff at both ends until it's over six feet long and glowing red. He turns to me and curls his palm, beckoning me closer. Like a tightrope walker, I take a deep breath and put one foot in front of the other to walk towards him. We're in the giant shadow of the looming white spire at the far end of the roof and, just as I near him, Nine turns and runs towards it.

I have no idea what he is about to do, so I stop walking to watch his next move. Without breaking stride, he sprints straight up the spire until he reaches the top. The spire is swaying in the wind and I'm dizzy just looking at him, teetering up there. Nine pulls the red staff over his head and, before I can register what he is doing, he hurls it. The second it leaves his hand, Nine dives headfirst towards me, and I'm faced with dodging two flying objects at once. I just manage to roll away from the sharp staff as it nears me, and I watch as it plunges into a metal beam at an angle. I turn to deal with Nine's approach and as he's about to tackle, I land a blow so hard I send him flying across the roof.

I reach over and yank Nine's red staff out of the metal beam. Henri never trained me with anything like it, but I twist it over my head and charge anyway. Nine stands and steels himself for my attack. I swing the staff across his body, but he parries it away with his wrist and immediately moves to kick my newly repaired knee. I pull my leg back so he misses, but he's able to get his hands on the staff. We both struggle to gain control of it, circling and kicking, dodging and blocking. He uses his telekinesis to float my feet off the ground. I start to resist but then realize I can use it to my advantage with the strong wind up here. Carefully timing my moves with a hearty gust, I flip over the staff; in a fraction of a second, I'm behind Nine with the staff against his throat.

'We should be on our way to New Mexico,' I say, pulling us towards the door that leads back to the elevator.

Nine head-butts me with the back of his skull, right into my nose, and I lose my grip on the staff. He grabs it as I stumble backwards and slam into an electrical box.

'Is that you talking, Johnny? Or, is it *Pittacus*?' he says mockingly as he swings the staff. My bracelet expands just in time to deflect his blow. The electrical box I'm next to has been sliced in half by his near miss. Sparks fly everywhere, including inside my open shield and onto me. When they bounce onto my shirt, I let the fire catch and spread. My shield shrinks, and Nine stares, stunned at the sight of me consumed by flames.

He shakes the surprise off. 'Why didn't you turn into a human fireball when we were on the same team?' he shouts.

The fire around my body crackles and hums in the strong wind. I walk towards him. He may think this is all fun and games. I don't. 'Are we done now?'

'Not quite.' He smirks.

I form a small ball of fire in my palm. I figure I'll make my lack of humor about the situation clear enough if I bowl the ball of fire at his legs, but he knocks it away with the end of the staff like a hockey player. I skip two more fireballs down the roof, each one faster than the last, but he uses his mind to push them to the side. The first one rolls off and ineffectually burns out; the other makes its way to the edge of a fan casing. The heat melts it away, and the high winds tip the whole cover off the enormous fan, leaving it exposed.

I raise my hands over my head to create a fireball the size of a refrigerator, but as it grows, Nine charges at me with the staff over his shoulder. He plants one end of the staff in the ground and vaults himself, feetfirst, at my flaming chest. He screams in pain as the soles of his shoes connect with my burning body, and I'm sent flying backwards. The world that had been reds and yellows is now grays and blues. On my final rotation, I realize I'm flying directly into the exposed fan. At the last possible moment, I spread my arms and legs out and catch myself, mere inches from its blades. The fan is powerful enough to nearly extinguish what's left of my dwindling fire before I dive off and roll away.

'Trying to cool off?' Nine asks, hands on hips, as if simply observing my technique. He's kicked off his half-melted shoes.

'I'm just getting warmed up!' I leap to my feet to ready myself to respond to his next move.

Nine sprints to his left and I follow. He jumps over some pipes onto the raised ledge. Again I follow. We are now both inches from a thousand-foot drop onto the street below. To my utter shock, Nine then steps off the ledge. I yell and lean over to grab him, but when I do, I don't see him sailing to his death. He's standing, horizontal, on a window with his arms crossed, that same, big, smile on his face. I've leaned too far, trying to grab him, and I frantically wheel my arms to regain my balance. But I can't catch myself and suddenly I'm tipping further over the abyss. Nine sprints back up the side of the building and hits me with a powerful uppercut to my jaw. I'm knocked backwards but I don't have the chance to land. Nine catches me by the neck, spins and holds me over the ledge.

'Now, Number Four. All you have to do to get me to set you down, all safe and sound, is say it.' He holds the staff with his other hand over his head. 'Say you're not Pittacus.'

I kick at him, but he holds me out, just out of range. I end up swinging back and forth like a pendulum.

'Say it,' he repeats, his teeth gritted. I open my mouth, but can't bring myself to deny what I feel with such certainty to be true. I believe I *am* Pittacus Lore. I believe I *am* the one who can and will end this war. 'You want to go running to New Mexico to find our ship. You can't believe for even a second it might be a trap. Then you talk about taking on Setrákus Ra, but you can't even beat *me* in hand-to-hand combat. *You* are not *him*. You're not Pittacus. So, let's stop the bull right now. Just say it, Four.'

He tightens his grip on my throat. My vision blurs. I look up into the cloudless sky and it turns red, just like the night the Mogadorians invaded Lorien. I see flashes of the faces of Loric who were slaughtered. Their screams ring in my ears. I see the explosions, the fire, all of the death. I see krauls with Loric children in their teeth. The pain I feel for all of them at that moment is so overwhelming that I know I can withstand whatever is done to me now, including Nine crushing my neck.

'Say it!'

'I can't,' I manage to squeak out.

'You've got to be delusional!' he yells, squeezing harder. Now I see the bombs falling on Lorien. I see the torn bodies of my people, my planet being destroyed. At the top of one mound of bodies, I see my dead father wearing his silver and blue suit. Nine shakes me violently, my feet swinging wildly. *'You're not Pittacus!'*

I close my eyes to escape the visions of carnage swimming in front of me, dreading whatever comes next. I can see Henri's letter in my mind: *'When the ten of you were born, Lorien recognized your strong hearts, your wills, your compassion, and in turn she bestowed the ten of you the roles you're all meant to assume: the roles of the original ten Elders. What this means is that, in time, those of you left will grow to be far stronger than anything Lorien has ever seen before, far stronger even than the original ten Elders from whom you've received your Inheritances. The Mogadorians know this, which is why they're hunting you so feverishly now.'*

Whatever it all means, I know Nine wouldn't actually kill me. Each member of the Garde is too important, Pittacus or not. More than anything, coming together and fighting as one, as the Garde we were born to be, is more important than any fight he and I might have. That's small comfort, given the fact that my body is still swinging when I feel the wind change slightly. The hand around my neck opens and my stomach drops as I start to fall. Could I have been wrong? Instead I feel my feet touch down in less than a second. I open my eyes and find myself back on the roof. Nine walks away, his head down. He snaps his wrist and the long red staff shrinks into a piece of silver. Over his shoulder, he yells, 'Next time, I drop you!'

19

I'm facedown in scorching hot sand. It's in my mouth, up my nose, I can barely breathe. I know I should get up, try to roll over, but my bones ache too much. I squeeze my eyes shut, trying to block the pain all over my body. I finally muster the strength to rise, but when I place my hands down to push myself up, the sand burns them. I let myself fall back.

'Marina?' I groan.

She doesn't respond. I still can't open my eyes, but I listen carefully for any signs of life. All I hear is the wind and sand whipping against my body.

I try to speak again, but can only muster a whisper. 'Marina? Somebody, help me. Eight? Ella? Anyone?' I'm so confused I even call out for Crayton. As I wait and hope for a response, I'm hit with the memory of Crayton's dead body. I see it all happening again. Ella's tears. The Mog attack. Hooking my hand inside Marina's elbow and Eight saying, 'Here we go.'

The sun is so hot above me my hair feels like a blanket of fire on my neck and shoulders. Finally, I manage to roll onto my back, and to lift my arm and shield my eyes from the blinding light. Slowly, blinking, I open them a bit at a time. I don't see anyone. Just sand. I struggle to my feet and hear Eight's voice echoing in my head: 'I really hope this works. I've never tried to bring anyone else.'

Well, it looks like it *didn't* work. Or, it worked, but not for me, for all of us together. Where did Ella and Marina end up? Are they together? Is Eight with them? Are we all in different corners of the world? Or am I the only one alone? My brain is frantically churning through all the different possibilities. If we've not only lost Crayton, but also been separated, torn apart, we are so much farther away from our goal. I feel *sick* with the frustration and panic. All we've worked for, everything we sacrificed to go to India and find Eight – it might have been for worse than nothing.

I'm alone under a cloudless sky and a sweltering sun, with no idea of where I am or how in the *world* I'm going to find another living soul, Garde or not. I scan every direction, hoping to see Marina stumble over a dune with her hand waving above her head, Ella not far behind, or a laughing Eight, cartwheeling across the sandy expanse, but all I see is a desolate desert.

I think about what Eight told us about how this teleporting thing works. Wherever it is that I've landed, I *know* I'm near one of the blue Loralite stones. Even if I don't have his teleporting Legacy, I'm hoping I could still use the Loralite in some way. I drop to my hands and knees and furiously start to dig. I have no way of knowing where the thing is, where to start looking, but I'm desperate. So desperate I barely notice the sand burning my fingers.

But the only rocks I find are tiny, cracked and ordinary. Out of breath, sweat pouring down my face and into my eyes, I finally stop and sit back. I can't afford to expend what little energy I have this way. I need to find water and shelter. I cock my head and listen to the wind, hoping for some kind of sign, but there's nothing and no one. Nothing but sand and dunes for as far as the eye can see. And that leaves nothing for me to do but walk. I look up at the sun, orient myself using my shadow, and start to trudge through the sand.

I walk north. With no protection from the blazing rays, my eyes stinging from my sweat running into them, and the pain of the hot sand whipping against my entire body, I feel vulnerable in a way I've never felt before. Everywhere I look, there is just an endless view of the same, and I know my body can't endure this intense sun for a long period of time. I struggle for a few more steps, then I turn invisible to escape the relentless heat. This will make it hard for anyone to find me, but I have no choice. Then I use my telekinesis to hover above the Earth, just to keep my feet away from the burning sand. The higher vantage point only confirms my long-distance assessment of sand, sand and more sand. I squint, hoping to see a road or sign of civilization of any kind each time I pass a dune. But the only thing that changes, the only variation in my endlessly sandy view, comes in the form of devilish flowering cacti and chunks of petrified wood. The clear, cloudless sky mocks me, offering not even a bit of white to manipulate into creating a thunderstorm. When I rip open the first cactus I come near, I am devastated to find it doesn't hold enough water to begin to quench my thirst.

Eventually, just as my energy and spirits are almost at their end, mountains appear on the horizon, giving me at least the prospect of some salvation. They look like they're at least another day's walk away, though it's hard to know for sure. They're definitely too far to reach today and that is enough to send my hopes plummeting. I know I need to find shelter.

I turn visible and hope someone will see me. I look up at the sky and see the first group of clouds of the day. My heart leaps and I feel a small surge of energy I did not know I even had. I concentrate on creating a storm, just a tiny one, above me. The rain is brief, but awesome nonetheless. It's the only reason I don't collapse and just give up.

I keep moving until I at last come across a low barbed-wire fence. Just beyond it I can make out a faint dirt road. It's the first sign of civilization I've seen, and I'm so overjoyed I can even pick up my pace to reach it. I follow the road for a mile or so before I reach a small hill, which I manage to get up and over. On the other side, miraculously, I see outlines of several small buildings. I can't believe it. Should I believe it? It has to be a mirage.

But, no. The closer I get, the more convinced I am these structures, these signs of life, are *real*. Unfortunately, the closer I get, I can also see the buildings are full of holes; crumbling, wooden skeletons abandoned to the relentless attack of the desert. These buildings represent what happens when you're stuck in a place like this. I've stumbled into a ghost town.

Before I let my disappointment bring me to my knees, I focus on what might have been left behind. Before the ghosts took over. Plumbing? A well? I stumble around, searching inside and outside the structures, trying to find some source of water. I have been reduced to that one, essential ingredient. I need to find water. Everyone needs water, so there *must* be some, somewhere, right?

No. Or, at least, there is none that I can find. I guess there must have been a well at some point, but there isn't one now. Buried by sand, ripped out by space aliens, who knows? The despair that comes over me is like nothing I've ever felt before. Alone, no water, no food, no proper shelter. I yell, as loud as I can, 'Is there anyone here? Please! Someone! Anyone!'

A wood beam creaks from somewhere on my right. It's not exactly the answer I'm looking for.

I look inside each building; as expected, each is emptier than the last. After I've confirmed just how alone I am, I pick the corner of what I believe was once a grocery store to rest for a bit. I try to imagine the building stocked with food and water, just to entertain myself. I pretend I'm going to cook a huge meal for the remaining members of the Garde. At the long table in my mind, Marina sits between

Eight and Ella. I put John at the head, with me at the other end. I imagine Nine and Number Five are with us. They kid around with each other, and share stories about all the places they've been. Everyone is laughing, congratulating me on the feast I've prepared, and I tell them all I'm just happy they could make it out here.

'What's your favorite memory of Earth so far?' I imagine Marina asking the table.

'Right now,' John says. 'This one, right here. Safe, with all of you.'

We all agree, raising our glasses to successfully finding each other. Number Five gets up, leaves the room and reenters with an enormous chocolate cake. Everyone cheers and plates are passed around. When I take a bite, it's the most amazing thing I've ever tasted.

Of course, none of this has happened. I'm just a lone, crazy person, sitting in an abandoned, broken-down grocery store in the middle of the desert. I must be crazy, because as I come out of my dream of feasting with the Garde, I realize I am chewing. Chewing air with a satisfied smile on my face. I shake my head and will away my tears. I have not battled Mogs, survived a Mogadorian cell and watched Katarina die to have it all end in the middle of the desert, alone. I pull my knees up to my chest and rest my forehead on them. I have to figure out a plan.

It's still sweltering hot when I leave the ghost town. I've rested from the sun for a while, but I know I have to keep moving before I lose all of my strength. I've walked about a mile towards the mountains through the burning sand when I feel the most intense cramping in my legs and stomach. I focus what little mental energy I have left on uprooting a few nearby cacti and manage to get a mouthful of water from them.

I concentrate on my Legacy and try to summon another thunderstorm from the few scraggly clouds overhead, but all I manage to create is a plume of sand that washes over me, burying me up to my knees.

For the first time, I'm not just nervous about what's to come; I'm scared I'm going to die out here. I have nothing left. The Elders chose me as a warrior to save our race, and I'm going to die in the middle of a desert.

I feel myself starting to panic, to truly lose it. I have just enough of a grip to know I can't lose it – I'm so vulnerable out here that it will be all over if I do. I'm so desperate I think back to last night, and my imaginary meal with the rest of the Garde. To keep myself focused I think about what I wish I could say to them right now.

Hey, Marina, how are things? Me? I'm in a desert heading to some mountain. I'm guessing I must be in New Mexico, based on what Eight said about where he was able to teleport to before. I'm growing weak, Marina. I don't know how much longer I can hold on. And I don't know where you are, but please, please find a way to get from wherever it is you landed and come and find me.

Ella? Do you know how sorry I am about Crayton? I know how much it hurt, watching him die, leaving him behind. I promise you, we will avenge his death, and I will be the one out front. If I make it out of this desert, I will avenge all of Lorien.

Eight, I couldn't find the Loralite. I see no sign of food, water, shelter, civilization, and I am alone. Can you tell me where the Loralite is? I want to get out of here; I want to find you guys.

I don't even feel stupid, chatting in my head to people who are almost certainly on the other side of the world. I close my eyes and desperately wait for someone to answer me. No one does, of course. So, I trudge on. It gets harder to place one foot in front of the other. I start to waver, listing to the right, then the left, almost falling but catching myself at the last moment. Eventually, though, I can't steady myself and I fall forwards. I resign myself to crawling and continue like this for a while with my eyes closed against the blinding sun. After a while I look up to check where the sun is in the sky and again think I'm imagining a mirage when I see a gate made of solid metal a few hundred feet away. It's over twenty feet tall, topped with spiraling barbed wire. Even from this distance, I can hear the hum of electricity. The fence is charged. This goes a long way towards convincing me it isn't a mirage.

Although I have no idea what's behind this gate, I need help, and I'm at the point where I don't care where that help comes from. I crawl over to the gate and manage to sit up. I wave my hands over my head, hoping it's monitored.

'Please help me,' I manage to whisper, my throat as dry as sandpaper.

The gates don't open and no one emerges. I let myself slide back down into the sand. I try to gather the last bit of strength I have to make one more go of it. I roll over onto my stomach and pull myself slowly up to my feet. I decide to test the fence. What's a little electricity after near starvation and life-endangering thirst? I look around and spot a small cactus. I float it up into the air, and drop it onto the fence, where it sizzles and pops. The charred remains fall to the ground, smoking.

I let myself fall first to my knees, then onto my side, then, finally, roll onto my back. I close my eyes. I feel blisters forming on my dry lips. I hear a faint mechanical noise behind me, but I can't lift my head to see what it is. I know I'm losing consciousness. There's a swirling echo in my ears and then a low drumming. A few seconds later, I swear I hear Ella.

Wherever you are, Six, I hope you're okay, she says.

A short laugh comes out of my mouth, followed by a sob. I'm sure there would be tears, if I had any moisture left in my body. *I'm dying in a desert, Ella*, I respond. *The one with the mountains. I'll see you on Lorien one day, Ella.*

I hear her voice again, but this time I can't make

out what she's saying. She is drowned out by a new noise in my head, choppy and loud. And then I feel it. It's a high wind that whips my hair over my face. I slowly open my eyes to see three black helicopters hovering over me. Men yell for me to put my hands over my head, but all I can do is close my eyes.

20

Ella is floating above me. She is in a panic, eyes wide, bubbles shooting out of her mouth. I'm trying to figure out what's going on, how she got here, why there is so much water. I try to reach for her hand, but my arms won't do as I ask them. What happened to me when we teleported? I can tell my face is numb, and there's a pain behind my eyes that's unbearable. My legs won't kick no matter how hard I try. All I can do is watch Ella float higher and higher above me, away from me. Where did all this water come from? My left shoulder begins to rock violently, and it takes a second to realize someone is shaking my arm. Then I see Eight, his black curls hovering over his head like a halo. He hooks his arm under my armpit and I try not to let his look of concern scare me more than I already am. He tries to swim us towards the surface, but the Chest under my arm weighs us down.

I let the freezing water enter my lungs. It's the only thing I can do. Eight kicks the Chest out of my paralyzed arms and yanks me upwards. We start to rise. I look around wildly for a glimpse of Six, but I don't see her.

When my head breaks the surface of the water, the first thing I'm aware of is a glaring, hot sun. Everywhere I look is water. I see Ella treading water nearby. A few minutes in the fresh air gets my limbs to start working, so I tread water as well. Eight appears fully occupied with cursing our luck.

'Where's Six?' I cry, coughing. I keep whipping my head around to see if I can spot her blonde head bobbing around on the surface.

'I couldn't find her down there!' Eight yells. 'I have no idea if she made it or not!'

'Why wouldn't she have made it?' Ella asks, a new panic rising in her voice.

Eight slowly rises out of the water until he's standing on the surface. It doesn't look as easy for him this time. He kicks the tip of a slow passing wave, pissed. 'Damn it! I knew I shouldn't have tried to teleport with so many people!'

'But where could she be? How do we find her?' Ella cries.

'I don't know. For all I know, she's still back at what's left of the cave.'

My limbs are still coming around slowly, and I'm struggling to just keep my head above water. 'What! She'll be killed if she's still there!'

Ella is also struggling to stay afloat. Eight pulls her over to him so she can get on his back, her arms wrapped tightly around his neck. 'Six could have ended up somewhere else, too,' Eight says, trying to sound more hopeful. 'I just don't know where, exactly.'

'Where are *we*?' I ask.

'That much I know.' Eight sounds relieved to have a definitive answer to something. 'We're in the Gulf of Aden. And that . . .' he points at the coastline in the distance that I didn't see before. 'That's Somalia.'

'How do you know?' asks Ella.

'I ended up here once before,' he says flatly. He doesn't elaborate, so there must be more to his story.

I don't know much about Somalia, other than it's in Africa and is in a perpetual state of brutal tribal and civil war, not to mention the poverty that keeps tempers high. I don't know if I have the strength to use my telekinesis or even to swim underwater to get to that coastline; I'm even less sure if I want to. I need to think.

'You know what? I'm going to go under for a bit. I can save some energy down there while we figure out what to do,' I say. As I go down, I hear Ella call out.

'Look for Six!'

Her words give me a surge of strength. Just the possibility of finding Six puts new energy in my dive. I go deep and open my eyes. The water is relatively blue, even this far away from land. There's movement below me and I dive further to find a small school of tuna. I slowly twist around in circles, looking for even a glimpse of Six's dyed blond hair, and more than twice I'm fooled by waving strands of seaweed. I look up and see the faint shadow of Eight's body on the surface. Feeling confident my strength will stay with me, I descend until I touch the bottom. Navigating my way along the sea floor and scanning the water ahead of me, I accidentally brush up against a mass of coral and cut my knee. The sharp pain stuns me for a second and I reach down and touch it, to heal it, and it takes longer than I expect for my Legacy to work. Whatever happens during teleporting must have some effect on our Legacies and our strength. Grateful that my breathing seems to be okay, I can only hope this doesn't last long – I don't want us to be vulnerable.

I keep moving and eventually find my Chest next to Eight's, and spot the large, blue Loralite stone a few feet away from them both. I try to pick up the Chests, but am too weak to budge them. I look up and see Eight's shadow still in the same spot and decide to ask for his help.

As I ascend I cut through a school of beautiful orange fish. I break the surface. 'No sign of Six, but the Loralite stone is down there, right next to our Chests,' I report. 'Let's get them and go. We'll teleport somewhere else, see if we can catch up to wherever Six has landed.'

'Don't we need to be *at* the Loralite to teleport? How will I get down there?' Ella asks. 'I can't hold my breath for that long.'

'You don't have to,' Eight says with a grin.

'Do you have a Legacy that turns you into a torpedo people can catch a ride on, too?' I ask.

'Better,' Eight says. He reaches into his pocket and grabs the green crystal he put there when his Chest was first returned to him. The crystal begins to glow, and then a crazy amount of wind starts to shoot out from it. Eight aims it at the ocean. A shallow crater forms in the water below him and he falls into it. 'Come on! Quick!'

Ella and I swim into the crater. Eight holds out his free hand and I take it; Ella grabs my other hand.

'Get ready. We're about to drop. Fast!' he says. 'You have to stay with me because the water will collapse behind us. When we get to the bottom, Ella, be prepared to hold your breath long enough for me to grab the Chests.'

'Everyone keep your eyes open for Six,' I say.

Ella squeezes my hand. 'If she's down there, we'll find her.'

Eight positions the crystal so it's aimed at the ocean floor. 'Here we go!' he yells. We fall fast, the wind from the crystal blasting a small circle of water out of our way until it unites again a few feet behind Ella. We're inside a bubble, shooting through the water. Eight howls in amusement; I can't help but join in.

Ella grabs my arm. 'Six is in trouble!' She says. 'She says she's in the desert!'

'What are you talking about?' I reply, as fish and sharks and squid pass us in a blur. 'How do you know that?'

Ella hesitates for a second before yelling, 'I don't really know! I just talked to her somehow in my head! She says she's dying!'

'If she's in the desert, then she's in New Mexico already!' Eight shouts.

'Eight, we've got to get there right away,' I cry.

We arrive on the ocean floor and try to run on the muddy bottom, but it's impossible to move quickly. Water rushes in behind our pocket of air and the crystal swiftly becomes useless, creating a small whirlpool in front of us. I look back to make sure Ella is okay and holding her breath. When I turn around, Eight has transformed into a black octopus. He swings two tentacles out and snatches up our Chests, and with two of his other tentacles he grabs our hands. Eight pulls us towards the glowing blue Loralite stone sticking out of the mud floor. Before I can look at Ella again, I'm engulfed in darkness.

21

Nine and I ride the elevator down in silence. I'm furious and utterly humiliated, and it's got nothing to do with the feelings welling up inside me. When we enter the apartment, Bernie Kosar jumps off the couch to ask if we are finished with all the nonsense.

'I don't think it's up to me. What do you say, Johnny?' Nine mutters. He opens the fridge and pulls out a slice of cold pizza. He flips the tip of it into his mouth, takes a huge bite and chews noisily.

I lean down and scratch BK's chin. 'I hope so, buddy.'

With a mouth full of pizza, Nine says, 'Pack up your doggie bags, BK, because we're hitting the road. We're heading back to Paradise city, where the girls are pretty. And, damn, Four, take a shower already. You smell like smoke.'

'Shut up,' I say, falling onto the couch. Bernie Kosar climbs into my lap and looks up at me with sad eyes.

Nine walks away, down the hallway. He calls back to me, 'A deal's a deal, man! We leave for Paradise in a couple of hours, so you may want to grab a quick nap after your shower. And, hey! It's a road trip! You can't be bummed about a road trip!'

I'm exhausted, but I slump towards my room. A deal *is* a deal. The bed moans when I fall onto it, but after a few minutes, I can't bear my own smell. I drag myself into the shower. The water can't get hot enough on my skin, a side effect of my Legacy. As I stand under the spray, so tired I'm swaying on my feet, I replay the fight on the roof in my mind. I try to figure out how I lost against Nine, but I can't. I'm so tired. I think I'm mumbling to myself. I turn off the water and listen to the drops fall onto the shower floor. I grab a towel as I stumble back to bed. I need to rest.

I climb in between the sheets and using telekinesis, turn off the light. I hear Nine's thudding steps as he moves towards the surveillance room and I close my eyes. Sleep blankets my mind for a second before I hear a noise. Nine is lightly tapping on my open door. I have my back to him and I don't move, even when he clears his throat and starts to speak. 'Hey. Johnny? I'm sorry that I can be such a dick. I could blame it on being locked up for so long, that does something to you. But, honestly, I'm pushing here because I really do think I'm right. We *need* to go to Paradise. *Now.* So I hope we can be friends. I want to be friends. And I'm glad you're here.'

I haven't moved a muscle the whole time he's speaking and I'm stunned by this moment of sensitivity. I'm not sure what to say, even as I flip over. He's a slouched shadow leaning in the doorframe. 'I'm glad I'm here, too. Thanks.'

'Sure.'

Nine slaps the wall twice, looks down at the ground, then turns and walks away. As his footsteps move down the hall, my eyes drift closed. After a few minutes, I hear faint whispers. I know a vision or nightmare is coming. I'm aware I'm in bed, yet I'm frozen in place. I feel myself floating, and when a dark doorway forms above me, I start to spin in the air incredibly fast. I rocket through the doorway and I'm moving through a black tunnel with my arms stuck to my sides. As the black turns to blue, the whispers grow louder, repeating the same thing, over and over, 'There is more to know.'

The blue tunnel turns to green, and green turns back to black. Then, bam, I fall out of the tunnel and my bare feet land on a familiar rocky floor. I swing my arms and find I have control of my body once again. I'm back in the arena at the top of the mountain. I whip my head around, looking for Sam, but he's nowhere to be seen. Neither is the other Garde member. The space is completely empty, even the bleachers.

But then, in the center of the arena floor, a black stone flips over, and on the other side crouches a large Mog soldier, wearing a ragged black cloak and black boots. His waxy pale skin shines and the sword he holds above his head shimmers, as if lit from within. When he sees me, he stands and points the sword at me menacingly. It's pulsing, as if somehow alive, an extension of the evil that wields it.

I don't hesitate. I rush right at him, my palms lighting up and emitting a powerful beam. When I'm ten yards away, I aim the Lumen at my feet and light them on fire. The flames climb up my body as I leap. The soldier jumps at me and when we meet, I burrow a smoldering hole right through his chest. He turns to ash before hitting the ground.

To my right, another black stone flips over; it's another sword-wielding Mog. Two more flip to my left, and I hear others appear behind me. The stone under my feet starts to vibrate, and I dive away just as it rotates to produce a Mogadorian holding a cannon. After punching a hole through the closest soldier on my left, I start launching fireballs, battling with a newfound strength. My red bracelet comes to life, blasting open to sever the head of the giant soldier. In a minute, I wipe them all out. My adrenaline is pumping, and I'm listening for more stones to reveal my next round of suitors.

A dozen stones flip in front of me, and then fifty on both

sides. The largest, best-equipped Mog soldiers I've ever seen surround me. I create a small ring of fire around myself and move backwards, the fire maintaining its perimeter until I'm against the wall of the arena. The fire burns between the Mogs and me. Somehow, though, I don't think my position is particularly secure.

I widen the ring of fire around me until it hits a row of soldiers. They catch fire, but don't turn to ash. In fact, they walk right through the fire with their weapons up. I throw dozens of fireballs, but this time they have no effect. Something red zips in the air over my head, and I watch it puncture the chest of a Mog soldier who continues to march forward. I recognize the item. It's Nine's staff. Nine drops out of the empty bleachers to the spot right next to me. Even in the middle of an attack, I feel relieved to see him. I immediately feel safer, more confident that even these fire-resistant Mogs will be defeated now that it is the two of us.

'Nice of you to join me!' I yell.

He stands right next to me but doesn't seem to hear my voice. 'Hey, Nine!' I try again, but he doesn't still react. He just keeps staring at the advancing Mogs.

When the soldiers are only a few feet away from us, the ground below our feet starts to tremble and quake. I try and hold on to the wall, but I can't keep my balance. Next thing I know, a tremendous *boom* shakes the opposite end of the arena and pieces of black rock rain down on us. Nine dodges a large boulder that slams into the wall behind me, leaving a giant hole that leads to the outside. Looking through, I can see blue skies.

From the swirling dust and flying debris a large stage rises out of the explosion. There, in the middle, is Setrákus Ra. *Like an evil rock star,* I can't help but think. The purple scar around his neck burns brightly above the three blue pendants on his chest. To my horror, the moment he appears, my fire goes out. I try to illuminate my legs with my Lumen, but my palms suddenly won't light. Setrákus Ra slams the end of his golden staff with the moving eye onto the ground and roars for silence. The soldiers in front of me snap to attention, turning from me and Nine to him. One by one, they rest their weapons at their sides.

'All of you have been chosen to end this fight!' Setrákus Ra yells. 'You will go forth and you will destroy the Loric children. When they are dead, you will bring me their pendants and their Chests. You will crush their human friends. *You will not fail me!'*

The Mog soldiers cheer and raise their fists in unison.

Setrákus Ra slams his staff down on the stone floor with another thundering bang. 'Mogadore will rule this galaxy! Everything, on every planet, will be ours!' The soldiers cheer and wave their weapons in the air.

'Together, we will fight. I will fight with you. Together, we will win this battle and annihilate all who live on Earth!'

I try again to light my Lumen but it still doesn't work. Then I try to lift a large sharp stone at my feet with my mind to launch at Setrákus Ra. It doesn't budge. My bracelet shield has retracted and shows no sign of kicking into action. My Legacies – and my Inheritance – have left me.

The soldiers have turned back around and once again aim their weapons at us. Without our Legacies, we're sitting ducks. We *have* to get out of here.

'Nine! This way!' I yell.

Finally, this seems to get through to him. He whips his

head around and looks at me. We move towards the hole in the wall. Standing in a ray of cold sunlight at the lip of it, I peer down into a valley, thousands of feet below. I look over my shoulder; there are Mog soldiers charging at us.

'We'll walk on the side of the mountain,' Nine says. 'Here. Take my hand.'

I grab his hand. We've only taken a single step down the side of the snowy mountaintop when we realize Nine's Legacy has failed him too. Instead of feeling the mountain beneath my feet, there is only air. We're falling. I look over at a shocked Nine, his long black hair whipping all around his face. Below us, two dark doorways are approaching fast. I prepare myself for a painful impact, my stomach doing backflips as I fly through the air. To my utter amazement, I go headfirst through the door on the left and I keep falling until I find myself in a dark tunnel alive with booms of thunder, cracks of lightning. The whispering starts again, and as the tunnel turns to green to blue and back to black, the hoarse voice I heard when the vision began speaks again: 'New Mexico.'

My eyes snap open and I sit up, my face damp with sweat. I rip off the sheets that cling to me. *New Mexico.* I leap up and charge down the hall towards Nine's room, determined to convince him once and for all. If I have to fight him again, so be it. I will keep fighting until I win.

I stop in front of Nine's door and turn on my Lumen, needing to confirm that my Legacies really haven't abandoned me. I knock and push the door open. I'm surprised to find Nine sitting up in bed with his head in his hands.

'Nine,' I say, flipping on the light. 'I'm sorry, I know a deal's a deal and you did beat me. But we have to go to —'

'New Mexico. I know, Johnny. I know.' He shakes his head. I'm not sure if he's trying to wake up or come to grips with his sudden reversal. Probably both. 'Just let me wake up a bit.'

'So, you've reconsidered?'

He plants his feet on the floor, one at a time. 'No, I haven't *reconsidered*. But when you're falling to your death off a mountain because your Legacies don't work and some ghost keeps repeating "New Mexico," you take the hint.'

'You had the same vision?' I ask. The comfort I felt when I saw Nine – it was because he was really there. It dawns on me that Nine and I have a connection and I should give him more respect than I have been. I have to stop seeing him as an adversary. Our lives depend on it.

Nine pulls on a shirt, and gives me a condescending look I know well. 'No, you idiot. Haven't you figured it out yet? I didn't have a vision *too*. We were in the *same vision*. It's been happening all week. Get a clue, would you?'

I'm flustered, and I don't hide it well. 'But whenever I talked about them you blew them off. You blew *me* off. You kept saying they're just dreams and all that. You could see how the dreams have been tormenting me, Nine! You've been acting like I'm nuts for taking them seriously!'

'First of all, you believe you're Pittacus Lore, so technically you *are* nuts. Second, I wasn't messing with your head. I did blow the visions off at first; mine *and* yours. Thought they were bullshit. When Setrákus Ra asked me to surrender, just like he asked you and that other kid, I figured the visions were a form of mind game or some trick, perpetrated by the Mogs. I didn't think we should trust them; I definitely didn't think we should do anything they suggested we do. In fact,

I thought the safest bet was to do anything *but* what they wanted. But this time . . .' Nine pauses. 'This time, it felt like a warning. A warning we should take seriously. Now, I'm pretty convinced that there is some serious shit about to go down, Four.'

As relieved as I am that he has finally decided to listen, I'm frustrated it took so long. 'That's what I've been trying to tell you! Okay, then, let's go! Have you thought about how we're going to get there? Oh, man, please tell me you and Sandor have your own helicopter or airplane tucked away somewhere!'

'Sorry, dude, they were on our wish list.' he yawns and stretches. 'But I do have a car in the parking garage. And I *love* to drive. Fast.'

Nine and I grab as much as we can from the weapons room, stuffing two large duffel bags full of rifles, handguns, and grenades. I pick up a rocket launcher but Nine says it won't fit in the trunk. We need the remaining space for ammo. Next, we race to the surveillance room to grab the tablet.

Nine sits down and starts punching keys at one of the computers. 'I have to shut this sucker down. Wouldn't want any of it to be useful to someone who isn't welcome. Do me a favor. While I'm dealing with this, check on the Garde with that tablet thing.'

I press the blue circle in the upper corner and wait. I see our two radiating blue dots in Chicago. Then I see one in northern New Mexico, and there's still one in Jamaica. I wait a few seconds for the other three to appear, but they don't.

'Um, Nine? I only see four,' I say, my voice rising in panic. 'There're only four blue dots!'

He rips the tablet out of my hand. 'Let me see it. They must somehow be off the grid,' Nine says. He doesn't sound so sure of himself all of a sudden. He presses the green triangle and the green pulsing dots show up on the map in New Mexico and Egypt, just like before. 'At least the missing three didn't take one of the ships.'

I look closer and press the blue circle again. I realize the blue dot in New Mexico is now at the exact same spot as the green dot. 'That Garde in New Mexico is on top of the ship, if that *is* a ship.'

'Hope whoever that is knows it would be one *lonely* flight,' Nine says. I shake my head at him and look back at the screen, trying to figure out what our next move should be.

Then it hits me. 'Wait. The government is involved in all this somehow, right? What else is in New Mexico? Area 51! Is that where this green dot is? The most well-known place for UFO sightings?' It's all starting to come together.

Nine pulls the keyboard closer and starts tapping even more quickly. 'Cool your jets, cowboy. First of all, Area 51 is in Nevada. Second, we *aliens* know that place is just a decoy. It's a meaningless airplane hangar, give or take.' A map of New Mexico appears on the main screen and Nine zooms in on the northern half. 'Okay, wait a second.' He looks from the tablet back to the computer screen. 'Now *this* is interesting. You weren't that far off, after all. We may not be headed for Area 51, but we *are* going someplace just as secret.'

'What do you mean?' I ask, while I wonder why I'm always playing catch up with this guy.

Nine pushes his chair away from the desk with an annoyingly satisfied grin on his face. 'Holy shit. It all makes sense now.' He stabs the screen with his finger. 'In this part of New

Mexico there's a town in the middle of the desert called Dulce. Is any of this ringing familiar? No? Dulce, as in the infamous underground Dulce Base, run by the one and only U.S. government. That *must be* where our ship is. Now I'm positive those are our ships, blinking away on that screen! In their perfect wisdom, the government feeds the rumors about Area 51 so all the UFO freaks stay away from the real deal in Dulce.'

I can't help but smile. 'So, now we're going to an underground government base?'

'I certainly hope so,' Nine says, shutting down the computer. He practically takes a bow, so pleased with himself for figuring all this out. 'Although it's supposed to be insanely secure and completely impossible to get into. And that's why it's the perfect place to hide our ship.'

'Or to hide the random aliens you find during the course of your travels,' I add.

It feels as if everything has been turned upside down since I woke up. We quickly get moving, piling the weapons, our Chests, and the supplies in the elevator. BK barely squeezes in with us as the elevator doors close. Nine surprises me with how gentle he sounds when he addresses the closed doors, 'You were a sweet home, Chicago. I hope I see you again.'

We descend rapidly. 'Hey, man,' I say. 'Remember, our *real* home is *so* much cooler.' He doesn't say anything, but I see his shoulders relax.

The elevator doors open into an underground garage. We pause and carefully look around before we start to unload. With the coast clear, Nine and I throw the bags over our shoulders and BK follows. As we turn a corner, I see we're headed for a car hidden under a dusty tarp. After the luxury of the apartment, I can only imagine what must lurk beneath it. I can picture a yellow Ferrari, or something equally flashy. Or maybe it's a white convertible Porsche or even a black Lotus.

Nine must have read my thoughts. He winks at me and yanks the tarp off to reveal our ride. There, in all its glory, sits an old, beat-up, beige Ford Contour. Not exactly the pimped-out ride I was expecting, but bling is now the least of my concerns; this thing doesn't look like it'll even start.

'Are you serious?' I ask, not even bothering to hide my disgust.

Nine looks at me innocently, even though he clearly knew what I was expecting. 'What? You were hoping for a Camaro?'

'Not exactly. But I was hoping for something with less rust spots. Something that looks less determined to die,' I say.

'Shut up and get in, Johnny,' he says, tossing his bags into the trunk. 'You ain't seen nothin' yet.'

22

I wake to the sensation of rocking back and forth. Everything hurts. My whole body feels fried by the sun: my throat, my skin, my feet and my head. My lips are so dry and burned, I can't even put them together. My eyelids are the worst of all, and they refuse to open, no matter how desperately I want to see where I am. The rocking and swaying continues and it dawns on me I must be in a moving vehicle. A wave of nausea rolls over me. I try to lift my hands to my head, but that's when I discover they're tied down. So are my legs. Now I'm wide awake, and I force my eyes open and look madly around, but all I see is darkness. I close my eyes again. The desert sun must have left me blind.

I try to call out for help, but all I can do is wheeze and cough. My ears pick up an echo, and I concentrate on the air around me. I cough again, just to hear the echo once more. It's enough sound to understand I'm in a tight space, and that the space around me is made of metal. It feels like I'm in a coffin, and I almost wretch.

That's when I start to panic. What if I'm not blind? What if I'm really dead? I can't be. I am in way too much pain to be dead. But I feel buried alive.

My breath starts to come fast and furious when a

man's voice stops my panic attack cold. It's loud and electronic, coming through a speaker. 'Are you awake?'

I try to answer him, but my throat is too dry. I tap my fingers on the bench and realize it's metal, too. A few seconds later there is a noise to my right, and I can sense something has been placed near me.

'There's a glass of water and a straw beside you. Take a sip,' the man says.

I turn my head and find the straw with my mouth. The skin on my lips cracks as I try to close them around the straw. When I take a sip of water, I can taste the metallic tinge of blood and I hear a low humming in my ears. It's the same hum I heard at the gate. The box I'm in must be flowing with electricity.

'What were you doing at that gate?' The man asks. Every time he speaks, I am struck by how neutral his voice is. It isn't friendly, but neither is it threatening.

'Lost,' I whisper. 'I was lost.'

'How did you get lost?'

I take another sip before saying, 'I don't know.'

'*You don't know.* I see. Your number is six, is it not?'

I cough and choke at the question, mentally chewing myself out for doing so. I'm usually cooler than this, but my mind is completely cooked by the sun. If he wasn't sure of the answer before, he is now. I resolve to get a grip, to stop making stupid mistakes.

The voice is back. 'Well, Number Six. You're pretty

famous around here. The footage from the high school in Paradise and the way you took down those helicopters in Tennessee was impressive. And then there's the incredible show you put on in D.C. last week, breaking John Smith and Sam Goode out of a federal facility. You are quite the little warrior princess, aren't you?'

I'm still stuck on how he could know who I am; now he's talking like he had front-row seats to my life? My body sways hard to the left, and I realize I must be in a moving vehicle that just took a turn, taking me who knows where. I push against the strap over my forehead – nothing happens. I try using my telekinesis, but as soon as I even start to focus my thoughts pain rolls through my stomach so bad I almost throw up again.

'What you need to do is relax. Trying to fight isn't going to get you anywhere. You're dehydrated and most likely have heat stroke. You're going to feel pretty sick for a while.'

'Who are you?' I manage to ask, painfully.

'Agent David Purdy, FBI,' he says. I feel slightly better knowing I'm in the hands of the U.S. government, not captured by the Mogs. I couldn't go through that again, knowing what was coming, especially now that the charm that protected me the first time has been broken. With the FBI, my chances of survival have just skyrocketed. No matter how aggressive they are, they aren't monsters. All I need right now is a little patience; the opportunity to escape will come. Purdy doesn't know that, probably assumes it can't be true. Right now, I'll just follow his advice. Relax. Rehydrate. Wait. I might as well see what else he's willing to tell me about what he knows about me, what he knows about all of this.

'Where am I?' I ask.

The speaker squeals before Agent Purdy answers. 'You're in a transport. It's a short trip.'

Again I try to use my telekinesis to undo my leg straps, but I'm still too weak and the attempt makes me nauseous again. I take another couple of sips of water to give myself time to think. 'Where are you taking me?'

'We've got a reunion planned for you with a friend, or maybe I should say a friend of John Smith's. Do you call him John? Or, do you call him Number Four?'

'I don't know what you're talking about,' I say. I pause before answering. 'I don't know anyone named John Four.'

All of a sudden, I remember what happened back in the desert, just before I blacked out at the gate. I felt half out of my mind, so much so I wasn't even sure the helicopters landing close by were even real. I remember hearing Ella's voice. No. I didn't just hear her voice; we *spoke* to one another. She asked, I answered. Given the fact that it's the FBI who has me, it's a pretty good bet there really were helicopters. If *those* were real, maybe I did communicate with Ella. Has a new Legacy kicked in? Just when I needed it most.

Ella? Can you hear me? I try again, just in case.

The FBI is holding me, some agent named Purdy has me locked up and we're in some kind of vehicle. Purdy says it isn't far, wherever it is we're going.

'How did you get to the desert, Number Six?' Purdy's voice interrupts. 'Weren't you just in India, with your friends? Remember that? Just like all the other kids, reading schoolbooks and being kidnapped at the airport.'

How does he know that?

'How did you know where the base was?' His voice is losing a bit of its neutrality. I think I hear just a hint of impatience.

'What base?' I ask. I'm having a hard time thinking straight.

'The one we found you dying outside of in the desert. How did you know where to find it?'

I try to turn invisible, but again, the moment I try testing my Legacy, my stomach erupts with a ferocious and immediate pain. I want so badly to curl up in a ball, but the straps hold me flat and the pain takes my breath away.

'Drink your water,' the agent advises again. His voice is back to its detached neutrality.

Just as I did the first time, I obey, take a sip and wait. The pain finally starts to dull, but then a powerful wave of dizziness washes over me. My mind feels like it's a car careening out of control, swerving this way and that. The thoughts, too many of them to be coherent, come fast and furious. The events from the last few days flash by me. I see myself taking hold of Marina's arm right before we teleported. I see Crayton lying motionless. I watch myself saying goodbye to John and Sam. I almost forget where I am. That is, until the voice forces me back to my present circumstances.

'Where is Number Four?' He is nothing if not consistent, this guy.

'Who?' I ask, forcing myself to focus on what he's saying. If I don't, I'm going to make another mistake like I did before.

All of a sudden, the calm voice is completely gone. He screams through the speaker, 'Where is Number Four?' I wince at the noise.

'Go to hell,' I spit. I'm not telling him anything.

Ella? Marina? Anyone? If anyone can hear me, you need to say something. I need help. I'm in some desert. All I know is I'm near a U.S. government base, and the FBI has me. We're going somewhere, but I don't know where. And there's something wrong with me. I can't use my Legacies.

'Who was with you in India, Number Six? Who were the man and the two girls?'

I stay silent. I picture Ella's face. The youngest Lorien left. I know how that must weigh on her. And now, she's without Crayton. It was just a day ago I was jealous of what they had, and now he's gone.

'What numbers were they? Who were the girls?' Agent Purdy sounds impatient, though his voice is calmer now.

'That's my band. I play the drums. They sing. I love *Josie and the Pussycats*, don't you? I like to watch retro cartoons. All the kids are doing it.' My lips crack and bleed again when I smile. I don't mind. I taste my blood on my tongue and smile wider.

'Six?' the man asks in a gentler voice. I guess he's going to try the Good Cop tactic. 'Was that Number Five and Seven you were with at the airport in India? Who is the older man? Who are the girls?'

Suddenly it's as if I can't control what comes out of my mouth. My voice doesn't even sound like mine when I say, 'Marina and Ella. They're sweet, sweet girls. I just wish they were a little stronger.' What am I saying? Why am I saying anything?

'Are Marina and Ella members of your race? Why do they need to be stronger? And what number is Marina?'

I catch myself this time before answering, shocked that I even opened my mouth to answer again. I concentrate all my energies to find my voice, to respond as I know I should. It's like I'm battling a war within me. 'I don't know what you're talking about. Why do you keep talking about numbers?'

Agent Purdy's voice blasts into the box. 'I know who you are! You're from another planet! I know you kids go by numbers! We have your ship, for Christ's sake!'

At the mention of our ship, my mind starts to spin. I flash back to the journey from Lorien. I see myself as just a kid, staring out the ship's windows at the emptiness of space as we travel towards Earth. I eat at a long white table and look at the other eight kids, each with their Cêpans. There's a boy with long black hair laughing and throwing food. A blonde girl sits next to him quietly eating a piece of fruit. The Cêpans at the end of the table watch the kids closely. I see a young Marina crying, her legs tucked up to her chest, sitting on the floor under a control panel. Her Cêpan is on her knees next to her, trying to coax her to stand up with her. I remember I got in trouble with a boy with short black hair.

The next face I see is a young Number Four. His blond hair is long and wavy. He's kicking the wall with his bare foot, angry about something. He turns around and grabs a pillow, slamming it to the floor. Four looks up, sees me watching, and his face turns bright red. I hand him a toy, something I've stolen from him. The guilt I felt back then rushes over me all over again, just as strong as it was when it first happened. The other faces in the room grow fuzzy.

Then I see myself in Katarina's arms when we landed on Earth. I remember the door of the ship opening.

Where have these memories come from? As hard as I tried before, I could never remember very much about our journey to Earth aside from a few small details. I've never had this vivid a flashback before.

'Are you listening to me?' Purdy yells. 'We have talked to the Mogadorians,' he says. That statement yanks me back to the present with a thud. 'Did you know that?'

'Oh, yeah? What'd they have to say?' I ask, trying to sound like I'm just making conversation, but I regret it instantly. Why would I admit knowing who the Mogs are? Before I can dwell on my mistake too much, my mind drifts back to the ship, to its doors opening, to the human with brown hair and large thick glasses standing, waiting to greet us. In his hands are a briefcase and a white tablet, and behind him sits a big box of clothes. Somehow I know that's Sam's dad. Sam. Oh, how I want to see Sam again.

'I want to see Sam,' I slur. Even though I don't want to say anything more, reveal anything else to the agent, I can't help myself. I hear my voice, feel my brain thick and sluggish, and instantly I realize there must have been drugs in the water. That's why I can't hold a thought in my head, why I keep drifting into my past, and why I feel such pain when I try to use my Legacies.

I kissed Sam. I should have kissed him for real but I was too worried what John would think.

John. I kissed John, too. I would really like to kiss John again. My stomach gets kind of squirmy when I play back the moment when John grabbed me by the shoulders and turned me towards him. He lowered his face to mine, but just before our lips touched, the house exploded. I can feel my chin tilt upward as I replay the moment again and again. Except this time, when the house explodes, we kiss. The kiss is perfect.

'Sam?' Agent Purdy asks, interrupting my thoughts. I was really enjoying remembering that kiss. 'I'm guessing you mean Sam Goode, right?'

Sam's face is now all I can see and my head is

spinning out of control. 'Yeah. Sure. I want to see Sam Goode.' I can hear my voice drifting off.

'Is he one of you? What number is Sam Goode?'

My eyelids grow heavy and I find myself falling asleep. The drugs are finally doing me some small favor.

'Six!' He shouts. 'Hey, Six! Wake up! We're not finished here!'

His shouts jar me so badly, I jerk up, only to be stopped by my restraints.

'Six? Six! Where is Sam Goode? Where is John Smith?'

'I'm going to kill you,' I whisper. My anger and frustration with being tied up and powerless is getting the best of me. 'When I find you, I am going to kill you.'

'I have no doubt you'll try.' The agent laughs.

I try to clear my head, to concentrate on where I am. Too quickly, everything begins to spin until I pass out.

The room is tiny and made of cement. There's a toilet and cement block with a mattress tied down on it and a blanket that's too short to cover me. I've been awake for two hours, maybe more. I'm having a difficult time putting thoughts together. I'm trying to establish some kind of timeline from when I found myself alone in the desert, to the gate, to waking up to my interrogation ride of horror. I need to figure out where I've been, how much time has passed and what information I let slip.

Unscrambling my brain isn't easy. Since the moment I regained consciousness in this cell, the overhead lights have strobed relentlessly. I feel a sharp, pounding pain in my head. My mouth is dry and I hold my churning stomach as I try to focus on the most important part of my recall, my conversation with the agent.

I manage to turn invisible, just to see if I can, but as soon as I do I'm attacked with that extreme nausea I felt on the ride, so I materialize immediately. Either the drugs are still in my system or this is being caused by something else.

I close my eyes for a few minutes to escape the flashing lights. They're so bright, it's impossible to block them out entirely. I remember Agent Purdy said he was in contact with the Mogadorians. Why would the U.S. government be talking to the Mogadorians? And why would he admit that to me? Don't they know the Mogs are the enemy? What I can't figure out is, how much does the government know about me, about my kind? As soon as the Mogadorians wipe out the Garde, the next thing they'll do is kill every last human on Earth. Doesn't the government know that? I'm guessing the Mogs have presented a very different picture of themselves.

I hear a man's voice come from somewhere above me. It's not Purdy, the agent who spoke to me in the container. I open my eyes to look for a vent or speaker, but I can't see anything with the strobe light flashing relentlessly.

'Prepare yourself for transport, Number Six.' A

small panel in the middle of the metal door opens with a clang. I stumble over and find a plastic cup of purple liquid sitting on a shelf. My insides gurgle at the sight of it. Why is it purple? Is it drugged, like the water I was drinking earlier?

'You must drink the water to be transported. If you do not drink the water, we will be forced to inject you with it by any means necessary.'

'Go to hell!' I yell at the ceiling.

'Drink,' the voice repeats. It does not invite discussion.

I pick up the cup and walk to the toilet. I hold the cup high and tilt it, making a big show of pouring it out. The last drop has barely fallen when the cell door whips open. Several men with batons and shields rush in at me. Acid bubbles in my stomach as I try and steel myself for a fight because I know I'm going to have to use my Legacies. I decide that this time, I can do it. And maybe I can use the flashing lights to my advantage.

I greet the first officer with an open punch to the throat. As a baton swings down at me on my left, I catch the attacker's wrist and give it a good twist. I hear it snap. He screams and releases the baton. Now, I have a weapon.

The officers form a circle around me but in the flashing light, our movements look like they're happening in slow motion and are hard to follow. I pick a man at random and attack, cracking my baton across both his knees. He falls and I pounce on his neighbour. The physical exertion causes sickness to

226

crawl up my throat, but I swallow it back down. Now that I've managed to push through once, hopefully it will become easier. I slam the butt of the baton on the man's temple. One of the remaining men hits me on the back of my head with something, and another one grabs a chunk of my hair and yanks. Using my telekinesis, I smash them against each other. The body slam makes both of them fall, and I kick them hard.

The once incapacitating sickness ebbs and flows, but my strength doesn't – it is *back*. Now armed with two batons, I fight off three more men. When they start firing Tasers, I freeze the sharp probes in the air before swinging them back towards the shooters. Finally, the doorway is clear and looks like it is staying that way. When I step outside the cell, I brace myself and turn myself invisible. The pain is the worst yet, but I know I can push past it. I just need to hold on for a little while longer, until I can get out, and find the others.

23

I come to facedown in wet grass. I lift my head and press my palms onto the ground to get my shoulders up. I hear Eight groan from somewhere nearby. Ella calls my name, but my head throbs too much for me to sit up and look for her.

'Six?' I whisper into the air. 'Are you here?'

'I don't see her anywhere, Marina,' Ella says, coming over and sitting down next to me. I lay my cheek back down on the grass and allow myself to just lie there for a few more minutes. Ella brushes a lock of hair off my cheek, but I'm numb and don't feel a thing. Sickness rises in my throat as I hear Eight continue to groan. Ella seems unaffected. I *never* want to teleport again.

I look around. My vision keeps doubling, and I struggle to bring it under control. Based on how green and lush it is, it's obvious we didn't land where we intended. 'This isn't New Mexico, is it?'

'Not even close,' Ella whispers.

I finally feel as if I can move, albeit slowly, and I look up at Ella. Her brown eyes are hard to read in the darkness, then I register it must be the middle of the night. I look past Ella and into the starry sky. I flash back to the blue ocean, to Eight turning into a black octopus. Then I remember what Ella said just before we teleported.

'Ella. Did I imagine it, or did you say you *talked to Six*?' She nods. 'With your mind, right?'

Ella looks away. 'I'm sure you think I'm nuts. I keep asking myself if it really happened. Maybe I just wanted it so badly. . . .' Ella shakes her head and looks down at me, her face serious. 'No. I did *not* imagine it. I *know* I spoke to her. She said she was in a desert. That *must* mean she made it to New Mexico, right?'

'Ella, you're not crazy. I believe you and I think you're right,' I say, pressing my fingers against my pounding temples, willing away the pain and the fuzz that keeps me from thinking clearly. 'You must be developing a Legacy. What we need to do now is figure out how it happened that time so we can do it again. '

Ella's eyes widen. 'Really? You think it's a Legacy? What's it called?' she asks eagerly.

'Telepathy,' Eight's voice comes from behind me.

I roll over, grimacing from the pain, and look up at Eight, who's standing on a huge stone slab held up by two even larger gray boulders.

I sit up, roll over onto all fours, and get unsteadily to my feet. Hands on hips, I turn around and realize this place looks awfully familiar. But it isn't because I've been here before. I know this place from all the pictures, from textbooks. I look back up at Eight. 'Are we seriously at –'

'Stonehenge? Oh, yeah.'

'Wow,' I whisper, slowly turning around again to survey the scene. Ella walks over to a stone that must be twenty-five feet high, her head tipped back as she drags her hand across the surface. I understand the impulse to reach out and touch it. I mean, it's *Stonehenge*. I can't help but join her. The stones are cold and smooth, and just touching them makes me feel like I'm three thousand years old. Some are in perfect shape while others look like they must be mere shards of what they used to be. We all wander around for a while, seeing up close what most people only ever see in textbooks.

'Eight? What *is* telepathy, exactly? Do you know how to use it, and how I can control it?' Ella asks.

'Telepathy is the ability to transfer thoughts from one being to another. You're able to communicate with someone else's brain. Go ahead, try it with me.'

Ella circles around and comes to a stop in front of Eight. She closes her eyes. As I watch, all I can think is how amazing it would be if Ella *has* developed this Legacy. It would allow us to connect the Garde, no matter where any of them are, anywhere in the world. After a few seconds, Ella opens her eyes and looks at Eight. 'Did you hear me?'

'I didn't,' Eight says, shaking his head sadly. 'You just need to keep trying. It always takes time to figure out how to work with our Legacies. Telepathy will be no different.'

Her shoulders sag in disappointment anyway. 'Your Chests are over there, by the way,' she says, pointing.

Eight turns to me, stretching from side to side. 'I just need a little more time to recover from that last one. I want to be as strong as possible when we try again for New Mexico, okay?' He climbs up on a nearby rock.

'I don't know,' I sigh. 'I felt so horrible when I came out of that last one. Injuries are one thing – teleporting makes me feel sick. I don't know if I can do it again. And what's to stop us from ending up back at the bottom of the ocean? Meanwhile, it sounds like Six is in serious trouble, and we're bouncing around from place to place. We may never land in New Mexico!'

'I know, I know,' Eight says, hopping down from a stone and brushing off the dust from his pants. 'I know how frustrating this is. But doing something is better than nothing. And the only thing we can do is keep trying until we get where we need to go. We three will stick together, we will keep trying and we *will* find Six.' I don't know where he gets his calm, his conviction.

Ella wanders off behind a grouping of stones as I say, 'You know, there are other ways of getting from one place to another. We could just find an airport and fly there from here.'

Eight scratches his chin, deep in thought as he starts to walk. I follow him to the center of the monument. 'If Six really is in trouble, an airplane isn't the solution. It would take us forever to get to her.' He stops for a minute and turns to face me. 'Besides, I see us finding her.' I look at him quizzically, but he just grins and shrugs. What does he mean?

'Eight. Did you have a vision? What else did you see? Who else did you see?'

He shrugs. 'I can't really tell you more than that. I just see it; or, I feel it. I think it's a Legacy I haven't figured out yet. The only way I can describe it is that it feels like a sixth sense.'

'Is that how you knew we were coming to India?' I ask.

'Yeah,' he says. 'I don't have any control over it. These flashes, images, just come to me.'

We continue to walk through the group of massive stones and find Ella off by herself, sitting against a rock. When we approach, she looks up and says, 'I keep trying to talk to Six again, but nothing happens. Maybe it never *did* happen.'

I kneel beside her and put my arm around her shoulders. 'Legacies take time, Ella. I know when mine appeared for the first time, it was usually when I was upset or in danger. They come at a time when they are of the most use, when they might save us. My Legacy that allows me to breathe under water came as I almost drowned. Also, the teleporting may have affected you, so maybe it will take a while to work again.' I give her shoulders a squeeze.

'It's true. The first time I teleported,' Eight says, 'my Cêpan was about to get run over by a taxi. I just appeared next to him, like that.' He snaps his fingers. 'It's the only reason I was able to pull him out of the way.'

'I miss Crayton so much, right now,' Ella says. 'He always helped me with this stuff. What if I'm never any help to the Garde? Sometimes, I wish I was never chosen by the Elders.' Her voice trails off and she slumps down, looking absolutely dejected.

'Ella.' Eight takes a step forward. 'Ella. Look at me. You can't think that way. We are *so* happy you're here. We need you. If you weren't here, we would be looking for *you*. You are exactly where you should be. Right, Marina?'

'Ella, do you remember what we used to say, back in the orphanage? We are a team. That means something important. We take care of each other.' As I'm talking, I realize that my aversion to teleporting is selfish. The only hope we have of finding the others is by getting to New Mexico. The safest, fastest way to get there is by teleporting, even if it means landing in the wrong place a few more times. I will not allow my fear to endanger anyone. When one of us is weak, the rest of us need to be that much stronger.

I give her shoulder another squeeze. 'We will get to New Mexico, find Six, and we will continue to fight.'

Ella nods but remains quiet.

We all wander off, lost in our thoughts. I know I need some time to clear my head, to be as strong mentally as I feel physically, before we move on. This place is so peaceful, and it's so quiet, that it's the perfect setting in which to think. An hour or so later, I walk into the center of the circle to see Eight leaning down and picking a stone up before dropping it.

'Eight! What do you think you're doing?' I yell, alarmed. 'Do you remember where we are? This is a sacred, historic, *ancient* place! You can't just kick rocks around! Put them back where they were!'

Before he even has a chance to return the stones, I use my telekinesis to do it myself. Stonehenge may not be my history, but it is someone's, and that deserves more respect than Eight is showing right now. I want to leave this place exactly as we found it.

Eight looks up at me, surprised by my anger. 'I'm looking for the Loralite stone. I know it's half buried around here, under one of these stones, and we have to find it if we're going to go anywhere,' Eight says.

'Well, just make sure you put them back *exactly* where you found them when you're done looking,' I grumble. 'Stonehenge is one of the most famous places on Earth. Let's not ruin it.' I am tired of leaving destruction behind.

Eight makes a big show of peeking delicately under a rock and returning it gently to its place. 'I would just like to say that Stonehenge is only here in the *first* place because of the Loric. Reynolds said we built it as a cemetery for those who died fighting on Earth.'

'Really? This is a graveyard?' Ella asks, walking up behind me and looking around curiously.

'It was,' Eight says, patting a large boulder. 'For thousands of years, at least. And then humans started poking around, doing all that research they love so much. There is nothing like a quest to understand everything, even if there is nothing to know. Whatever. I will *honor* the placement of the rocks.' He continues to move as if tiptoeing through a bed of tulips.

'Let me help.' I walk carefully among the stones, helping Eight look for the Loralite, floating several rocks inches above the ground before setting them back down exactly as they had been. As I move on to another group of stones I hear shouts in the distance. I lean around a stone to see two men in uniforms running towards the monument, flashlight beams bouncing in the darkness. Ella and I duck down behind the biggest, closest rock formation.

'Shoot,' I whisper. 'Everybody hide.'

We can see the beams from their flashlights scan the ground, and whenever one gets close to us, we shift our position around another stone just in time.

'I know I heard something out here. Kids' voices,' the smaller of the two guards says.

'Okay. Well, where are they?' the other guard asks, looking around. There is a distinct note of disbelief in his voice.

Both men are silent for a moment. I peek around the stone to see the larger guard looking around, annoyed by the lack of evidence of intruders. Then something catches his eye, but I can't see what it is. I'm worried. What could he have found? 'Bill? Come over here and look at this. Where do you think these came from?'

'Huh. Don't know. They sure weren't there earlier,' the other says.

I nearly jump out of my skin when Eight materializes next to me. 'They found our Chests,' he whispers. 'I'll just toss the guards into the pasture, okay? We need to find the Loralite, so we can get the hell out of here, and that's not going to happen until those guys leave. And I am *not* letting them leave with our Chests.' His voice is grim.

I'm about to say no when my brain begins to buzz. After a brief echo of static I hear Ella's voice in my head: *I can distract them while you find the Loralite.* I look over at her in shock, eyes wide.

Ella squeezes my hand and whispers, 'I can distract them –'

'I already heard you,' I interrupt. 'Ella, I heard you in my head!'

She smiles widely. 'I *thought* it worked this time. Wow! I did it!' she whispers excitedly.

'Hey, you two, keep it down,' Eight whispers. 'Do we have a plan?'

'I have an idea,' Ella responds. Shrinking herself into a six year-old, she runs wide, out past the outer circle of the stones, then walks back towards the men. She puts on her best little girl voice as she calls out, 'Daddy? Where are you?'

'Hello?' One of the guards calls back. 'Who's out there?'

Eight teleports away while I watch Ella. She is standing

still, shielding her eyes from their flashlights. She's quite the actress. She sounds legitimately lost and worried. 'I'm looking for my daddy. Have you seen him?'

'What in the world are you doing out here, little girl? Where are your parents? Do you know what time it is?'

As they approach her, Ella starts to sob, stopping the men in their tracks. 'Now, now, just calm down, no need for tears,' the larger one says in a soothing tone.

Ella turns up the waterworks and says, louder now, 'Don't touch me!'

'Hey, hey, nobody's touching you,' the other says in alarm. They are looking at each other, both confused and at a loss as to what to do with her.

'Psst, Marina,' Eight whispers. He's behind me with a Chest under each arm. 'We have to find the Loralite. Now! She can't hold their attention forever!'

We run into the center of Stonehenge. Eight and I start checking under every rock we can find, as quickly as we can. There are only a few left to check when we hear the men coming back towards us, Ella in tow, still sniffling.

'Okay, I think it's time for another distraction,' Eight says, disappearing again. He reappears by the outer circle of stones, plants his hands on an upright slab, and pushes hard. All I can do is watch in horror, frozen to the spot. The huge stone wobbles and then slowly tips backwards, then the horizontal slab on top falls too, and that's when Eight starts yelling, 'Help! Help! The stones are falling over! Stonehenge is falling down!' I will *kill* him. I clench my fists at my side, which is when I realize I still have a small rock in my hand. I lean down and carefully, pointlessly, return it to its spot.

The guards break into a sprint towards Eight's voice, and when their flashlights catch the falling stones, they scream in panic. The smaller guard runs to get in between two vertical stones, but it's too late. They connect and collectively tip to the right. The horizontal slab that was over them lands on the ground with a thud. My mouth falls open as the stones tip, one by one, going over like dominos.

'Code Black! Code Black!' the large guard screams into his walkie-talkie, then tosses it to the ground. He wraps his arms around one of the massive vertical stones remaining upright, trying with all his might to stop it from going over with the others. But it's pointless. The massive stones keep falling.

Eight appears back by me and tips over two small stones, and suddenly a faint blue glow lights up his legs. 'I found it! Over here!' he whispers excitedly. I'm relieved to hear he's found the Loralite, but I'm too focused on the demolition of Stonehenge to be excited. I can't believe he did this. I'm furious. Ella runs past me as I dart under one of the few slabs still in place and use my telekinesis to slow down the boulders in motion.

The larger guard slams his back against a stone that's next in line to tip, and the other guard joins him. I wrap my mind around their stone and hold it steady. When it's hit with another falling boulder, I don't let it tip. The guards slide away from the stone and fall to the grass, shocked by their sudden show of strength. Next I reverse the domino effect so the fallen boulders push each other back up, and I stabilize them in their original positions. Then, using what little strength I have left, I slowly lift the horizontal slabs off the ground and set them back on top of the boulders.

The guards watch all this, mouths agape, too stunned to respond to the crackling, concerned voices squawking from their walkie-talkies.

'Marina,' Ella whispers. 'Hey. Marina, we need to go. Now. Come on.'

I walk backwards towards the center of the monument, relieved and able to leave, now that I've managed to put everything back together.

I stalk over to Eight and yank my Chest from him. Still furious and unable to look at him, I grab hold of his hand. Ella carries Eight's Chest while clinging to his other hand. We stand, joined together, over the blue Loralite. The last thing I hear before the darkness comes is the larger guard – defeated and ready to be done with this particular adventure – responding into his retrieved walkie-talkie, 'False alarm.'

24

I hide behind a row of lockers in a long dark hallway
while I turn visible. The pain from using my Legacies is so intense I curl myself up into a ball,
pressing the two batons into my ribs to get some
relief. I push my sweaty head against the cool cement
wall and try to catch my breath, hoping the pain will
subside quickly. I've been going up and down hallways, but I worry I'm just running in circles. So far,
I've found an empty hangar and a lot of electronically locked doors. I know from when Sam and John
were caught by the police before that our telekinesis
doesn't work with electricity. I think about John and
Sam, Marina and the others. I hope they're okay; or,
at least, in less pain than I am. I picture John and
Sam waiting for me at our rendezvous point. We
were supposed to meet there in a few days. What
will they think when I'm not there? I am so
frustrated – and scared – I feel breathless. I know
this kind of thinking isn't helpful, so I try to refocus
my attention on how to get the hell out of here.

Almost on cue, an alarm sounds. The bleating
overhead feels relentless as soon as it begins. I know
what this means and I know I need to get it together.
Fast. Everyone is looking for me. Armed soldiers zip
down the long hallways in small open vehicles. Each

time one passes, I'm tempted to pluck the men out, hop in, and take off. But I'm sure I wouldn't get very far and I'd give up the one advantage I have right now. They don't know where I am.

I've stopped trying to communicate with Ella. Clearly, I was just delusional. I'm on my own. I need to stop talking to myself and find something to blast through a door and get out of here. I think I'm underground. I just wish I knew how deep.

The lights go on in the hallway. As I discovered earlier, I know this means the motion-sensors have been triggered. A moment later, I hear a vehicle coming my way. I clench my stomach, turn invisible, and get the anticipated wrench of pain. Tears silently flowing down my face from the agony, I press myself up against a wall and watch the cart crawl towards me carrying three soldiers. As it passes in front of me, I hit the driver in the face with one of the batons. Man, do head wounds bleed a *lot*. Nose, mouth, forehead, all gushing geysers. His (seemingly) spontaneous injury causes him to slam his foot on the gas pedal and veer straight into a wall. The driver is out cold and the other two soldiers spill onto the cement floor. They take in the driver's face and see absolutely nothing around that might have caused it, and grab for their walkie-talkies. But I'm expecting this, and I've stepped into position to slam the closest man's head into the hood of the vehicle and kick his legs out from underneath him. The third soldier starts over to see what happened, and I slam his head down too. Then I grab one of their badges and run.

I need to figure out where to go from here and I need to do it fast. I can't stay invisible too much longer.

I use the swiped badge to get past an electronically locked door and find myself in a hallway completely different from the others I've seen so far. I have to stop the pain, so I turn visible and immediately feel relief. I look around and try to figure out where I am. The hall is wider than the others, with a high ceiling that's domed and carved out of sandstone. Two thick yellow pipes crawl along the ceiling, flanked by drooping electrical lines. I come to a turn in the hallway and peek around the corner. I don't see anyone, so I flatten my back against the wall and ease around the corner. I'm facing a red door with a sign that reads: DANGER. AUTHORIZED PERSONNEL ONLY. SHUTTLE ONE.

I try using my telekinesis to open the door, pushing through the pain, but another electric lock keeps it shut. I'm about to try the badge again when I hear footsteps coming fast in my direction. I turn invisible again, but it makes my stomach churn so violently I fall to the floor. I can't survive another round of this, no way. Around the corner someone yells, 'I think I hear something this way!'

From the ground, barely able to stay invisible, I grab a guard by the ankle as he runs by. He goes facedown onto the floor, giving me enough time to swipe my stolen badge through the electronic lock. The door pops open and I slip inside.

I'm on a grated metal platform, high above three sets of train tracks that disappear down a circular tunnel. A three-car tram, plastered with several different symbols of the U.S. government, sits empty on the set of tracks closest to the platform. Outside the door behind me, I hear the guard I disabled yelling to a group of men who have just arrived on the scene. I stumble down a narrow set of stairs and jump inside the open doors of the tram, pulling down on the first lever I see.

My head snaps back as the tram takes off like a rocket. The circular tunnel blurs with red lights and long dark shadows, and twice I zip under grated platforms like the one where I entered without slowing down. The tracks suddenly dip and curve to the right, and then I'm rolling high over a long canal filled with water. I'm hoping this will shoot me out into the desert. Instead, the tram slows down and stops below another platform. There must be points at which there are automatic stops. The doors open and I jog up the stairs. I've let myself turn visible again and appreciate how pain-free my stomach is, knowing it won't stay that way for too much longer. I'm going to need my Legacies to get out of here.

I take a deep breath and carefully try the door at the top of the stairs. It's unlocked. Slowly, I open it just a crack to peek and see what is on the other side. My eyes have barely focused when the door is slammed open, clipping my shoulder painfully. I'm now face to face with a guard with a familiar weapon hanging from his shoulder – a Mogadorian cannon. As soon as the guard reaches for it the cannon buzzes to life with a spark of lights. But before he can press the trigger, I dive at him and we crash into a stone wall. The guard rushes forward and tries to grab me by wrapping his thick arms around my waist. Instead, I move just out of his reach and tackle his legs, pulling them out from under him. His skull makes a horrible cracking sound when it hits the ground. I cringe, but I can't stop to think about it. I quickly shove his body just through the door into the tunnel and close it. I grab his cannon and bolt.

I look around to get my bearings. There are enormous, smooth columns holding up the ceiling of the winding tunnel, and I weave in and out of them, keeping an ear out for more guards. My mind is racing, sorting through what I've seen, trying to piece it together. First on the list, *why* did that soldier have a Mogadorian cannon? Did he get it from a captured Mog? Or are the Mogs supplying the government with their weapons? The tunnel forks and I slow, trying to decide which way to go. I see nothing to help me choose, so I think of the last time I encountered a fork in a road. It was in the Himalayas, the one that surprised Commander Sharma. I go left.

The first door I spot on the left is all glass. Through it I can see scientists in white coats and masks moving around what look like large gardens brimming with tall green plants. Hundreds of powerful bright lights hang low over them from the ceiling.

A red-haired woman in a dark suit enters through another door and walks over to one of the guys in a white coat at the front of the room. Her right arm is in a sling and she has bandages on her cheek. She watches the scientist pour a vial of liquid over a section of the closest garden. I am stunned to see the plants instantly grow several feet taller and their tips split open. White vines spread in every direction, creating a thick canopy over their heads. The scientist writes something on his clipboard, and then looks up to talk to the woman. I don't have time to duck out of the way and we make eye contact through the glass door. I slowly raise the Mog cannon at him and shake my head. I have to hope he considers himself a noncombatant and wants to stay out of the action. No such luck. I watch him slip his hand into his pocket. Damn. He's triggering something. There's a noise over my head and a thick sheet of metal nearly hits me as it falls in front of the glass door, protecting it. Alarms sound and I know the whole area is going into lockdown. I can't get captured. I brace myself for the pain about to take over my body and make myself invisible.

Just in time. Soldiers pour into the tunnel and I inch along the wall to avoid them. The pain and the wave of sickness doesn't come. Whatever drug they gave me must have worn off. The relief I feel is profound, though I don't have time to enjoy it. A door clicks open on my right. Without thinking, I jump through it and find myself in a narrow white hallway lined with more doors. Halfway down the hall a lone soldier is backing out of one of them.

'Please. Just shut *up* already,' he calls into the room. 'And you should really eat something.'

He pulls the door shut and starts to turn and walk away. But I'm right there and drop him with a right hook to the jaw. I see his keys hanging from his belt, pull them off and frantically shove them into the lock of the door he just closed, one after another, until I find the one that works. I am guessing whoever he was talking to is no friend of his, and I could use an ally right now. I push the door open to see if today is the day I make a new friend.

I suck in my breath, shocked at what I see. I don't know what I expected, but it wasn't the girl I see cowering in the corner. She's covered in grime and there are thick red welts on her wrists, but I recognize her instantly. Sarah Hart. John's girlfriend, and the one who turned John in to the police the night we went back to Paradise.

She pulls herself shakily to her feet, using the walls on either side for support. She is steadying herself to face whoever walks through the door. The fear in her eyes tells me only bad things happen when the door opens. I remain invisible long enough to drag the unconscious soldier from the hall inside the room. Leaving him just invites others to investigate, and I don't need any company. I shove him into a corner, hoping that he's out of sight if there are cameras in here. I close the door.

'Sarah?' I say quietly.

She spins around, looking towards my voice but visibly confused. 'Who is that? Where are you?'

'It's Six,' I whisper. She gasps quietly.

'Number Six? Where are you? Where's John?' she asks, her voice shaking.

I'm still speaking softly, not sure if we're alone. 'I'm invisible. Just sit back down like you were and pretend I'm not here. Put your head down so we can talk. I'm betting they have you on camera.'

Sarah's sinks back down into the corner, pulling her knees to her chest. She lowers her head, her hair falling forward and blocking her face entirely. I walk over and sit down next to her on the floor.

'Where's John?' she whispers.

'Where's John?' I can't keep the anger out of my voice. 'Right now, you can forget about John, Sarah. You should know where John is; after all, you set him up, right? Because of you, he went to jail. And then, *I* got him out. What I want to know is, what are *you* doing here?'

'They brought me here,' her voice trembling.

'Who brought you here?'

Sarah's shoulders shake as she cries softly into her knees. 'The FBI. They keep asking me where John is and I keep telling them I don't know. You need to tell me where he is. I have to tell them or they're going to kill everyone I know!' She sounds desperate.

I can't say I'm very sympathetic. 'That's what happens when you switch sides, Sarah. You knew how

John felt about you; you knew he trusted you. And you used that to help these people. And now, they're using you. Now, quickly, tell me what you told them about John!'

'I don't know what you're talking about,' Sarah says, and she starts to sob even harder. I can't help it; it kind of breaks my heart seeing her like this. What have they done to her? Her long hair covers her face and arms and she looks so small and young. I feel my anger melt away and I rest my hand on her back.

'I'm sorry,' I whisper.

She catches her breath at my touch and turns her head to look in the direction of my voice. I can just make out her blue eyes; they're red and bloodshot. To give her the strength to do what we need to I make myself visible for a split second, show her the Mog cannon in my hands, and disappear again. I see a tiny smile cross Sarah's face before she turns her face back to her knees. She sighs, takes a deep breath and in a much firmer voice says, 'It's good to see you. Do you know where we are?'

'I think we're in New Mexico in an underground base. How long have you been here?'

'I have no idea,' she says, wiping away a tear that has fallen on her leg.

I stand up and go over to listen at the door. I don't hear anything. I know I'm wasting precious minutes, but I have to ask. 'I don't get it, Sarah. Why did you turn John in? He's in love with you. I thought you cared about him.'

She flinches as if I've slapped her. Her voice is wobbly, but she looks me right in the eye when she responds. 'Really, I have no idea what you're talking about, Six.'

I have to close my eyes and breathe a few times to keep my voice from rising, to keep my anger from returning. 'I'm *talking about* the night he came over to profess his undying love for you. Remember? Your phone buzzed at two a.m., and the police arrived a minute later? *That's* what I'm talking about. You broke John's heart when you turned him in.' She starts to raise her head to respond, but I make a noise to remind her to keep her head down.

She resettles her head on her knees and speaks in a flat voice. 'That's not what I was trying to do. I didn't have a choice. Please. Where is John? I need to talk to him.'

'I'd like to talk to him too. I'd like to talk to all of them! First, though, we have to figure out a way out of here.' My voice is urgent.

She sounds defeated when she speaks again. 'There is no way out of here. Not unless you want to fight a thousand Mogadorians.'

'What?' I circle back to her. What is she talking about? This is a U.S. government facility, not a Mog base. 'You've seen them? The Mogs? They're here?'

A glazed look washes over Sarah's face. She no longer looks like the girl I met in Paradise, the human girl who John fell in love with and was willing to do anything for. I don't even want to think about what the FBI and the Mogs have done to her. 'Yes. I see them every day.'

I feel as if the wind has been knocked out of me. It was one thing to suspect this was the case – another to have it confirmed. 'Well, *I'm* here now,' I announce, trying to make one of us feel more confident. 'I promise, the next Mog you see will have my foot up his ass.'

Sarah laughs quietly into her legs. Her shoulders relax a bit for the first time since I walked in. 'Sounds good to me. Six, please, can you tell me where John is. Is he okay? Will I be able to see him?'

I know she's worried about Four, but her constant questions about him are beginning to really annoy me. 'To be perfectly honest, I haven't seen him recently, Sarah. We split up. He went with Sam and Bernie Kosar to get his Chest back, and I went to Spain to find another one of us. We were supposed to meet up in three days, but I don't see that happening right now.'

'Where? Where are you supposed to meet? I need to know. It's killing me, not knowing where he is.'

'Right now, it doesn't matter where we were supposed to meet because *I won't be there,*' I explode. 'We need to focus on how we're going to get out of here.'

Sarah flinches at the anger in my voice. She tries again. 'Where are the others? Where's Number Five?' Sarah asks.

I ignore her – she is clearly not listening to me. I walk back to the door and put my ear to it again.

I hear footsteps – definitely more than one person – coming down the hallway. I consider my options. I can either lure them into the cell or I can take them down where they are. Either way, I know I need to deal with them, turn Sarah invisible, and pick a direction for us to get out of here.

Sarah stands up. 'What about Numbers Seven, Eight and Nine? Where are they? Are they together?'

If she doesn't quiet down, she's going to get us captured, or worse. I hiss at her, 'Sarah! Enough! Stop!' I put my ear against the door again and instantly know something is wrong. It sounds like the hallway is packed with men. We're trapped. I spin around to tell Sarah, but she looks like she's in the middle of a seizure. I am frozen seeing her body convulse and flop around the floor of the cell.

'Sarah!' I let myself become visible and run over to try and keep her head from slamming down on the cement floor. Has she been drugged?

Sarah's body starts to shake so fast she becomes a blur. I can only watch helplessly as a white outline appears around her body. I reach out to touch it but before my fingers reach it, the line turns black. I focus on Sarah with my mind to try and stop her convulsions with my telekinesis, but as soon as I try my brain feels like it's burning, like an enormous amount of dark energy is invading my skull. The next thing I know, I am falling backwards, holding my throbbing head, my eyes squeezed shut. When I open them again, I can't believe what I'm seeing. Sarah Hart is growing taller, and darker, until she's at least seven feet tall. Her blond hair shortens until it's a short black buzz cut. Her face morphs into a demonic monster's. A purple scar appears on one side of her now thick neck; then it slowly elongates until it reaches the throat. When the scar finally stops growing, it begins to glow.

Did I just watch Sarah turn into Setrákus Ra? I've never seen him, but I've heard enough to have a pretty good idea of what, or who, I'm looking at.

The door bursts open and I am momentarily blinded by a flash of blue light. The next thing I know, a dozen Mog soldiers rush in, cannons up and ready.

I try to turn myself invisible, but nothing happens. I don't have time to figure out why. I grab the cannon I had set down to help Sarah, jump up, and fire it at one of the Mogs. He falls to my feet in a cloud of ash. I keep shooting, killing two more, but as I turn to find my next victim, I'm yanked backwards and choked by my pendant. I can turn my head enough to see I'm being held by the beast who was once Sarah. He spins me around, swats the cannon out of my hands with his other massive paw and yanks me towards his face. Up this close, I can see his dark skin is a sea of small scars, like he's been raked by razor blades.

I focus my mind on lifting my weapon off the ground but it just sits there. None of my Legacies are working! Without my Legacies, I'm vulnerable. I'm worse than vulnerable. I've got nothing to fight with. But I am not giving up.

'Tell me where they are!' Setrákus Ra roars. He pulls my chain tighter around my throat. I watch his purple scar brighten as he asks, 'Where are they, Number Six?'

'It's too late,' I whisper as bravely as I can. 'We're too strong now and we're coming for you. Lorien will live again and we will stop you.'

The slap is so hard that I can't feel the side of my face and my ears are ringing. I force myself to keep staring at him. He curls his cracked lips to reveal two rows of sharp, crooked teeth. He's so close that my vision is slightly blurred, so I look for something I can concentrate on. I pick a tooth that's broken in half and leaking a thick black liquid. I'm not sure why, but this has the strange effect of making him less scary. It's just so gross.

'Tell me where you're supposed to meet Number Four in three days.'

'On the moon,' I say.

'You will die in front of them. I will kill you myself.'

I don't respond. I don't acknowledge he's even spoken as he tightens his grip. The pendant John and I found in the well in Ohio, the one that was on the massive skeleton, cuts into the back of my neck as it is pulled tighter and tighter. As he pulls the chain even more, I think of John's face as we trained together, I see the Garde sitting around the white table on the ship and I smile. I'm proud to have been chosen by the Elders. Out of respect to them, I will not beg for my life.

'So, there you are, Number Six.' I know the voice

immediately. Agent Purdy. I open my eyes to see an old man. He has a cast on one arm and his face is covered in bruises. When he walks towards me, I see he's limping.

When he gets close enough, I spit at his leather shoes. Setrákus Ra laughs right into my ear.

Agent Purdy looks over my head to speak to him. 'Did you get the information you were looking for? Do you know where they are?'

Setrákus Ra growls and I'm whipped against the wall as an answer, my knees striking the cement first. When I hit the ground, I'm immediately pulled back to my feet by the pendant chain. I can feel my ribs have taken some of the impact; I think a couple of them are cracked. I'm having difficulty breathing. I try again to use my mind to lift the cannon on the floor, but it doesn't budge.

'So nice of you to join us here, Six,' Purdy says. 'I see you've met Setrákus Ra.'

'You're a coward,' I whisper. Legacies or no, I am going to take him down or die trying.

'Coward? *You* are the one who runs from me,' Setrákus Ra objects dismissively.

I stare hard into his maroon eyes. '*This* is cowardly. You must think you won't be able to kill me if I am at my full power. And that is what I call a *coward*.'

Setrákus Ra's scar glows again, the brightest yet. To my surprise, the chain around my neck loosens. 'Put her with the girl,' he says, pulling the pendant over my head. My stomach drops when I see it

255

hanging from his hand. He looks at me, and smiles. 'I will fight you, Six. Alone. And you will die. Very soon.'

I'm dragged out of the cell and the top of my feet sweep across the cement. Then something hard hits the back of my head. I close my eyes – better for them to think I'm out cold so it's easier to focus on where they're dragging me. One right and two left turns. I hear a door open and I'm pushed forward. I stumble until I hit something soft. Or until something soft hits me. I haven't opened my eyes yet when I feel arms wrap around me. When I open my eyes I'm surprised, for the second time in an hour, to see Sarah Hart.

25

Our beige Ford Contour barrels down the highway with Nine behind the wheel. I stare at the long rows of corn in the fields and I try to picture what they'd look like from space. I can't stop thinking about our ship sitting somewhere in the New Mexico desert. After all these years, after all the running and hiding and training, everything is nearly in place. Members of the Garde have developed their Legacies and are coming together, Setrákus Ra came to Earth to fight, and when it's all over we will have a ship to fly us back to Lorien.

'I'm bored,' Nine says. 'Tell me a story. Tell me about Sarah. How hot is she, anyway?'

'Forget it. She's out of your league,' I say.

'Four, if *you* could get anywhere near her, I'm pretty sure I'd have a shot. Especially in *this* car.'

This car. Nine let me wallow pitifully when I first saw it sitting there. I mean, given everything else that I'd seen about how Sandor and Nine had lived, it was understandable that I pictured our ride as something with a whole lot more bling to it. Turns out, looks can be deceiving. The Ford was just hiding its assets.

From the outside, the car does look like something most likely found on cinderblocks. But inside it has to be the most technologically advanced thing I've ever seen. I feel like James Bond. There's a radar detector, a laser jammer, and bullet-proof tinted windows. When Nine wants a break from driving, the car does the driving for him. With the push of a button, a gun turret with large barrels pops out of the hood. This, of course, is controlled with the steering wheel. Nine demon-strated all of it on a lonely stretch of highway in southern Illinois, squeezing off a few rounds at an abandoned barn. My firsthand experience of cars was limited to the beat-up pick-ups and other throwaways Henri found for us – the kind of cars we would have no problem ditching at the last minute. He never would have gone for something like this. There would be too much evidence if it got left behind. It just goes to show again how different each Cêpan was.

Nine takes his hands off the wheel and puts them together like he's praying. 'Please, I'm begging you. Just tell me again what she looks like. After this many hours of corn, I would do anything for something pretty to think about.'

I look back at the fields, lips pressed together. 'No way.'

'Dude, you'd think she hadn't, you know, turned your ass in to the police. Come on! Why are you so protective?'

'I don't even know if she *did* turn me in. I don't know who to believe anymore. But if she did, I have to think she had her reasons. Maybe she was lied to or pressured into it.' So many questions about Sarah have been running through my mind. If only I could see her, talk to her.

'Yeah, yeah. Forget that stuff for a minute. Just tell me what she looks like. I really want to know. And I promise not to say a word.' I can tell he's not going to give this up. 'I swear on the Loric code, if there is such a thing.'

'Of course there's such a thing! You and Sandor were just too busy living this cushy life, playing with your toys, to bother with anything as basic as Loric code,' I retort. We ride in silence for a few minutes. 'Okay, I'll tell you this about Sarah.

You know when you're talking to a beautiful girl and she's focused only on you and everything is going great?'

'Yeah.'

'And you think you're with the hottest girl in the state, maybe in the country, *maybe even on Earth*. Just by walking in a room, she lights it up. Everyone wants to be her best friend, wants to marry her, or both. Can you picture her?'

Nine's smile widens. 'Yeah. Okay. I can picture her.'

'Well, that's Sarah. She's the hot girl who lights up the room. She treats you like you're the most important person she's ever met. When she smiles at you, oh man, it's the best, and nothing else matters. On top of all that, she's the sweetest, smartest, most creative person I've ever met. And she loves animals and once –'

'Dude. I don't *care* if she's nice to puppies. Just give me her deets, her look, her style.'

I've never known anyone so relentless. I sigh. 'Blond hair, blue eyes. Tall and thin – and you should see her in this one red sweater she has. It's not even fair how gorgeous she looks in it.'

Nine howls at the ceiling, waking Bernie Kosar up in the back seat. I point at him. 'Hey! You're not supposed to say anything, remember? On the Loric code?'

'Okay, okay, okay,' Nine says. 'Thank you for that tidbit. She sounds like a total babe. Now, tell me about Six.' He rubs his hands together, grinning in anticipation.

'No way!'

'Aw, come on, Johnny.'

I laugh. It's impossible not to want to talk about her. 'Okay. Six. Let's see. Well, first of all, she's the strongest person I've ever met.'

He snorts. 'Give me a break. I'm sure I could kick her ass.'

'I don't know, man. Wait until you meet her.'

He fixes his hair in the mirror. 'Huh, I can't wait.'

'And she's got long black hair, and she always looks like she's pissed off –'

'Have you ever noticed, there's something kind of exciting when a girl is mad at you? ' Nine muses, tapping his chin as if he were really giving it deep thought.

I suddenly feel guilty. I shouldn't be talking like this, with Nine of all people. And I definitely shouldn't be comparing Six and Sarah this way, as if it's a competition – especially since they hate each other. Sarah hates Six because of everything I said about Six the night she turned me in, and Six hates Sarah because I risked our lives going to see her when Six needed my help. And because she thinks Sarah betrayed us. 'I don't feel right talking about Six. I think I'll just let you meet her, come to your own conclusions.'

Nine shakes his head. 'You are such a wuss, dude.'

For a while, we ride along in silence. Road signs announce where we are. I check the tablet again, grateful for Nine and Sandor's love of electronics. If I couldn't plug it into the car's computer, I would have no way to see if the three Garde members have reappeared. I see the blips representing me and Nine in eastern Oklahoma; there's still one in New Mexico, and a fourth is moving quickly north over the Atlantic Ocean. The other three showed up in England, and I still don't know how they could have gotten there so quickly from India. I decide to give myself permission to check again in five or ten minutes.

I look out the window, examining the signs as they go by. We're more than halfway to New Mexico when I notice the gas gauge is perilously close to EMPTY. I point to it and Nine pulls in to a truck stop. He asks me to open the glove compartment. Two rolls of hundred-dollar bills roll out and into my lap.

'Damn,' I say, catching them.

'Let me have one of those, will ya?' Nine asks.

I peel off a bill and hand it to him. He pops the gas tank and climbs out of the car. I put a few of the bills in my pocket and tuck the rest of it back in the glove compartment. Exhausted, I pull the lever to recline the seat, put my head back and close my eyes. Bernie Kosar leans forward and licks my cheek, making me chuckle. I am bone-weary tired, but I fight the sleep that tries to wash over me. I can't deal with what comes with sleep. I'm sick of taking on Setrákus Ra in my dreams.

I let my mind wander to Sarah and Six; I hope they're both okay. Then I think of Sam. I still can't believe I abandoned my best friend. I tell myself I had no choice. The blue force field had incapacitated me to the point where going back in would have been suicide. No matter how true all of this is, it still feels bad.

I'm startled from my thoughts by the loud click of the gas pump finishing its fill. I breathe deeply, eyes still closed, to appreciate every last second of silence before Nine gets back into the car. Except, the silence continues. Nine doesn't hop in and start to chatter away. I open my eyes and look back at the pump, but no one is there. Where is he? I look around the gas station. Nothing. I'm immediately worried. I get out, Bernie Kosar hopping out behind me, and lock the doors.

First I head inside the station – he's not there. Next, I go out to the parking lot which is full of semi-trailers. With my advanced hearing, I pick up Nine's voice, and I can tell he's good and pissed off. Bernie Kosar and I run towards his voice, weave around several trailers, and find him standing between two young guys with blood on their T-shirts. In front of Nine are three big truckers, all of them shouting in his face.

'*What* did you just say to me?' the trucker in the middle asks Nine. Under his yellow cap, a bushy red beard covers the man's face.

'Are you deaf?' Nine says, over-enunciating as if speaking to an idiot. 'I said, You have girl arms. I mean, look at your wrists.' Why does he insist on *looking* for trouble?

'Uh, what's up?' I interrupt, walking over.

The trucker on the right, a tall guy wearing aviator sunglasses, looks at me. He points his finger in my face and yells, 'Mind your own business, asshole!' As I join the group, the trucker on the left spits a long stream of brown juice at my feet.

'As far as *I've* figured out,' Nine turns to explain to me, 'these fat guys are angry at these little guys. The little guys were hitchhiking and caught a ride with one of them, promising money they didn't have. So now, the fat guys are trying to beat up the little guys with their puny girl arms.'

I turn to the truckers, the fat guys, and try to make nice. 'Okay, well, none of this has anything to do with us, and we need to get on the road. So, guys, let me apologize for my friend, who clearly doesn't know when to mind his own business.'

'Yeah,' the bearded trucker growls at Nine. 'Just get the hell out of here, punk, and let us deal with these lowlifes.'

I take my first real look at the hitchhikers. They smell like they've been on the road for a while. They couldn't be more than eighteen, probably younger. As the truckers move towards them menacingly, they glance at each other with real panic in their eyes. Next thing I know, Nine is stepping in front of the little guys and saying, 'I don't care who promised what to who. You touch these kids again and I'll break *all* your goddamn arms.'

I squeeze in between Nine and the three now truly pissed-off truckers, holding both sides back. Bernie Kosar barks threateningly. 'Okay, okay, just stop.' I turn to Nine, willing him to listen to me. 'We can't do this right now. We have some-where *very important* we have to get to. *Now*,' I say. I dig into my pocket and turn to the truckers. 'Listen, how much did these guys say they would give you?'

'A hundred bucks,' the one wearing the aviators says.

'Fine,' I say, pulling one of the bills out of my pocket. The truckers' eyes widen at the sight of such a big bill and I instantly know things just got worse.

'Why would you give *anything* to these guys, Johnny?' Nine asks.

I feel the meaty hand of a trucker on my shoulder. He squeezes my shoulder as he says, 'Did I say a hundred bucks? I meant a thousand. *Johnny*.'

'That's crazy!' one of the hitchhikers shouts. 'We never said we'd give you any money!'

I spin back to the truckers, waving the bill like it was flag. 'A hundred bucks, guys, just take it. Consider it a tip for good service, or payment in lieu of a beating, I don't really care what you call it. Just take it!'

'I said a thousand,' the man on the left says, spitting again, this time directly on the top of my shoe. 'Are you deaf?' A low growl starts deep in Bernie Kosar's throat.

Nine moves forward, but I push him back and turn to face him. 'No! It's not worth it, man!' I put my face right up in his. He has to understand how serious I am. I will not let him do this. 'Please. Think of what Sandor would want you to do. He'd want you to walk away. *I* need you to walk away.' I whisper.

'You guys aren't getting *shit*!' Nine yells over my shoulder at the truckers.

I use my body to shove him backwards, towards the car. I spin around just in time to see the bearded trucker pull a knife out of his pocket. 'All of your money. Now.' The other two men step up to flank me.

'Listen,' I say, lowering my voice, trying to get control of the situation. 'You will take the hundred bucks and you will walk away. If you don't, I'm not going to hold my friend back any-more. Believe me, you don't want that. You have no idea what he can do and you don't want to know.'

I'm not entirely surprised when the answer comes in the form of a fist. It comes from my right and I easily dodge it. I grab the trucker's wrist, and throw him down. BK looms over him, still growling, and the man shrinks back.

'My turn!' Nine says gleefully, pushing me out of the way.

The bearded trucker swings his knife wildly at Nine, who steps lightly out of range. On his next swing, Nine ducks under the blade and hooks his arm beneath the man's armpit, slam-ming him to the ground. He kicks the knife out of the trucker's hand and it goes skidding under a truck. 'Dude, you should listen to my wise pal over there. You *seriously* do *not* want to mess with us.'

'All right, all right. We're done here,' I say, placing my hand on Nine's shoulder. 'And now, we're *all* going to walk away. Let's go.'

I hear the hammer of a gun click. We freeze. The trucker with the aviator glasses waves a .50-caliber Desert Eagle at us. I don't know everything about guns, but I know this one packs a very big punch. He sounds pretty serious when he asks, 'Which of you wants to die first?'

Of course Nine steps forward, crossing his arms over his chest. 'Me.'

He raises the gun towards Nine's face and laughs at what he thinks is just bravado. 'Don't tempt me, punk. Killing you would be the highlight of my day.'

'Well, then, shoot. No reason to put off the highlight of your day. You don't look like you get a lot of them.' Nine says. I sigh, knowing this is all going to end badly. And after, there will be attention we don't need.

At this point things begin to move really fast. First, a sudden and very loud blast from a nearby truck startles the gun-touting trucker, who fires off a shot. Nine stops the bullet with his mind, just inches from his nose. With a grin and a tilt of his head, he spins the bullet midair and sends it racing back at the shooter. He sees the bullet coming his way and turns tail and runs as fast as his legs will take him.

I turn to look at Nine. This guy is having *way* too much fun. I know what he's going to do and I know it is a bad, bad idea. 'No. Nine. Don't do it,' I say, shaking my head, knowing he is going to do it anyway.

Nine laughs and feigns innocence. 'Do what? This?'

He and I both turn to look at the bullet that is still hovering where Nine stopped it near the trucker. He gives a little chortle and sends the bullet racing after the fleeing trucker, right into his ass. He goes down, screaming his head off. Nine turns to the other truckers, including the one BK has decided to let off the ground. They look like they are about to pee in their pants they're so scared. Nine smiles at them and I know he's still not done messing with their heads. He says to the two truckers, 'You know what? I think you two should make up for your rude friend. Here is what you are going to do. You are going to reach into your pockets, *very slowly*, and take out your wallets. Then, you are going to give every dollar you have to these nice guys here. You know, for their trouble,' he says, motioning to the hitchhikers. 'I don't think you want to hear what I'll do if you do not cooperate. Quickly.' Both truckers nod and reach into their pockets.

The hitchhikers look totally stunned by all they've just seen. 'Uh, thanks, man,' one of them says.

'No problem,' Nine says as the money is exchanged. Everyone's hands but ours are visibly shaking.

'Just so you know, we never promised that guy any money. They were trying to shake us down. We're absolutely broke,' the other says.

'I believe you. And, you're not broke anymore,' Nine says, smiling. 'Let's just say, I know what it's like, on the road and on the run. It can be hard for a kid to figure out a way to get some cash.' He turns to me for confirmation. I smile at the kids but look back at Nine and make it clear I am more pissed off than I've ever been. He shrugs. 'Hope the next ride you catch goes better!' He turns and walks away, and BK and I follow.

We get to our car, climb in, and pull away in silence. After a minute or two, Nine reaches over and flicks on the radio. He drums his fingers on the wheel in time to the song.

'What the *hell* were you doing back there?' I yell, punching his shoulder. 'And don't give me any crap about the poor little boys and the mean, mean trucker men, either! You're just entertaining yourself and showing off! And you know what? That's putting us *both* in danger, not to mention keeping us from getting where we need to go. C'mon, Nine! Get it together!'

Nine is gripping the steering wheel so tightly his knuckles are white and I can see his jaw is clenched so hard his muscles are twitching. 'I was *not* showing off and I was *not* entertaining myself.' I wait for him to continue, to explain, but it's clear he is not going to say anything else. What does *he* have to be mad about?

'What, you were just standing up for two humans who were getting pushed around? Even though you said humans aren't worth the time or energy?' He flinches when I throw his words back at him.

'I don't like bullies. No one has a right to take or to hurt, just because they can. I wasn't going to let them do that. And I made damn sure they wouldn't do it again.' His voice is flat. He looks over at me, at the surprised look on my face, and turns back to the road. 'Don't know why you look so shocked. I'm a humanitarian, man.'

I shake my head. Every time I think I have Nine figured out, he does something to turn it around and I end up liking him even more. I shrug, lean my head back, and turn to watch the landscape whip by the window. I drum along with the music on my armrest. 'I didn't know, that's all,' I say.

He relaxes into his seat and smiles in a satisfied way that is more like the Nine I'm used to. 'Yeah, well, now you do, man. Now you do.'

26

My head is in Sarah Hart's lap, the real Sarah Hart, and she strokes my hair with her fingers. I stare blankly at the ceiling. I reach up and touch my neck. The cut that runs all the way around it is deep. I want to sit up, but my bruised ribs and knees won't allow it.

I'm humiliated by how easily I was overtaken by Setrákus Ra. How weak I was in the face of his tremendous strength. I've killed so many Mogadorian soldiers. I've cut off their heads while mowing them down with weapons I controlled with my mind. Since I received my Legacies, I have always been ready to fight, no fear, no matter who or what I faced. Until now. Setrákus Ra tossed me around by my pendant like I was a rag doll. I was helpless against him. He even made my Legacies disappear. I had the opportunity to kill Setrákus Ra, to save Lorien and end the war, and I was swatted down like an annoying gnat.

'Six? Can you tell me if John is still alive?' Sarah asks cautiously. 'I know you're in pain, but can you tell me that?'

'Yes. He's alive,' I whisper. I can feel her sigh with relief against me.

After a pause, she asks, 'Are you okay?'

'I don't really know,' I say. I turn my head so I can look up into Sarah's tired eyes. I try to smile. I'm exhausted. My eyelids are already fluttering when I open my mouth to speak, 'He was you, he tricked me into thinking he was you, the monster.'

Sarah takes this in without any sign of confusion. She shakes her head and looks away. 'I know. He showed me. A couple of days ago he came into my cell. I thought he was there to take me back to the room where . . .' She trails off for a minute, then clears her throat and straightens up. 'This room with all these machines and strobe lights. I feel like I'm crazy in there and everything hurts. It's hard to explain. But he wasn't here to take me anywhere. He just stood there, not saying anything. Then he started jerking around, like he was having a seizure. Then he started to shrink, and, bam! – it was like I was looking into a mirror. When he finally did speak, it wasn't his voice. It was mine. I tried to hit him and rip out his eyes, but he beat me so badly that . . . Well, the first time I could stand was when I caught you when you were thrown in here.'

'I'm flattered.' I try to laugh, but it gets caught in my throat. 'No, seriously, thank you.'

'Well, you're *welcome*.' She's smiling down on me, and I think she must have been terrified. I was more scared than I've ever been just now, and I was born and raised to do this. This is my life. It isn't Sarah's, not by a long shot.

'I don't get something. How did he know so much about you? How could he trick me for so long?'

'They know everything, Six,' she says, her voice deadly serious.

I slowly begin to roll out of her lap, to push myself off the ground. I try to ignore my ribs begging me to stay down. 'What do you mean, everything? About who? And what do *you* know? About any of this?'

Sarah looks away. 'What little I know, I told them all of it,' she says after a minute. 'I couldn't help it. They kept taking me to that room, strapping me down, and they injected me with drugs. They asked me the same questions, over and over; after a while my mouth moved even though I told it to stop. I just couldn't stop talking.' Sarah puts her face in her hands and sobs. 'I told them everything, repeating whole conversations word for word.'

I sit against the wall and let the pain wash over my body. 'If John sees Setrákus Ra and believes it's you, I don't know what will happen.'

Sarah suddenly sounds frantic. 'We have to get out of here! We have to stop him! Is there any way we can warn John?'

'I don't know if I'm ready to break out of here.'

'What? Why?' she asks, shocked.

I stagger to my feet, clutching at my ribs. 'Now that I've met Setrákus Ra, I want another chance at him. He let me live, and now, I'm going to kill him.' This would sound more lethal if I weren't swaying slightly, but I mean it from my very core.

Sarah stands, and I get a good look at her for the first time. Her face is covered in dirt and bruises, her blond hair limp on her shoulders, but she's still beautiful. The bottom of her red sweater is torn and she's not wearing any shoes. She's swaying a bit herself. She stares at me, incredulous. 'Look at yourself, Six. You're hurt. You're *really* hurt. Do you know what you're even saying? It would be nuts for you to fight him alone. John will come; just wait for him. Please. He'll come, and he'll rescue us, *and* Sam. I know he will.'

'Sam's here? Are you sure? Have you actually seen him?'

Sarah clenches her jaw. 'They tossed him in here with me once. He was unconscious, all cut up and bruised. Like me.' Then the energy drains out of her and her voice drops. 'But I know I can't believe anything I see or hear anymore.'

Picturing a bloody Sam in this very cell makes my stomach twist with anger. What happened in that Mog cave? I punch the cement wall, surprised to see it chip away. My strength is returning. No pain. My Legacies are coming back. I look directly into Sarah's eyes. 'Sarah, did you turn John in that night at the playground? You need to tell me.'

Without hesitation she answers. 'Absolutely not. I love him. Yes, I was confused about, well, about everything and it was a lot to take in. But I would never betray any of you, especially John.'

I see her tear-filled eyes, and know she's telling the truth. 'Even though he's an alien, you still love him? You don't care?'

Sarah smiles. 'I can't explain it. I can't explain how love feels to me, how it fills me up inside and keeps me going, but I know that it's strong and beautiful and I know it's how I feel about John. I love him, and I will always love him.' Just saying the words aloud has her standing up straighter; she looks stronger and more determined.

Her conviction moves me. I think about what happened between me and John, the kiss and everything. I don't love John like Sarah does. She clearly believes John is the only one for her, in the entire universe.

'I've been having these flashbacks, you know, about our trip to Earth. He and I were always fighting,' I say, my voice soft.

'You were?' she asks, hungry for anything I can tell her.

'Well, not really fighting so much as me pushing him around and taking his toys.'

We laugh and she takes my hand. I'm sorry she's here because of us. I'm not going to let her down. She has so much faith in what we do, who we are, I can see it on her face. 'I'm going to get you out of here, okay? I'm going to get you back to John,' I say.

'I hope so,' she says softly.

'And we'll find Sam and get him out of here too; then we'll meet up with Seven, Eight and Ten, find Five, and we'll figure everything out as a team.' Her hand in mine gives me even more strength, more certainty than ever.

'Hang on. Number Ten? I thought there were just nine of you guys.'

'There are a lot of things you don't know, things we've learned recently,' I say, touching the cut around my neck. It still hurts, but feels like it's already starting to heal. I wonder vaguely if I'm gaining a new Legacy.

Sarah hugs me, but our moment is brief. The door whips open, and a dozen Mog soldiers march into the room, cannons aimed at my chest.

'Turn invisible,' Sarah whispers under her breath. 'Go.'

I test my ribs and roll my neck. I feel better than I did five minutes ago. It has to be good enough. 'No. I'm done running.'

The red-haired woman I saw in the garden room limps into the cell. I look at her arm in the sling and the bandages over her cheek, and can't help but wish I was the one who did all that to her. Anyone who would join up with the Mogs and torture kids in a secret bunker, deserves everything she got, and more. Does she know who the Mogs really are? What they intend to do? The woman purses her pale lips and stares at me. 'So. You're the one who will fight Setrákus Ra?'

I step forward. 'Yes. Who are you?'

'Who am I?' she asks, shocked that I would dare to ask such a thing. I guess she isn't used to people questioning her right to be anywhere, asking her to explain who she is.

'Yeah, *you*, asshole.' Does she have me confused with someone who has any respect for her *position*? 'I asked you a question. Who are you and why the hell would you be working with *them*? Do you know what the Mogadorians are going to do? What their plan is? They will destroy Earth, but only after they get what they want. And you are not only helping them, you are putting out the damn welcome mat! Did they tell you why they're here? Did you even ask?' I am furious and desperate; this woman has got to listen to me. She needs to understand what is at stake here.

Her face remains unchanged. 'I know all I need to know. They are *here* because they're looking for you and your friends. In exchange for our help, they will help *us* with matters that are vital to our security. And I'll let you in on a little secret. I look forward to finding that Number Four again, and his freak alien friend. I have first shot at them, and I will take it, with pleasure.'

Sarah and I exchange a glance. Alien friend? Who is she talking about? Has John met up with another Garde?

'What *things* are the Mogadorians going to help you with?' I ask.

'Well, for starters,' she says, motioning to the Mog's cannon, 'we get these. Thousands and thousands of alien weapons with capabilities impossible to create here on Earth, that none of our enemies have access to. With their technology, the Pentagon will be light years ahead of any other army on Earth. We will be invincible.' I'm disgusted and I make sure it shows. 'Setrákus Ra has also been supplying us with iridium, a chemical that's incredibly rare on Earth, and we've made scientific breakthroughs with it that will make this country billions of dollars. Also, the United States government is very interested in finding other life-sustaining planets, and the Mogadorians have already shared information about that.' When she stops talking, she rocks back on her feet, and crosses her arms over her chest defiantly.

'Did they tell you what they do when *they* find other life-sustaining planets? I'll tell you what they do. They destroy them,' I shout in her face. 'You picked the wrong side, this time. My friends and I are trying to stop them.'

'That's enough. Your presence is requested by Setrákus Ra. This way. Now.' The woman moves aside to let me to pass.

I know I could take this woman and every one of these soldiers. But that would just delay getting to what I really want – to defeat Setrákus Ra. 'As tempting as it is to kill you all right now, I think I'll save you for Number Four and his freak alien friend,' I sneer. 'If Ra wants to do this now, let's go.' I push past her and walk out of the cell.

'Six!' Sarah calls after me. 'Please! Be careful!'

I walk down the hall, my enemy flanking me. We walk down hallways, through several doors, and after a few minutes, I'm standing inside a huge room. It's big enough for an army of tanks. It's also big enough for an epic fight.

The door slams and I hear it lock behind me. It's so dark now that I can barely see two feet in front of me, never mind the other end of the room. I walk towards what I think is the center of the room, testing my telekinesis as I go by levitating off the ground. The pain I felt earlier is gone. When I think I'm in the middle of the room, I close my eyes and turn around, feeling the air with my mind. I sense there are about two dozen or so beings silently entering the room. I'm disappointed. I wanted this to be one on one.

When I open my eyes, they've almost adjusted to the dark. I wish I had Marina's Legacy to be able to see in the dark, but I can make out enough for now. There are Mog soldiers lined up against the back wall. They're wearing ragged black cloaks and black boots, and whip their swords across their bodies. They're bigger than most of the Mogadorians I've fought before, but I know I can kill them just the same. A door opens behind me, and another dozen soldiers enter.

'Hey! What is this? Setrákus Ra!' I yell to the ceiling, turning around to make sure the Mogs can all see me and know they do not have some cowering human here. 'I thought you wanted to fight me!'

A section of the wall explodes in the back of the room, and the Mogadorian leader appears. The three Loric pendants swing from his grotesque neck. I plan on taking all of them back. Setrákus Ra opens his arms and yells, 'You must first earn the right!'

I guess this is the command to charge, because all at once, the soldiers let out a battle cry, and rush at me. I start at my right and begin to pick them off, one at a time.

27

Wind, hot sand and punishing heat, along with a pounding headache, welcome me to our next teleporting destination. I try to shield my eyes from the blinding sun as I lie on my back, recovering. Welcome to New Mexico.

'Oh, yeah,' Eight groans, but he sounds satisfied. 'We made it.'

I smile but stay where I am to give the pain in my head time to lessen before I try to move.

'Ella?' I call out.

'I'm right here, Marina,' she calls over. 'Look where we are! New Mexico!'

'Finally. Can you try communicating with Six again?'

'I already have. No luck yet.'

I slowly stand up. Eight is on his hands and knees at the bottom of the sand dune, dry heaving. The teleporting seems to have affected him more severely than it did the last couple of times. Ella has her hand on the back of his neck. The two Chests sit nearby. I rotate 360 degrees and all I see in every direction is sand, sand and more sand. And the occasional cactus. 'Which way should we go?'

Ella and Eight climb up the dune and stand next to me. After a minute, Ella points north and says, 'Look! Six said something earlier about dying in a desert with mountains.'

Squinting, I see where she's pointing. The faint outlines of mountains ripple in the afternoon haze.

'That's where we're going then,' Eight says. 'We can cover the distance in short hops once my teleporting comes back. For now, we walk.'

We pick up the Chests and head north. 'Ella,' I say, 'you need to keep trying Six. If you can't reach her, maybe you can try Four, or even try one of the others, Five or Nine.' We've lost so much time just getting here. Maybe Ella can find something out that will save us some time now.

Nine examines the map he's brought up on the screen in the middle of the steering wheel. He looks around at the endless desert surrounding us. The car's GPS has picked up an underground tunnel nearby; now we just need to find the entrance. When I press the green triangle on the tablet, it shows we're only a mile or two from the ship. I push the blue circle and shout, 'Nine! They're here!'

'Who's here?' Nine asks, scanning the horizon.

'The other three blue dots. They're here in New Mexico!'

Nine rips the tablet out of my hands and lets out a loud hoot. 'Holy shit, bro. This is really all about to go down.' He looks at me, his eyes shining.

'I think this is it. The beginning of the end.' As much as I'm looking forward to finally getting a chance to do what we need to do, it's dawning on me that this is going to be the fight of our lives.

'This right here, *this* is when we rise to the occasion,' Nine says. 'You will fight harder than you ever have, Four. You're going to be a beast. And me? I'm going to rip Setrákus Ra's head off, wrap it up and send it back to Mogadore with a giant red bow on it. And then Lorien is going to rise from the

280

ashes.' His voice is shaking with emotion, with all the pent-up anger and fight he has been carrying around with him.

Bernie Kosar barks from the backseat and Nine turns around to look at him with a smile. 'You, too, BK. You, my friend, are going to kick some major ass.'

I imagine what it will feel like to meet up with all the Garde members, something I haven't let myself do for so long. I look out over the horizon. My mind is clear and open to all possibilities. It feels good. And that's when I hear a girl's faint voice echo in my head. It's soft and broken like a bad radio signal at first, but it becomes clearer.

Four? Number Four? Can you hear me?

'Yes, yes! I can hear you!' I yell out loud, whipping my head back and forth. 'Who is that? Where are you?'

Nine looks at me, confused. 'Um, dude. I *hope* you can hear me. I'm right here.'

'Not you. I heard a girl. Did you hear her? A girl was just talking to me.'

Number Four? It's Number Ten. Can you hear me? This may be hopeless, I don't know if I'm talking to anyone. Maybe I'll never figure this out without Crayton.

'There it is again,' I say excitedly. Nine is looking at me like I've completely lost my mind. 'Nine! She just said something else! Did you hear her? She said she's Number Ten! I think she's in my head somehow.'

'Number Ten! The baby from the second ship! Well, don't just sit there staring at me! Talk back to her, dumbass!'

That's easy for him to say. She didn't know if it was working. I'm guessing it's a new Legacy kicking in — for both of us! — it takes training to know how to make a Legacy work when, and how, you want it to. I know I don't have much time to waste figuring it out. I take a deep breath and block out the noise in my head and around me, and focus. I try to re-create the feeling I had right before I heard the voice a few minutes before. I feel calm, open, and somehow . . . connected.

I can hear you, I try saying in my head. Nothing. I wait a moment and try again. *Number Ten?*

Number Four! You can hear me?

'She heard me!' I laugh out loud and look at Nine, victorious.

'Tell her we're about to ride into town and save the day,' Nine says. 'Tell her we'll swing by and pick her up on our way to Lorien, wherever she is.'

Where are you? I hear her ask. *I'm with Seven and Eight in the desert, in New Mexico. We're trying to find and rescue Number Six.*

'What's she saying?' Nine yells. I know it's making him crazy not being able to hear our conversation, but I can't talk to him now. I need to concentrate on hearing Ten's voice, on responding to her.

What do you mean? Where is Six? We're in New Mexico too. I'm with Nine and we're in the desert looking for an underground base.

I look out at the mountains. 'We have to find that tunnel, fast,' I say to Nine.

'Did she say where they are?'

'She just said she's here, in the desert, with Seven and Eight and they're trying to rescue Six. That must be who we saw show up on the map earlier. I know I shouldn't worry — if anyone can take care of herself, it's Six. But still — I'm worried.'

'She's got to be inside Dulce. Let's go find her.' Nine's

fingers speed over the screen. The map changes color and looks to be scanning the area, finally zooming in on the trunk of a five-pronged cactus about a quarter mile away from where we are. Below it, I can see the outline of an underground tunnel. 'Ha! Nice try, you sneaky government bastards. Tell Number Ten to get her butt over here!'

Can you tell me where you are, Ten? We found a tunnel to get inside the base where we think Six is being held. We're in a brown car, pulling off on a side road.

After a pause, she says, *We can teleport to you. How do I find you?*

'They don't know how to find us,' I report to Nine.

'Maybe we can send up a signal somehow? Damn it! We should have brought that rocket launcher!' He hits the steering wheel with the palm of his hand and stares out the window, shaking his head.

'We don't need a rocket launcher,' I realize, jumping out of the car. I aim my palms into the blue sky and light my Lumen, swaying the beams back and forth.

Look for the beams of light in the sky, I instruct Ten. I don't hear anything for a minute. I hope we haven't lost our connection.

We see them! Ten finally says.

'They're on their way,' I yell into the car, keeping my Lumen in the air. I want to give them as much time as possible to see exactly where we are. 'We just need to sit tight.'

'I'll try,' Nine says, studying the screen on the steering wheel again, but already starting to twitch. 'Man, I can't believe we found them!'

I finally turn off my Lumen and climb back in the car. I almost can't believe this moment has come, that we're about to fulfill the destiny the Elders laid out for us. We're coming together to defeat the Mogadorians and resurrect Lorien from its hibernation.

Suddenly, we hear the unmistakable noise of a helicopter.

'Um, Johnny?' Nine says. 'They're not getting here by helicopter by any chance, are they?'

'Shit,' I say. Bernie Kosar jumps into my lap, putting his front paws on the door to look out the window. The three of us watch several helicopters climb into the sky from the hazy horizon. The cluster of choppers moves together and stops to hover directly above us. I use my mind to focus on the one out front and send it spiraling off back where it came from. Then I bring it down, hard enough that it won't go up again anytime soon.

'It must be the Feds. They're getting on my nerves almost as much as the Mogadorians. They must have been looking for us and saw your lights!' Nine yells. The gun turret in the hood of the car pops up. Nine aims, then shoots warning shots to the right of the remaining choppers, then the left. As soon as he stops shooting they lower down, hovering just above us. I'm about to get rid of another one with my telekinesis when Nine lets out a yelp.

'Check out the road,' he says. I look to my left and see an enormous dust cloud rising from a long line of black vehicles. Bernie Kosar barks and scratches at the door. I open it and he changes into an enormous hawk and ascends into the sky. I run around to the trunk of our car and open it with a pound of my fist. I unzip one of the duffels and pull out four automatic rifles, dropping two next to Nine's door. Gunshots are already firing from the faraway vehicles, and I scramble on top of the car and take aim while Nine continues to unleash a barrage at the incoming helicopters. Out of the corner of my eye, I see Bernie Kosar swoop into the side of a helicopter. He's got one of the pilots with his talons. He yanks and pulls at him, using his powerful beak to rip out the safety belt holding him in the seat. When the pilot is free BK drops him onto the sand below. His helicopter falls and bursts into flames on impact. The caravan of black cars swerves around the wreckage and I hold down the triggers of my two guns, taking out the front tires of the first two cars. It doesn't stop the convoy, but at least it slows them down.

The remaining helicopters spread apart in the sky and come at us from different angles. Pockets of sand explode all around us. One helicopter flies directly overhead, and I roll out of the way of its line of fire.

I struggle to clear my mind. It isn't easy, but I'm getting the hang of what it takes for me to go inside my head to communicate. I take a few deep breaths and quiet my mind. *Number Ten? Where are you? We're under attack.*

We can hear it, she says. *We're coming.* Her thoughts are calm, with an edge of worry. It feels good just to hear it, though, to know others are on their way.

I shift around and see two black helicopters bank left and head in the opposite direction, firing missile after missile at a new target. That has to be them! I can only redirect three of the rockets, but someone else deflects the rest.

'Ten and the rest are almost here!' I yell down to Nine through the driver's window. Next thing I know the gun turret on the front hood has exploded, sending hot metal flying over my head. I roll off the roof of the car just as it's split in half by a new hail of bullets.

Nine jumps out of the car and grabs the two rifles I set in the sand by his door. 'Looks like we've got a real fight on our hands. I've been waiting for this my *whole life*.'

The helicopters circle back and line up over the faraway vehicles, forming a united front. Nine lifts his palm and the lead black truck is suddenly ripped straight up in the air like a shuttle rocketing into outer space. Nine flips his hand and the car falls back down again. We can hear the men screaming from where we are. The car comes to a stop right before it hits the ground, then smashes down hard. We watch the men scramble out on shaky legs and look for somewhere to run. At the sound of the impact, Bernie Kosar, still in the form of a hawk, dives and lands behind the twisted car on the road, and transforms into a beast. The trailing vehicles swerve into the desert to avoid him, some spinning completely around. Bernie Kosar roars.

Nine ducks into the backseat of the car and throws our Chests into the sand. Opening his, he pulls out the string of green stones and the silver staff, and as he jogs backwards towards the chaos, he yells, 'You wait for the others. BK and I will be right back!'

I shout back, 'Don't look like you're having too much fun! And make sure you don't blow up the entrance to the military base!' A helicopter swings in from my right, and just as I yank on its nose with my mind, something rips into my left leg. I fall headfirst into the sand, blinded by pain. It feels all too familiar and I roll on the ground screaming at the top of my lungs. I know what this means. A scar is searing itself into my leg. Another member of the Garde is dead.

Everything stops. The thought of another one of us dying sweeps through my body and I'm paralyzed by grief so deep it feels like I'm sinking into the sand. There is one less soldier to reclaim Lorien, one less soldier to fight to save Earth and every living thing on it. Two missiles slam into our car, blowing it to bits.

Gunfire rains down on me and just in time my bracelet expands into a shield. I take some solace in the fact that my Inheritance is in tune with the dangers that face me – although I don't know why it didn't protect me from the first onslaught of gunfire. The bullets are hitting close and constant. When I finally manage to examine the new scar wrapped around my ankle, I'm shocked to see two gaping bullet wounds instead. I don't know that I've ever been so happy to be wounded and bleeding. I'm so relieved that it's not another scar that I don't even care that my hands are covered in blood. As I apply pressure to stop the bleeding, the desert goes strangely silent. My bracelet retracts.

I manage to flip myself over and look up. Standing over me are three teenagers. The boy is tall and tan with curly black hair, and the two girls hold Loric Chests. I recognize the boy immediately from my visions. He nods and smiles, saying, 'Nice to see you again, Number Four. I'm Eight.' Before I can respond, he disappears.

One of the girls is short with auburn hair and tiny features. She looks no older than twelve, and I know this must be Number Ten, the Garde from the second ship. She drops the Chest and kneels by my side. The other Garde, a tall girl with shoulder-length brown hair, sets her Chest down and, without saying a word, kneels beside me as well and lays both her hands on my wounds. An iciness rushes over me and my body convulses on the desert floor. Just when I think I am about to pass out from the pain, it's gone. I look at my ankle and see my wounds are completely healed. It's amazing. The girl stands, offers me her hand, and pulls me to my feet.

'That's one hell of a Legacy you've got there,' I manage to say.

'John Smith.' She's staring at me and looks kind of star-struck. 'After all this time, I can't believe you're standing here in front of me.'

I'm about to respond, but over her shoulder I catch sight of a missile screaming towards us. I shove the girls to the ground, falling on top of them, and a dune behind us erupts like a volcano, sending a sand cloud high over our heads. When it dissipates Eight reappears next to us.

'Everything good here? Everyone ready to fight?' he says.

'Yeah, we're good,' the taller girl says, nodding towards my leg. Ten had said she was with Seven and Eight, so this must be Number Seven. Before I can introduce myself properly, Eight disappears for the second time.

'He can teleport,' says Number Ten, smiling at my look of wonder. I can hardly believe that so many of us are finally together. I smile back at her.

In the distance, I can see Eight again, fighting alongside Nine and Bernie Kosar. They wreak havoc on each approaching vehicle; flipping and disabling heavy military equipment like cheap plastic toys. Nine's glowing red staff slices open the underside of a low-flying helicopter. Eight teleports next to a black Humvee and flips it over with his hands. Two helicopters swing low and collide into a fireball.

A new sense of urgency comes over me to get to Six as fast as I can. 'So I'm guessing you're Seven and Ten; what can you do?' I say as I find our rifles in the sand and hand them each a gun.

'You can call me Marina,' the girl with the brown hair says. 'And I can breathe under water and see in the dark and heal the wounded. And I have telekinesis.'

Call me Ella, I hear Ten's voice say in my head. *Aside from my telepathy, I can change ages.*

'Awesome. I'm Four, that nut job with the long black hair is Nine, and the beast is my Chimæra, Bernie Kosar.'

'You have a Chimæra?' Ella asks.

'I don't know what I'd do without him,' I say. What's left of the brigade finally separates, and a dozen vehicles bounce off the road and race towards the three of us. A small plume of smoke escapes from the top of one of the vehicles, and I turn the rocket it just fired around with my mind, slamming it into a sand dune. The other trucks and SUVs keep speeding ahead.

I start picking up pieces from Nine's destroyed car and whipping them towards the oncoming brigade. I launch tires, doors, even a mangled seat at them. Marina does the same, and we're able to stop three or four vehicles from advancing. Still, there are a half dozen or more to deal with.

Suddenly Eight, Nine and BK pop up in front of us. Eight lets go of Nine's hand and reaches forward to shake mine. 'Number Four.'

'You have no idea how happy we are that you guys are here,' I say.

Nine shakes Ten's and Seven's hands, and says, 'Hello, ladies. I'm Number Nine.'

'Hi,' Ten says. 'You can call me Ella.'

'I'm Number Seven, but I go by Marina,' she offers.

I wish there was time to talk to these people I've waited so long to find, to hear their stories, to know where they've been hiding, to know their Legacies, and what's in their Chests. But there are more helicopters on the way.

'We can't stay here and defend this same piece of desert forever,' I say. 'We have to get to Six!'

'Let's take out these bad boys,' Nine says, pointing to the oncoming cloud. 'And then we can find Six and get on with it.'

We all turn to watch the approach. Several new helicopters now dot the sky. I look over at my fellow Garde, and each one looks ready to fight. We've never had so many of us together. Never before have things looked so possible. After all this, we're never splitting up again.

'They'll just keep coming,' I say. 'We should just go get Six.'

'Okay, Johnny. The tunnel is that way,' Nine says, pointing behind us. 'I'll take up the rear and deal with anything that needs handling. You know, snap a few necks, shake things up a bit.'

Those of us with Chests pick them up. I take the lead, heading in the direction Nine pointed. I scan for traps and move everyone towards the five-pronged cactus. Seven and Eight are on my heels, with Ten close behind them. There is a steady stream of gunfire behind us as Nine does his thing. He sounds like he's having a party with himself back there, hooting and hollering. Only he would consider this fun.

We pick up the pace and don't stop running until we get to the cactus. Nine gleefully fires shot after shot while Eight and I try to deal with the prickly plant, the only thing that stands between us and where Six is being held. The map showed that the tunnel is right where the cactus stands. Finally, we manage to blow it to pieces using our telekinesis. Beneath it is a thick brown door with a metal handle in the middle of it. As I stand there looking at the entrance to the tunnel, the other Garde by my side, I remember what Nine said earlier: 'I've been waiting for this my whole life.' We've all been waiting for this — waiting for the moment when we'd find each other, when the nine of us would rise up and defend the legacy of Lorien against the Mogadorians. As it turned out, all nine of us didn't make it, but I know that the six of us who are left, as well as the addition of Number Ten, will do whatever it takes to survive what's to come.

28

An enormous Mog charges at me, gleaming sword swinging. I duck under the blade and connect my fist with his throat. He drops his weapon, gasping for air. No sooner has the metal clanged to the ground than I pick it up and behead him. A cloud of his ash engulfs me as three more charge. The ash hides me. I crouch low, slicing Mog legs off at the knees as soon as they approach. When I stand, another massive Mog tries to get me from behind. I backflip over him, driving my sword through his midsection as I land. I step through his cloud of ash to find myself surrounded by a dozen more. I don't see Setrákus Ra.

I turn invisible. After ripping through another round of Mogs, I look again for Setrákus Ra. I see him at the far end of the room and don't hesitate. I run straight at him. More Mogs appear; I lose count of how many. I leave them all a pile of dust. When I'm within thirty feet of Setrákus Ra, he raises a fist and points it at me, almost as if he can see me. Blue electricity shoots from his hand and crackles along the ceiling of the room and I feel myself turn visible. Once again, he's taken away my Legacies. I knew this could happen, but I feel a pang of loss anyway. Still, I'm ready for whatever he has for me.

Soldier Mogs come at me from all sides, but I just

keep moving towards Setrákus Ra. When a Mog steps into my path, I rip my sword through his neck. Another grabs me from behind and I cut off his arm. Another comes screaming towards me and I shove my sword through his midsection. At this point, I'm so focused on where I will ram my blade through Setrákus Ra's neck that I barely notice killing off the Mogs.

The next thing I know, he's right next to me and he grabs my neck. He raises me up with one hand until my feet are dangling off the ground and once again our faces are only inches apart.

'You fight well, little girl,' he breathes into my face. I wince from the stench.

'Give me my Legacies back and you'll see how well.' My voice is strangled.

'If you were as strong as you think you are, I wouldn't be able to take them away in the first place.'

'Don't give me that, you coward! If you're so sure you can take me, why don't you do it? Show me how big and tough you are. Give me back my Legacies and fight like a man!' I shout.

His voice echoes as he bellows, 'You use your powers, and I'll use mine!'

He tosses me back into the middle of the room, but I barely notice the pain of the impact when I hit the floor. My sword clangs to the ground and skitters away. A soldier sends his sword spinning at me at high speed. My first instinct is to try to stop it with my mind, but my Legacies are still gone. Even so, my strength and reflexes are with me, full force.

I am going to kill Setrákus Ra, with or without my powers. I reach out with both hands and slap them over the oncoming blade, trapping it inches from my chin. The next second I'm tackled around the waist and, as I fall onto my back, I rotate the sword between my palms and sink it into the attacking Mog. I'm covered in a blanket of ash as I hit the ground. More Mogs come. I'm destroying them with their weapons, and the justice of that is awesome. I feel stronger with every one I reduce to nothing. I'm also more pissed off. If I have to go through every Mog on Earth to get to Setrákus Ra, I'll do it.

Setrákus Ra is just standing there, watching the show. He roars so loud I can feel the vibrations in my chest. My years of training were all leading up to this moment. The only way I could feel stronger is if the rest of the Garde were here; we should be fighting him together. I shake off the thought. I will take him out for all of us.

After I finish off the last soldier, Setrákus Ra moves into the middle of the room to where I stand. He reaches behind his back and produces a massive double-headed whip that he snaps against the ground. It lights up with orange flames.

I don't even flinch. There is nothing he can do to scare or stop me now. I race forward, yelling, 'For Lorien!'

He flicks the whip over my head, sending a thick blanket of flames over me. I dive under its edge and roll in the direction of his feet. As I dodge his stomp-ing boot, I see several scars branded around his ankles. I register them but don't have time to think if there's a connection between his scars and mine. My sword slashes his calf just above the highest scar on his left leg and then I spring to my feet. The mark I made immediately hardens and fades to another scar. He is completely unaffected by the wound, he doesn't even limp a single step.

He snaps the whip at me again and I try to cut off one of its two tails but when the flames touch my sword, the blade melts. I throw the remains of the sword at him. He raises his hand and halts the weapon in midair. It twirls and glows and as he stretches open his fingers, the melted blade climbs back above the handle, reforming into a gleaming sword again. He smiles and lets it fall to the ground.

I dive for the sword, but when I reach down to grab it, his whip snaps across the top of my right hand. My skin boils and opens and, instead of blood, a hard black substance appears in the gash. I look at it and know I should feel unbelievable pain, but I'm numb. I stagger forward and finally get hold of the sword. Weapon in hand, I circle back around to face the Mog leader. But something is terribly wrong with my right hand now. It won't move.

Setrákus Ra cracks his whip again and I jump out of the way as it flies past me, leaving a trail of flames in its wake. When he raises his arm to pull the whip back over his shoulder again, I see an opening and take it. Gripping the sword in my left hand, I rush at him and plunge it deep into his ribcage. I yank it downwards, ripping his waxy skin apart until the sword is lodged at the bottom of his torso. I fall backwards, looking up at him and desperately hoping I've delivered the final blow, that I've ended the war.

No such luck. Though Setrákus Ra grimaces for the first time, instead of turning into a pile of ash he just reaches down and pulls the sword out of his body. He examines the blade, watching his thick black blood dripping off of it. Then he puts the blade in his mouth and bites down on it, breaking it in half, and lets it drop to the ground. It's like he's playing with me. What's going on? I rise to my feet, calculating quickly what my next move should be. Step one is avoiding Setrákus Ra long enough to figure it out. I wish, more than ever, that my Garde was standing with me.

Ella? Can you hear me?

Nothing.

I continue to back away from Setrákus Ra, trying to put more distance between us to give myself a fighting chance. That's when I notice my right hand is starting to tingle. I look down and see the skin around the whip's wound has turned black. As I watch, the discoloration spreads to my knuckles and fingernails; in a matter of seconds my entire right hand is black up to my wrist. The tingling sensation vanishes. My hand feels incredibly heavy. Like it's turned to lead.

I look up at Setrákus Ra. The purple scar on his neck begins to pulse with a bright light. 'Are you ready to die?' he asks me.

Ella? If you're coming, now is the time. In fact, it's now or never.

I want so much to hear her voice in my head, telling me that she and the others are just outside the door. We should be together, fighting Setrákus Ra with our Legacies, the gifts the Elders bestowed upon us, until there is nothing left to him but the worthless, powerless, pile of ashes all of the other Mogs have become. Instead, I'm here alone, my hand injured and useless, playing cat and mouse with Setrákus Ra. And he's just standing here in front of me, fire whip in hand, having rendered my Legacies useless, toying with me. *What* is going on?

I take one more look around at the desert, then reach for the wheel on the brown door and give it a spin. After one rotation, I decide to speed things up and just yank it off its hinges. A steel ladder goes down into a black hole.

'I can see in the dark,' Marina volunteers. 'I'll go first.' I stand aside to let her get by.

Marina climbs down the ladder into the darkness and drops out of sight. Eight tosses her Chest down after her.

'It's about twenty feet down. Looks like there's a long tunnel,' Marina calls up. 'All clear so far. I don't see anyone.'

Nine looks at Ella and me and says, 'Ladies first.' Ella starts down the ladder, and when she disappears, Nine smirks at me and says, 'Well, okay, but I was referring to you, Four.'

I shake my head at him. He's nothing if not consistent. He gestures for me to go down next. 'You know I love you, man. Get in there.'

Using telekinesis, I let Bernie Kosar down first, back in his

298

beagle form, then tuck my Chest under one arm and awk-wardly climb down using just the other hand. It's musty and cold inside the tunnel. Ahead of me, I can hear Ella and Marina walking and BK's toenails clicking on the cement. I turn the Lumen on in my free hand and sweep the con-crete tunnel for a few seconds, getting my bearings.

I use my Lumen to illuminate the distance between our location and a sharp turn far up ahead, then I turn it off. 'Marina, you can see to keep us moving, right?' Eight and Nine have now caught up with us. She nods and we all start to follow her down the dark passageway. We haven't gone very far when I almost slam into Ella, who has stopped dead in her tracks.

'Oh no! I finally got through to Six. She needs us! She says it's now or never!'

'Let's pick up the pace, people!' Nine calls out from the rear.

We run as fast as we can through the dark. I flash my Lumen every few seconds to keep us from running over each over. We make a sharp turn and I wave my hands again to light up the tunnel and reveal what's ahead. The next hundred yards slope downward, and my Lumen lights up a concrete door at the end. I slide my chest down ahead of me until it slams against the door. Still sprinting, I turn on both of my palms to give us all a better view.

Nine quickly rips open his Chest and pulls out the yellow ball covered in small bumps. Like a magician, he holds it in his fingers and then whips it at the door. It bounces just a few inches off the metal before expanding while turning black. Long, razor-sharp spikes explode out of it and the door is blown inward on impact. The spikes instantly retreat until it's just a yellow ball again, lying innocently on the floor. Nine leans down, grabs it, and tosses it back into his Chest, which he closes with a loud snap.

'I was hoping that would happen,' Nine says admiringly. If I were him I'd have taken advantage of my Chest of wonders to see through the door first, to know what we were about to get to. But this is no time to critique anyone's decisions.

We all bolt through the doorway. As soon as we enter, motion-sensor lights come on above us. Red lights flash and sirens blare, attacking our senses. At the end of this shorter passageway, we come to another large concrete door. This one rises as we approach it, revealing dozens of enormous Mogadorian soldiers with cannons and swords up and ready to use.

'Mogs? What are they doing here?' asks Eight in disbelief.

'Yeah. Bad news; the government and the Mogadorians have teamed up,' I say.

'Easy pickings,' Eight says. Nine nudges me and makes an exaggerated gesture of approval at our new-found Garde member.

I feel a surge of adrenaline pump through my body that I've only felt in my visions. All of a sudden I know what to do. I look over at the others.

'Follow my lead!' I yell. They nod back at me. I drop my Chest, light the Lumen in both palms, and rush straight ahead. The last thing I see out of the corner of my eye is Ella scooping up my Chest.

Just like in my vision, I aim the Lumen at my feet as I run and they catch on fire. The flames climb up my legs and engulf my body just as I reach the first soldier. When I jump, I'm a fireball that burns right through him. He turns to ash and I keep running.

The Mogs I pass swing around 180 degrees to shoot at me, but my flames offer the perfect protection. I lower my head and run with my arms stretched out, effectively keeping any other soldiers away. Marina, Eight, and Ella are on the heels of the soldiers, picking them off from behind as I race ahead. Nine has run up onto the ceiling and is battling the Mogs from above. I toss fireballs at the closest ones to me and in a matter of seconds, they're all torched, leaving a thick cloud of ash and smoke hanging above. I slow my pace when I see the last one go down. When we reach the back of the room, I launch a large ball of fire at the door, blowing it to pieces. I take a second to admire how well that worked, BK even getting his share of Mogs, though this is clearly neither the time nor the place for self-congratulation. Maybe Nine's rubbed off on me. We all turn to see what's next.

Setrákus Ra has done something to me. I can't move at all and stand rooted in place. At first, I wonder if it's just all the punishing battle or the bizarre wound on my hand, or both. Then I realize there is something seriously wrong, something stopping me from being able to move. I force my chin up to look at Setrákus Ra looming before me. Setrákus Ra has produced a golden cane with a black eye on the handle. He holds it out and the eye opens, blinks, rolls left and then right before it finds me. Then the eye slowly closes, and snaps back open to emit a crazy-bright, blinding, red light. As the beam crawls over my helpless body, it leaves behind a weird, buzzing sensation on my skin. I really need to move. I need to get away from that creepy light, away from whatever it's doing to me, but I'm immobilized. My hand weighs a ton. I am vulnerable and I need to get control – of the situation, of myself. But I can't.

The light from the eye is now purple and it rolls over my face. I lick my lips and taste something burned. Setrákus Ra moves towards me until he's a few feet away. I close my eyes and tighten my jaw, thinking of John and Katarina and Sam and Marina and Ella. I see Eight and Henri and Crayton, and even Bernie Kosar. I will *not* give Setrákus Ra the honor, the pleasure, of looking at him while he kills me. Something hot and soft touches my forehead, like a blast of air. I steel myself for whatever is about to happen; brace myself for the certain agony it will bring. When nothing happens, I open my eyes to see Setrákus Ra just standing there. Well, not exactly. There are bands of red and purple light shining out of the head of his cane and crawling up and down his massive body.

Setrákus Ra starts to shake and a white light outlines his shoulders and arms. He falls to his knees, convulsing, his huge head jerking up and down. Then his dull, waxy skin pulls away from the muscle and bone. When the skin snaps back down onto his shrinking body, it has a new, olive tone. Long blond hair grows out of his scalp until he has a full head of hair. When he looks up at me, I am more desperate than ever to attack but I still can't move. He's me – gray eyes and high cheekbones and dyed blond hair.

'For me to be you, you must stay alive,' he says in

my voice, 'but only for now.' He lifts a palm into the air and, as if there was one magnet in the ceiling and another in my now-black hand, I shoot off the ground, slam against the ceiling, and dangle there, fifty feet off the floor. I feel a painful buzzing in my brain. I try again to call for Ella in my head, but I can't even hear myself think. When I touch my free hand to the one stuck to the ceiling, it, too, turns black. The heavy stiffness that weighed down my hand is now spreading. The thing I can move at this point are my eyes. My entire body is now black. Black rock.

29

Once again I take the lead. Marina trails me and a growling Bernie Kosar runs alongside her. Ella still has my Chest, with Eight and Nine following close behind. My fire has made me invincible, and my flames instantly consume every Mogadorian soldier that comes charging around a corner or through a door. The fire has not only taken over my body, but also my mind. I have never felt so confident, so determined, so ready to defeat our enemies before.

'She still hasn't responded to me!' Ella yells as we enter another hallway filled with sirens and flashing lights. 'I don't know if she can hear anything I'm saying.'

'Well, she isn't dead yet because we don't have any new scars,' Nine says, sticking out his leg as if to admire it.

My fire is getting higher and wider, licking the walls and ceiling of the corridor as I pass through. It's hard to describe my energy, how I am barely able to contain it, like I might explode with it. I'm ready to fight Setrákus Ra and I know the others feel the same way. Nine and Eight are like wrecking balls swinging down the hall, pounding soldiers into oblivion, bouncing from one Mog to the other, and Marina is fighting fearlessly, using all means available to toss soldiers into the air. Ella, with fewer powers revealed, looks on a bit enviously as we swat away the soldiers. I wish I had the time to stop and tell her how vital she is, how important her ability to communicate telepathically was to our all coming together. How she, as the youngest Loric, represents our long life and the power of our Garde. We're ready to take back Lorien and that's only possible because of everything we bring to the fight, each one of us. The hallway splits off and we need to quickly decide which way to go. Separating is never going to be an option again.

'Okay, Fire Boy, which way?' Nine asks.

Marina steps up and says, 'This way.' Her ability to see in the dark is better than the limited view my Lumen offers, so I extinguish my fire and we all follow her to the left.

Marina doesn't even hesitate at the entryway of a long wide room filled with tall brown columns. Neither do the rest of us. We have our weapons ready when we first hear the noise of people marching in on the far end of the room. I nudge Marina's arm. 'Hey, can you see who that is?'

'Yeah. I'm guessing they're government soldiers. They're definitely not Mogs. There are a lot of them. I don't know, twenty, thirty? There could be more than that.' She turns and moves towards them. We all do the same. We can toss them aside easily, twisting their guns with our telekinesis. We blow through the big room, pass another corridor door, and turn left, where we find a dozen government soldiers dressed in black, protecting a heavy metal door. As soon as they see us, they step into formation to fully block the passageway and start firing. As if prearranged, Marina and Eight both raise their hands, stopping the bullets as they are fired, inches away from their barrels. Immediately, Nine joins the action and uses his mind to rip the guns out of the soldiers' hands and lifts the soldiers up, dangling from the domed ceiling. We each grab a gun.

Nine wedges the tip of his staff into the doorframe they were guarding and rips it off its hinges.

Behind the doorway is another hallway, this one lined with doors on both sides. Nine runs ahead to each of the doors and briefly presses his ear to each one.

He reports one unmanned control room after another. Further down the hall we find what look like empty prison cells. I wonder if we're getting closer to finding Six. She could be behind any one of these doors.

I spot a trail of blood in front of one of the doors. From ten feet away I rip the door out of its frame. The cell is pitch black inside. Before I have a chance to use my Lumen, Marina pushes by me. 'There's a person in here!' she cries.

We hear a whimper from the back corner and I flash my lights into the darkness. There, scared and dirty, is someone I thought I would never see again. Sarah. I fall to my knees, my lights glowing dimly. I open my mouth to speak, but only a squeak comes out. I try again: 'Sarah.' I can't believe she's sitting in front of me. I can't believe we found her.

After a quick glance up at me Sarah hugs her knees to her chest and looks afraid. Afraid of me. She drops her head into her knees and sobs. 'Please don't do this to me, please don't trick me anymore. Not like this. I can't take it, I can't take anymore.' She's shaking her head over and over. I don't think she's even registered I'm not alone. I can feel everyone standing behind me, cloaked in darkness.

'Sarah,' I whisper. 'It's me, John. We're here to take you home.'

Nine hangs back, but I can hear him say to someone, 'So this is the famous Sarah; girl looks good, even dirty.'

Sarah pulls her legs to her chest even more tightly and peeks over her knees. She looks so vulnerable and scared; I just want to scoop her up. But I move slowly, ready for anything. This could be a trap. I haven't come this far only to act without thinking. When I touch her shoulder, she screams in panic. I can feel everyone behind me flinch with the sudden noise, the sheer terror in her voice.

She presses her back against the wall, her hair sticking to the rough concrete. Then she lifts her face to the ceiling and cries, 'Don't trick me anymore! I've told you everything. Please don't trick me anymore!'

Marina steps forward so she is standing next to me. She grabs my arm and gives me a shake, then pulls me to my feet. 'John, we can't stay here; we have to get moving. We need to take Sarah with us!'

Sarah finally looks beyond me and sees the others. I watch her take in Marina standing there, looking down at her. Her eyes widen and she looks back at me, then she looks around at the others who have stepped closer. Tears streak the thick layer of dirt on her cheeks. 'What's happening? Are you really here? Are all of you really here?'

I kneel down next to her again. 'It's me. It's us. I promise. Look, even Bernie Kosar wants to say hi.' He trots over and licks her hand, his tail wagging.

I lay my hands on hers, and when I see the bruises running up and down her wrists, my eyes fill with tears. I press her fingers to my lips. 'Sarah, listen to me. I know I left you once. I promise you, I will never do that again. Do you hear me? I will *never* leave you.' She is still looking at me as if I might disappear or turn into a fire-breathing monster.

A thousand other things I've been thinking about for so

long race through my mind and I struggle to say more. I flash back to our last conversation at the playground, moments before the police took me away. 'Hey, Sarah. Do you remember when I said that I think about you every day. Do you remember that?' She looks at me and nods. 'Well, I did and I do. Every day.' She allows herself a tentative smile. 'Now do you believe it's really me?' She nods again. 'Sarah Hart, I love you. I love only you. Do you hear me?'

She looks so relieved, it makes me want to pick her up and tell her it's over and I will keep her safe. Always. She kisses me, her hands on each side of my face.

'Four, come on! We have to move,' Eight shouts. He and the others have moved to the door, anxiously looking both directions of the hallway.

There's an explosion in the hallway and Eight runs out to see what it is, followed by Ella and Marina. 'What the hell is taking so long, man?' Nine shouts to me, gesturing madly towards the door. 'Stand the girl up and let's get going! Sarah Hart, it is *awfully* nice to meet you, but we *really* need you to move! Now!'

Nine rushes over and helps me get Sarah to her feet. Once she's fully upright, he gives her a quick hug. She looks surprised by the warm welcome, and I have to wonder about the wink he gives me over her head. 'Sarah freaking Hart! Do you have any idea how much this jerk talks about you?' I smile at Sarah, then Nine.

'No,' Sarah laughs quietly, leaning into me and winding her fingers through mine.

'Okay, okay. Come on, you two,' Nine says, turning to head back to the door.

I stare into Sarah's blue eyes. 'Before we go, I have to ask you something. And you need to understand that I *have* to ask it. You're not working for them, are you? The government and the Mogs?'

Sarah shakes her head. 'Why does everyone keep asking me that? I would never betray any of you.'

'Wait. Who's everyone? Who else asked you that?' I ask.

'Six,' Sarah says, looking surprised I would even need to ask. Her blue eyes widen. 'You didn't find her?'

'You've seen Six?' Marina speaks up, excited. 'When? Where?'

'She's fighting Setrákus Ra,' Sarah says, starting to panic again. 'They took her away a while ago.'

'What? No way! That's *my* fight!' Nine yells.

'Don't worry, man, if we move fast, maybe you can get a piece of him,' I say. Then I look down the hall to find Eight, Marina, and Ella running back towards us.

'That way,' Marina shouts.

I grab Sarah's hand and pull her behind me. Everyone races down the hall where we find Bernie Kosar standing in front of a metal doorway that's the size of a loading-dock entrance, barking uncontrollably.

This time Nine does use his rock to look through the door. Like before, a white cone of light appears, then we can see right into a huge room. 'Looks like there's something going on in there. I see movement in the shadows,' Eight says. 'I'll teleport through and scout it out.'

'Wait a sec, Eight.' I hold up my hand to stop him. 'No scout. We should just do this, all of us.'

Eight looks at me for a second, then nods. 'You're right. This is for all of us.'

When we're all gathered at the door, I look down the line of determined faces. Even Sarah. She's gone from weepy res-cue-girl to warrior in a heartbeat. Pretty impressive. Of course, she hasn't got a *clue* what we are pretty sure is about to happen. It's likely this is going to be an epic battle, if not *the* battle. I have a feeling in my gut that everything has led up to this moment. This could be what we've been working towards.

'Whatever's inside, whatever happens,' I say, lighting the Lumen in my palms, 'we *will* kill Setrákus Ra, no matter what.' I'm saying this for me, not them.

'We're all on this, dude,' Nine says.

I hold a glowing palm over the door, and just as I'm about to blow it inwards, a woman with red hair and an arm in a sling comes hobbling through a door at the far end of the hall. She and I gasp at exactly the same time; then she turns and darts back through the door.

'Wait! Agent Walker!' I shout after her.

'Walker? Are you kidding me?' Nine asks, incredulously. 'The chick soldier who tried to capture us?' The others just look on, confused for a beat, before Eight speaks up.

'I'll get her for you,' he says, and then disappears. When he materializes a moment later he's got her, arms twisted behind her back. The first thing I do is rip off the gold badge on the front of her shirt.

Nine plucks the badge out of my hand and makes a great show of examining it carefully. 'Well, well, well. Who do we have here? Special Agent Walker?' Nine laughs. 'Lady, you look awful!' He hands the badge back to me as if it suddenly has cooties.

'Do you know how pathetic you are?' I yell. 'Cutting deals with the Mogs, doing their dirty work, for what? They are going to *destroy* you!'

311

'I'm doing my job,' she says stiffly. Eight has a tight grip on her. 'We are doing what's best for this country.' She stares back at me defiantly, but I know we will make it clear how much she has to fear from us soon enough.

Sarah points at her. 'I've seen you before. John, she was there when Six was taken away.'

Nine grabs Agent Walker by her shirt's lapels like some gangster from a movie. Eight never loosens his grip on her arms. Nine shoves his face right into her face. 'I want this one, I get to kill her.'

Walker is now frantically struggling to back away from Nine and free herself of Eight. 'Wait! I know where your ship is!' Special Agent Walker pleads. 'I know you want it and you'll never find it without me.'

'Our ship is here?' Marina asks, clearly uncertain if she can trust what Agent Walker says.

The agent narrows her eyes. 'I'll show you if you let me go.'

'What do you think, Four?' Nine asks.

'John? What happens when you find your ship?' asks Sarah, grabbing my arm.

'We don't have time for this!' Marina says. 'I know Six is inside this room. The fact that this woman will say any-thing to keep us from going in tells me I'm right! Forget about her! Who cares if or where our ship is, until we have Six!'

Nine says, 'I'll handle her.' Walker floats up into the air and hangs by her belt hook on the light fixture high above us, red-faced with fury. Nine looks at us, winks and flicks the fingers of one hand behind his back, blowing the door open. 'Marina's right. Six and Setrákus Ra come first. Shall we?'

He smiles at Sarah. 'You're pretty badass from what I've

heard from Johnny here,' he says, handing her Walker's Mog cannon. 'Think you can handle her?'

Sarah takes the cannon. 'If she moves from that light, I'll blast her. Gladly.'

I look at the rest of the Garde. 'It's time.'

We rush inside. We don't have to figure out who's doing what. We just know. It's quiet and dark and an awful stench permeates the air. All I can think of is the arena that kept appearing in my visions. Is this it? I look around, trying to see if I can tell. The center of the large room is dimly illuminated. Nine runs into the circle of light and yells, 'Time to come and play, Setrákus, you piece of shit!'

'Where's Six?' Marina says. She joins Nine in the center of the room, along with Eight. They quickly drop their Chests and start to look around.

'You guys! There's something up on the ceiling,' Ella says, her voice echoing around the room. I look up to see a small formation of rocks hanging from the ceiling.

I shine my Lumen on the object, and bathed in its glow, it almost looks like a statue. 'This isn't right. I don't know why, but there's something wrong here,' I say in a low voice.

While we watch the shadows for any sign of movement, Nine uses his anti-gravity Legacy to run up onto the ceiling and look at the rock formation. When he starts to get close I hear a familiar voice yell, 'Stop!'

I whip around to see Six standing alone in the doorway. A loop of thick rope hangs from her hip, and in her hand is a jagged blue sword. She looks unharmed. Now *that* is the Six I remember; confident and strong. Did she do it? Is it possible that Six has already killed Setrákus Ra?

'Six! Oh, my God, it's you!' Marina cries. 'You're okay!'

313

'It's over,' Six says. 'Setrákus Ra is dead. That formation on the ceiling is Mogadorian poison. Stay away from it.'

The relief in the air palpable. Eight teleports to Six's side and wraps his arms around her in a huge hug.

Six was always the strongest of us, stronger than even me or Nine. She just saved Lorien, Earth, and possibly the universe. I want to pick her up, put her on my shoulder, and parade her back to Lorien.

I start towards her too, but Ella grabs my wrist and pulls me back. I hear her in my mind. *John. Something's wrong.*

The next few moments happen in what feels like slow motion. Six pulls the jagged blue sword back and thrusts it forward. Horrified, I watch Eight become rigid, then the tip of the sword breaks through the middle of his shoulders. He slumps forward. Six pushes Eight's body off her sword and he falls to the floor, motionless.

'No!' Marina screams from behind me and rushes towards Eight.

I'm paralyzed with shock until my instinct to fight kicks in. I look down and a massive fireball has formed in the palm of my right hand. Whatever confusion I was just feeling has cleared and I know what I need to do. This can't be Six. And whoever this really is, I need to kill them.

'Six,' I say, rolling the fireball on the tips of my fingers. 'What did they do to you?'

She laughs and raises her other hand into a fist. Blue lightning shoots out between her knuckles and spreads along the ceiling of the room. My fireball disappears. What's going on?

'Four!' I look up to see Nine flying through the air from above me. His anti-gravity Legacy must have failed him too.

I manage to catch enough of him to stop him from slamming down on the ground and help him get to his feet.

Marina stands protectively over Eight, guns aimed and ready to fire. Eight is still on the ground and I can't tell how badly he's injured. At least I know he's alive, since I don't have a new scar. Marina lets loose a burst of bullets, but they stop inches from Six's face and drop uselessly to the concrete. I try to light myself with my Lumen again, but nothing happens.

With her sword held high, Six's body starts to convulse and blur with a quick flash of white. She grows taller and her long blond hair shrinks into a small patch on top of a large skull. Her face elongates and morphs, and somehow I know she's changing into Setrákus Ra even before the glowing purple scar appears on his neck. Two battalions of Mog soldiers silently emerge from doors on the sides of the room and flank him. Without a word, Nine, Marina, Ella, and I move closer to one another, standing over Eight, to make it clear we will face him together.

'All of you in one place. How convenient for me. I hope you're ready to die,' he snarls.

'I think you have that wrong,' I reply.

'That's what Number Six thought, too. But *she* was wrong. Very wrong.' He smiles, his revolting and stained teeth glinting in the dim light.

Nine looks over at me and rubs his hands together, all eager anticipation. 'Johnny boy, have we discussed how important oral hygiene is to me?' He looks back at Setrákus Ra, 'Dude, brush your teeth before you even think about threatening me!' He extends his glowing red staff, turns to Setrákus Ra and charges. Thankfully we still have the power of our Inheritance.

30

Out of the corner of my eye, I see Nine charging Setrákus Ra. I turn back to Eight, to see if I can heal him. I keep my hands on Eight's chest wound, waiting for my Legacy to start working again. Nothing. I beg Eight to hold on, to fight through the pain, but his brown eyes roll back, and his breath becomes more and more shallow. Panicked, I flash back on the drawing from the Loric cave, the one where Eight is killed by Setrákus Ra's sword. Is the prediction coming true? I desperately keep pressing my hands all over his chest.

'Marina!' John shouts. 'We have to get you and Eight out of this room, now! I have a feeling if we can get away from Setrákus Ra, our Legacies will start working again. If I'm right, you can still save Eight.'

'He's almost gone,' I manage to choke out. 'It might be too late no matter what we do.' I can't bring myself to tell him about the cave drawing. I wonder if Eight is able to think about any of this, to remember the drawing, to know what this moment might be. I hope not.

'Then we should hurry,' he says, handing me a Mog cannon and picking up Eight. 'Shoot anything and everything that's not one of our friends.'

We try to cover the hundred or so yards to the door as quickly as we can, while keeping an eye on the others who are locked in battle. With every Mog I turn to ash on the way, I feel stronger and stronger. I try not to think about where Six – the real Six – is, or what's happened to her. I *knew* that wasn't Six. I wish I had killed that *thing,* even before it revealed itself. I scan the room. Nine is fighting Setrákus Ra, clearly treading water, his staff clashing with Ra's sword. As strong as Nine is, it almost looks like Setrákus Ra is toying with him, just waiting for the right moment to strike and kill.

Every ounce of confidence and strength I felt a moment ago drains out of me. There are simply too many of them and too few of us. And we are without our Legacies, which means we're just *kids*. Kids fighting an organized, alien army. I hate to leave the others, but I know John is right. I know I need to get out of here if I'm going to have any hope of healing Eight. And saving Eight is the only choice.

We're almost at the door when two dozen Mogs come right at us. Some of them have cannons, some of them have swords, and they all appear terrifyingly unstoppable. I try to shoot them, but the cannon blasts I send their way don't even make a dent in the advancing mob. There are just too many of them. John manages to set Eight down just outside the door, then he joins me, charging them and wielding his sword. I fight alongside him. I will not let John down no matter how bad the odds appear. We protect one another and we draw strength from each other when we feel weak. It's why we've survived this long, and why we will win. We are stronger when we unite.

John mows the Mogs down, one at a time, methodically and fast. I shoot steadily as I maneuver to block the doorway and protect Eight. I duck outside the door to check on

Eight's condition. I feel his pulse, which is faint, and I can tell my Legacy has not returned. I lay my hands on him and whisper fiercely, 'You can't die, Eight. Do you hear me? I am going to heal you. My Legacy will return and I will heal you.'

I realize the Mogs that had charged us are all gone – destroyed – and the abrupt silence startles me.

'We have to hurry. More will come,' John says urgently.

We hear a deafening scream – through the door we can see Bernie Kosar has transformed into a beast and is surrounded by Mogs who are trying to slash at him, but he jumps in and out of their reach. The Mogs can't get him, but he isn't able to do much damage to them, either. We step back into the room in time to see Setrákus pull out a whip. Its tips begin to flame and he strikes Nine in the arm. The wound immediately begins to turn black. John turns to say something to me when I hear a shot. Before I can even tell what happened John's body convulses and he falls to the ground.

I'm stuck to the ceiling, entombed in black stone. I watch as the rest of the Garde fight for their lives and I can't even feel my own body, never mind let them know I'm up here. I'm helpless and it's killing me. I've trained every moment of my life learning how *not* to be helpless. Setrákus Ra is no great fighter. He's only taking us down because he is able to render us powerless. I want to be standing down there with his head in my hands for all of the Mogs to see. I would make sure they witnessed the destruction of their leader, and then I'd leave them in the same pile of ash.

Am I watching the dream of Lorien die? We thought we were so strong and so smart and so prepared. We thought we were going to end the war and fly back home to Lorien. We were fools, arrogant fools. We knew of Setrákus Ra, the great and terrible Mogadorian leader, but we didn't know anything about how he fought, the powers he would bring to the battle. In retrospect it seems obvious that he would have the power to take our Legacies.

I wish I could communicate with my fellow Garde – I'd be able to direct them well from this vantage point. For one thing, I can see that while the Mogs are stupendously strong physically, they bring little if anything in the way of mental technique. These guys are almost as dumb as the rock I've become. They reveal their movements before they act. Their plan of attack is easy to read because they don't have one. This is a game of numbers and brute force, and that is an enemy that can be beat if you know what you're dealing with. But when you're in the thick of it, it's impossible to see. I wish I could tell the Garde to focus all of their energies and strength on Setrákus Ra. Otherwise I fear the battle will be short, the Mogs almost sure to win.

I watch Bernie Kosar get slashed. He's transformed himself into an enormous beast, the same kind he became back in Paradise. His body is thick and muscular, his teeth and claws are sharp and jagged, and two curled horns have sprouted from his head. I see Setrákus Ra hit Nine with his whip and Nine's arm turn black, which I can only assume means he'll be in the same position as me soon. John has been shot, and he goes down writhing in pain. Marina picks up a cannon and starts firing on the advancing Mogs.

Ella's sneaking out of the room. Does she have a plan?

I'm distracted from watching Ella by the sound of BK roaring in pain. I see he's fallen to his knees. Though he's still fighting, still killing Mogs, he's bleeding heavily from his wounds. It's agonizing watching him slowly destroyed, in so much pain.

I'm bleeding out; I can feel my blood and my strength running out of me and there's nothing I can do about it.

Wave after wave of Mogs just keep coming. I have no idea how many we've killed so far today, but it doesn't seem to make any difference. Without our Legacies, it's like trying to stop a tsunami with a pile of Swiss cheese.

Marina is behind me, firing on the Mogs. I look over at Bernie Kosar and see the Mogs have ropes around his horns and are dragging him out of the corner.

'Coward, you're nothing but a coward! You have to paralyze us just to beat us!' I hear Nine scream. I see him in the center of the room, one of his arms black and hanging heavy and useless, as Setrákus rears his whip back.

Setrákus Ra smiles. 'You can call me whatever names you want. It's not going to change the fact that you're about to die.' He snaps the whip forward. Nine tries to block the flaming tips with his staff, but with only one arm, it's impossible. One of the tips hits Nine's hand, sending the staff flying, and the other tail of the whip hits Nine's face. He screams out in pain as his hand and face both start turning black. Setrákus advances on him. I have to do what I can before I'm totally useless, or dead, so I start firing my cannon at Setrákus Ra from my position on the ground. At best, I'm a distraction, but I will do whatever I can. He stops each one of the projectiles I fire in midair, and tosses them aside like they're nothing.

I hear a new source of cannon fire. I turn towards the door and see Sarah moving into the room, firing on Mogs, Ella behind her. Sarah. She hasn't been trained. There's no way she can survive a battle with the Mogs and Setrákus Ra! 'Sarah!' I scream. 'You've got to get out of here! This is not your fight!'

Sarah ignores me and keeps moving deeper into the room. Nine is trying to move away from Setrákus Ra, but his arms, both of which are now completely black, weigh him down. His face is quickly turning as black as his arms. Setrákus strikes Nine again, this time getting him with both tips of the whip right in the middle of his chest. Nine cries out and Setrákus shouts, 'I had heard you might be my greatest challenge, but look at you, you are *nothing*!'

As Setrákus Ra brings his whip back once more to deliver a fatal blow to Nine, Ella darts out from behind Sarah and throws something at him, something that looks like a small red blur. It hits Setrákus in the arm and he looks down, shocked, before letting out a deafening roar.

I feel something change inside of me. It's immediate and enormously powerful, like someone plugged me into an energy source. I focus on my hands and try, just once more, to light my Lumen. To my amazement, it works. Our Legacies have returned.

From behind me I hear Marina cry out and she races over

to Eight, who's still just outside the doorway. I see her run her hands over his chest, working on his wounds. She looks at me through the doorway. 'What just happened?'

I shake my head. 'I have no idea, but now we've got ourselves a real fight.'

My palms glowing, I turn towards the center of the room where Setrákus Ra is clawing at his arm, trying to pull out the small red object Ella threw at him. He finally succeeds and turns to snap the whip at Ella and Sarah, who is still firing the cannon. They don't move out of the way fast enough and the whip makes contact. They both go down.

As soon as the dart hits Setrákus, I feel the change. My Legacies are back. My strength is starting to return. I have a chance to get out of here and help the others.

I start struggling within the black casing and can now feel myself move slightly within it, but not enough to break out.

As I continue to struggle, I look below me. John is with Sarah and Ella, both down. He's left a trail of blood behind him as well as piles of ash. Marina has run back outside to Eight. Bernie Kosar is still in the corner, but now he is tearing apart the Mogs that were dragging him a second ago. In the middle of the room, Nine is still facing off with Setrákus Ra and he's been able to break his hands and face free from the black rock that was taking over his body.

Seeing that gives me hope that I can break out of my own stone prison and I continue my struggle until I feel the casing start to give way. I'll be out

323

soon. I am frantic to free myself. The only thing I want right now is to show Setrákus Ra what it feels like to have a real fight on his hands.

Just when I was giving up hope that I would ever be able to help Eight, my Legacy returned. I put my hands on the wound in the center of his chest and feel it start to work. With every second that passes, his heart beats stronger and stronger. I've never felt anything so good in my life, that steady *bump bump bump*. If I weren't in the middle of the fight of our lives, for our future, I think I would start crying right now, but I stay strong, and keep my emotions in check.

I look down and see Eight's eyes flutter open, then look up at me. 'You need to know . . . Six tried to –' he starts to say.

I cut him off. 'That wasn't Six. It was Setrákus Ra. I don't know how, but it was him.'

'But . . . ?' The confusion in Eight's eyes makes my heart break.

'Eight, I can't explain everything right now. How do you feel? Can you stand? We have to get in there, join the others and fight. Are you ready? I need to heal John and I need you to run interference. Got it?'

He nods and I start to get up, but there's just one thing I need to do before it's too late. I look into his eyes, his beautiful brown eyes, take a deep breath, and kiss him. He looks shocked as I pull back. I shrug at him and smile. 'Hey, there's no time like the present, right?' Before he can say or do anything, I turn to find John. I need to heal him, fast. He took three cannon blasts protecting me. If I don't get to him now, he'll die.

324

There's a trail of blood where John dragged himself across the floor, and Eight and I follow it. A heavy cloud of smoke is hanging in the air from all the cannon blasts. When we get to John he's on his knees, shooting balls of fire from his hands at a massive gang of Mogs trying to get to Ella and Sarah. As we move towards him, the Mogs fire at us. But now that I'm able to use my telekinesis I can deflect their shots, and Eight begins fighting back too. I run to John's side and begin to heal his wounds. He's breathing heavily and is very pale. He's lost so much blood.

'John! You need to stop for a minute so I can heal you!' I have to shout to be heard over the chaos and commotion. I grab his chin and force him to look at me.

He shakes his head, trying to release my grip, 'If I stop, the Mogs will kill Sarah and Ella.'

'If you don't stop, *you'll* die. Eight is healed now, he can do defense while I work on you. Please! John! We need you.' I feel him stop struggling.

I look more closely at the wounds on his legs. They're similar. Both legs are bleeding steadily from gaping holes. I work on the right one first, and can immediately tell Four's thigh bone is also broken. He can't help but scream while it kneads itself, but the sound is absorbed by everything else going on. His hands ball into fists as I continue.

The second leg isn't as bad and I'm able to heal it more quickly. John is already breathing easier. I reach for his arm and yell into his ear, 'You are looking a whole lot better!'

I place my hand on the wound on John's upper arm and can feel the muscles, the bicep and tricep, have been shredded. It's going to take a minute or two for them to heal.

Eight is still firing away at the constant stream of Mogs, but they are coming almost faster than he can keep up with.

I feel John's muscles finally knit together and he's healed. He looks at me and I nod. He leaps to his feet and races over to help Eight protect Ella and Sarah, who are still down.

I feel strong. Good. Sarah and Ella did something miraculous that got us our Legacies back, made it possible for us to fight, but now they're both hurt. I will turn every last one of these Mogs into ash for hurting my friends.

I rush towards them, whipping balls of fire from my hands at the Mogs. I know it should never feel good to kill a living creature, but right now, it feels *great*. Now that I'm up Eight is teleporting all over the room, appearing in front of Mogs and slicing them to pieces with a sword. Nine is still fighting Setrákus Ra, but the two of them are moving so fast they're just a blur. I need to get in there and fight, but I also need to stay here and help Sarah and Ella.

Suddenly, one of the Mogs advancing on me turns in a different direction. He's not aiming his cannon at me. It's pointed directly at Sarah and Ella, who are still lying motionless. He fires and their bodies start to convulse, and I begin to scream.

I watch in horror as Ella and Sarah's prone bodies are hit with Mog cannon fire. John reaches them and I rush to his side. He's kneeling next to them and holding their hands as their bodies shake. We're too late.

After all of this, after we made it this far and we all found each other at last, it looks like we're about to lose another member of the Garde. And Sarah. John just found her

326

again, and he's going to lose her. I close my eyes as well, bracing myself for another scar to burn itself into my leg, a scar for Ella. I know this one is going to hurt the most.

But nothing happens. Is there something different about Ella that her death won't cause a scar? That can't be. I open my eyes and look at John, who's still hunched over Sarah and Ella, still intently squeezing their hands.

I look closer at the girls and can't quite believe what I'm seeing. Their wounds – cannon blasts to their bodies and hideous burns on their faces – are healing. 'What's happening? How are *you* doing this?' I ask John, looking at him in wonder.

'I have no idea,' he says, shaking his head. 'I didn't know I could do this. I saw Sarah on the ground and I wasn't going to let her die, or Ella. Not another one of the Garde. I won't let that happen, especially now that we're together. I took their hands and thought about how much I wanted their injuries to heal, how much I wished I could heal them . . . and it suddenly just started to happen.'

'You've developed a new Legacy!' I cry, squeezing his shoulders.

'Or, I just wanted it so badly, a miracle happened. Whatever it is, they're both healing.' He lets out a laugh, filled with exhaustion and relief. John looks to the center of the room, where Nine continues to fight. 'Marina, this is not the time we're going to bring Setrákus Ra down. Even though our Legacies have come back, I don't think we can defeat him just yet, and I don't want to take the chance of losing another Garde member. We have to find Six. Then we need to figure out a way to get the hell out of here, regroup, and come up with a plan. We'll kill him together

327

or die together. But we do it on *our* terms, when we *know* we're ready to do it.'

We hear a moan, and look down at Sarah and Ella. Their eyes are open and color is coming back into their cheeks. John leans over and kisses Sarah.

The casing is finally breaking off. I flex my arms and kick my legs and start to fall as the last of it crumbles. I use my telekinesis to lower myself to the ground.

I lie there for a second, trying to catch my breath. The smoke is so thick my eyes are watering. All of a sudden, a huge explosion rocks the room. An alarm goes off, red lights flash, and a piercingly loud siren fills the air. I can see John's Lumen burning and I make my way through the haze towards it. Ella, Marina and Sarah are standing next to him, and as I get closer Eight appears, teleporting to Marina's side. Bernie Kosar has turned back into a beagle and he limps over to John.

Ella cries out when she sees me and throws her arms around me. I return her hug and then look at John. Seeing his face again is like a dream come true. He touches my arm. 'You okay?'

I nod. 'What about you?' I ask, and I know I sound as exhausted and beaten down as I feel.

'We're all alive so far – but where's Nine?' he replies, looking around as we all realize simultaneously that the battle sounds have disappeared. We run towards the center of the room, towards the area where Nine had been battling Setrákus Ra, keeping him at bay. Nine is lying on the ground, motionless, and Setrákus Ra is nowhere in sight. Marina falls to her knees next to him and frantically starts running her hands over his body while I spin in circles, trying desperately to see through the haze to make sure Setrákus Ra isn't hiding, waiting to capture and kill us when our backs are turned. Aside from the shrill sound of the alarms, the room is eerily quiet and I realize there are no Mogadorians anywhere.

'He's alive!' Marina cries. 'He's just stunned.' Nine sits up, shaking his head groggily.

'What happened?' he asks.

'I was going to ask you that,' Eight says. 'There was an explosion and everyone but the seven of us have disappeared.'

'I don't know – I didn't see where he went. One second I was trying to hold my own, fighting him off, the next thing I knew I was here on the ground.'

'What do we do now?' Sarah asks.

'We have to get of here,' says John. 'Setrákus Ra could reappear at any second, and this could be a trap. Even though this is a government base, it clearly isn't safe.'

'Anyone know a way out of here?' I ask. They all look at each other grimly.

'We have to go back the way we came in,' says Eight. 'My teleporting Legacy won't work with so many of us.'

'Okay,' John says. 'We don't know what we'll face on the way out and we may have to fight our way through more Mogadorians, or human soldiers, but we need to stay together now. We're never splitting up again.'

Nine steps over and stands next to me, then looks me up and down. 'I don't believe anyone introduced us, proper like. It's nice to officially meet you, sweetheart. I'm Nine,' he says, winking at me. I roll my eyes and John snickers.

I look around for a second. It's a miracle we're all together, all still alive. Every living Loric on Earth but one is standing within a few feet of each other.

We're alive and we're fighting and that means we still have a chance. And we *will* meet Setrákus again, and soon. Next time, he will *not* get away from us.